Homo Thugs

Edited by
Shane Allison

I0691934

Herndon, VA

Herndon, VA

Contents

HOMO HOMIES
Bearmuffin

Midnight in Downtown Los Angeles. Skid row. Thunder rumbled in the distance. The ominous sky flickered with intermittent flashes of lightning. I sure had picked one hell of a place to run out of gas.

My car had stalled a few blocks away. Now I stood on the corner of 3rd and Main Streets in front of the *Jalisco* bar. I'd heard it was a great place to pick up horny Mexicans. So, I decided to investigate it with the possibility of writing an article on skid row nightlife for a gay blog. Its red neon sign crackled and flickered, casting a weird red glow on the surrounding squalor. Shouts and loud laughter punctuated the *mariachi* music blasting from the jukebox within.

My cell was dead, so I made for the bar to use the phone. But, I was suddenly confronted by a stranger wearing a brown Pendleton shirt and baggy khaki trousers. He was wearing Raybans, so I couldn't see his eyes.

The pungent odor of marijuana drifted my way. The stranger lit up a joint. He toked off it and offered it to me.

"I got some dank nugg," he said. "You interested?"

"No, thanks," I said looking at his crotch. I wasn't here for drugs, but I sure could have used a hot cock between my lips: so much tastier, fun, and legal to boot. This young Hispanic tough certainly had the right combination of rugged musculature and super hot machismo that would give a rise to any red-blooded gringo's cock. He seemed chill.

Suddenly, we both heard a siren wailing and becoming louder and louder. A police car turned the corner and stopped in front of the bar with a screech. The young dude sprinted towards the dark alley, but a burly officer jumped out of the squad car and grabbed the Mexican.

"Okay, Chavo," the officer said. "I got you now!"

The cop jumped behind the stud to grab his arms. Chavo stood proudly without flinching as the officer slapped a pair of handcuffs on him.

"The guy's okay officer," I blurted out. "He was just trying to bum some change, that's all." The powerfully built blond officer turned to fix a commanding scowl at me, and for a moment it seemed as if he was about to arrest me. But, the burning glare became a broad, sinister smile.

"Hey, buddy. You asshole! What brings you to skid row?"

Luckily, this particular officer turned out to be an old friend of mine, Matt Quinn.

"Just doing a little research."

"Well," Bob said, "you certainly …" Just then a dispatch came over the police radio, and Bob was momentarily distracted as he took the call. Meanwhile, Chavo gave me a quick glance and then looked at the ground where he had kicked his stash to one side. I purposely dropped my wallet and used it a ruse to pick up the small plastic baggie, which I quickly pocketed.

Bob finished taking the call and turned to face us. "I know it's none of my business, Bob," I said, "but don't be so hard on the guy. Like I said, he was just bumming some change."

"Don't worry tough guy, there ain't going to be any police brutality here." Yeah, it was the same old Bob Quinn. And just as ornery and sarcastic as he had been in the Marines.

He turned to Chavo and faced him. Bob ran his left hand slowly up and down his long nightstick as he looked intently at the Mexican stud with a self-righteous smirk. "Me and Chavo go a long way back, don't we stud?"

Chavo ignored the officer. He looked right through him.

"Hands on the car, dude," the cop said. "Let's see what you got for me tonight."

Chavo did as ordered. It seemed more than a routine search as the officer slowly worked his hands over the stud's body from his ankles, along his sturdy thighs and up to his buttocks. When Bob slipped his hands between Chavo's legs, he held it for what seemed a few moments too long as he patted the dude's crotch and ass.

"Bet you got the stuff stashed up your butthole."

Chavo glared at the officer with a look of complete and utter hatred twisting his dark, attractive face.

"Okay, Chavo," Bob said. He removed the cuffs. "Looks like you're clean. Lucky you made a friend here. Otherwise, I'd run you in."

Chavo said nothing. He clenched his fists as Bob climbed back into the car. But, this was no mere display of street macho bravado. Chavo seemed proud of his Hispanic heritage, and his face reflected what I supposed was his seething anger at being so humiliated in front of me.

Quinn snorted, "If you're doing your research on the scum of the earth, you've come to the right place, pal." With a screech of burned rubber, the officer sped off.

Chavo spat on the ground. "Fucking asshole. *Chinga tu madre!*" He turned to me. "Thanks man, you're cool."

"Want to join me for a beer?" I said.

"Later, maybe," he replied. "I got some business to take care of."

I handed him the tin foil packet. "Here's your stuff."

Chavo laughed. "Fuck it, man. You keep it. You might want to party." Chavo turned on his heel and then stopped to give me a sexy glance. "You know something," he said, pointing a finger at me. "You're one cool dude." Then like a swift panther, Chavo disappeared into the dark shadows of the alley.

It was hotter than a tropical rain forest inside the bar. A couple of Mexican cowboys had their arms around each other and were singing to the music. At the back, a pool game was in progress. A few drag queens stood by the juke box gesticulating wildly and talking in street Spanish.

I took a seat at the bar. An ample, heavily rouged woman appeared before me. Her dark auburn hair was piled high in a sixties beehive. Her penciled in eyebrows arched high up onto her forehead. Her boredom was tinged with a touch of disgust. I quickly sensed that the last thing she wanted to do was to serve a beer-thirsty gringo like me.

"*Dos Equis*," I said.

She handed me a brew.

"You got a phone I can use?"

"You a cop," she asked coldly.

"Why?"

"You not a cop, *no problema*."

With a toss of her hair, she indicated where the phone was at the back by the pool table surrounded by a group of young dark studs engaged in a lively game.

I made my call to the auto club. The dispatcher said it would be a few hours before anybody could arrive. I wasn't the only one with car trouble that night.

I lit a cigarette and checked out the action by the pool table. That's when I noticed a hot looking young *hombre* in a black muscle T-shirt with the words "*Ensenada*" lettered over his humpy pecs. He rested against the jukebox. It looked as if he was watching the pool game, but I felt his eyes on me as well. From underneath a pair of grey sweat pants that hugged every sensuous curve of his well-muscled thighs, I saw a thick, obviously uncircumcised cock pulsating at the crotch.

The stud ogled me with an alluring gleam in his hazel eyes. He took a swig from a bottle of Corona and smacked his lips. A mini-skirted drag queen made a move towards him and asked for a quarter for the juke box.

4

He pointed to some change on the table. The surly queen picked up a couple of quarters. She punched out a few selections and returned to the stud. With a hand on his thigh and her lips brushing against his ear, she whispered something in Spanish. A hot proposition, no doubt. The stud smiled and shook his head. The queen hissed, tossing her head up with a curse and left to join her sisters at the bar.

I stayed by the phone to watch the pool game. From time to time, I glanced at the dude who had now moved a hand down between his legs and rested it upon the ever-thickening bulge within his sweats. Then, he massaged his cock with smooth strokes until it became one huge lust-filled cock, restlessly beating underneath the cloth.

He smiled at me. His eyes widened with enthusiasm. He slipped the tip of his tongue over his upper lip crowned by a bushy mustache. The dude nodded toward the men's room at the back. I waited till he had gone in and then followed him and locked the door.

There was hardly room for a toilet, let alone a sink in that shoebox of a men's room. The dude pissed in a urinal half-full of already smelly piss. I paused a moment just to trip out on the piss squirting from out of his splendidly bronzed uncut cock. The macho stud turned to face me. His eyes looked intensely into mine. He offered his fully extended cock to me. Without hesitation, I fell to my knees before that hot Hispanic dude. I took his magnificent cock into my mouth.

I kissed and licked his cock along the sides. I felt those huge veins burned and pulsate with lust against my tongue. Then, I took it down to his nuts. I sucked furiously on his dong, deliciously tangy with dick-cheese, and then worked on his huge, sweaty nuts. The deep rich scent of musk and raunch coming from his musky crotch rushed up my nose while I sucked on his meat to work his cock up to a frenzy.

Just as I thought he was about to pop his Mexican rocks, he pulled his cock from between my greedy, precum soaked lips. With a seductive gleam in his eyes, the dude pulled down my zipper to grab my cock. He ran his hands along my cock, playing with it as if it were his toy, until it was as hard and throbbing as his own. Then he turned around to bend over and spread his cheeks.

Such an offer was too much to refuse. I plunged my cock up his hot ass. He groaned and grasped the edge of the toilet. I gripped his waist firmly as I plunged my cock into his hot stinking ass. I reached for his solid pecs. I grasped each nipple and gave them a hard yank.

The dude's head bent back. He bucked against my engorged cock surging up inside his sweaty ass.

It wasn't long before the *hombre* was ready to come. "*Ay, cabron!*" The dude shouted. I grasped the base of his cock. His cock veins blazed with lust. I squeezed it hard. It quickly erupted. A full load of hot jizz spurted over my hands. "Fuckin' A!" I yelled as I shot my wad up his ass. His burning cock continued to explode with a stream of jizz that gushed between my hands and spattered all over the toilet floor.

But, our encounter had just begun. The hot *hombre* quickly stuck his finger up my ass and worked it up my hole. This time, it was my turn to bend over the toilet. I got a firm grip on the wobbly toilet seat. He crammed his face against my cheeks. He ran his rough tongue over each globe as he licked each buttcheek. Afterwards, he spit on my asshole and began to suck on it with his rough tongue. As the dude snaked his sweet brown tongue up my shithole, I grasped the iron security bars covering the window. I looked out into the almost pitch black alley. There was a flash of lightning. A police car slowly pulled up. Suddenly, the headlights were extinguished, and it stopped. To my amazement, Bob Quinn sat behind the wheel. Chavo sat next to him.

Chavo lit up a thick joint, which he passed to the cop. Bob took a long deep drag. The young stud got out of the car and leaned back against it. He unzipped his pants and pulled out his already rock hard cock.

Lust and desire shone on the cop's face. He sprang from his seat. His eyes saw nothing but the proud cock Chavo sprouted before him. Quinn fell to his knees in front of the young stud. He quickly clamped his lips around Chavo's dick and swallowed it to the hilt. He fisted his own cock as he gave Chavo super head. Quinn was no longer just a cop. Now he was a cocksucker, too. Just like the rest of us.

Quinn was too busy with sucking Chavo's cock to notice the fifties model Chevrolet that pulled up into the alley and blocked his car.

6

Five menacing dudes jumped out and stood in front of the two men. They had blue bandannas tied around foreheads and wore Raybans. A couple of the guys had hair nets pulled over their slicked black hair. All of them wore brown Pendleton shirts and tan khaki trousers split at the bottom over black patent leather shoes. This had to be Chavo's gang.

"*¿Que pasa ese?*" One of them called out to Chavo.

Bob made a sudden move to get up, but Chavo gave him a swift kick in the nuts.

The cop fell to the ground with an agonizing cry. Chavo grabbed Bob by the collar and pushed his face into the dirt.

"Okay, pig," he snarled. "We're going to give my homeboys a little show."

Chavo tore off his headband and blindfolded the stricken officer. Chavo's homeboys quickly formed a circle around the two men. When Bob made a feeble attempt to get up, he was kicked back to the ground by one of the gang members. Chavo then stepped into the middle of the ring formed by the lusty dudes. The young men began to attack Bob. They ripped off his shirt and blue gabardine trousers. He tried to fight back, but he was no match for the angry dudes who ripped off his T-shirt and flung it next to his shoes and socks. They left the poor cop bare-ass naked. Chavo took the shorts and stuffed them into Bob's mouth.

"You broke the rules, pig!" Chavo yelled. He stood over the cop triumphantly. Like a game hunter who had just bagged his prey. "You humiliated me in front of your friend, asshole. And now you've got to pay!"

"Cuff him, Flaco," Chavo barked to a half-naked, six-foot tall muscle-bound gang warrior who had just taken off his Pendleton.

A bevy of tattoos peppered his sturdy forearms, proud pecs and thick biceps. Flaco took Bob's handcuffs and cuffed him. Chavo pulled Bob's nightstick from its holder.

"Just going to warm up your stinking asshole a little, officer, sir," Chavo sneered. He rubbed the tip of the nightstick along the cop's trembling ass crack. "Just warming you up, pig!"

Bob squirmed and bucked, but the dudes held him down. Chavo penetrated Bob's ass with the stick. Muffled groans issued from the cop's mouth. But the gang members laughed as Chavo slowly worked the entire length of the nightstick up Bob's ass.

"Hey guys. Check this out." Chavo laughed. "Too bad we don't got a camera. This sure would make a great picture to send to his pig buddies." Chavo's homeboys howled with laughter at the sight of a cop with a Billy club stuck up his ass.

"Joker," Chavo said. "Get the pig's belt and warm up his ass for me."

Joker, lean and muscular and as dark as the devil, pulled the belt from around the waistband of his trousers. With a sharp crack, he whipped it against the squad car. Then he dealt Bob a couple of well-aimed blows at his ass.

Joker struck the cop on his back and face. And, Chavo fucked the cop with the nightstick. The gang members broke out some six packs. The air soon hung thick and heavy with the smell of marijuana as they passed several joints around. With savage glee, they watched Joker savagely whip the blond gringo cop. One of the drunken dudes threw down his beer can to unzip his pants. He pulled out an impressively huge and thickly veined cock. A huge stream of piss struck Bob right in the face as the young gang drenched the cop with their urine. By now, the rest of the gang all had their cocks out. They were either jerking off or pissing on the cop's face.

"Let's see if you're ready for a real man's dick, asshole!" Chavo's cock jutted out proudly and fully erect. He placed the wide cockhead shiny and slicked with precum against Bob's quivering butthole. Then he slammed it home.

"Fuck him, Chavo," the men screamed wildly. "Fuck that pig!" Ram your *verga* up his pig ass." They yelled wildly as Chavo grabbed Bob by the hair and butt-fucked the cop with brutal and merciless power hammer thrusts.

As I watched this incredible scene, my hot hombre had just finished eating out my ass. He gave me a good whack on the behind. Then he placed his huge cock head against the puckered opening of my hole. Slowly, he penetrated my hole until my hot ass was full of his hot

8

throbbing stud cock. As I watched Bob getting fucked, the dude grabbed my waist and began to fuck me super hard. Strange, but as the stud plowed and hammered his hot Hispanic cock up my hole, I felt as if I were the assaulted cop, and it was Chavo who was fucking me.

Chavo stopped to remove the shorts that had been used to muffle Bob's screams from the cop's mouth. The brutal fucking had transformed the once proud and sarcastic officer into a whimpering and whining little boy.

"Please, Chavo," he begged, almost out of breath. "For chrissakes, you're ripping me up."

"Yeah, you love it, pig! Tell me you love it." Chavo hissed into the cop's ear. "Tell me how much you love my spic cock up your fuckin' gringo ass!"

"Yeah," Bob murmured.

"Yeah, what, asshole?" Chavo barked as he whacked Bob on the thighs with the nightstick.

"I love it, Chavo," Bob cried out.

"Now tell me you want more."

"More," Bob gasped.

"More what, asshole," Chavo cried. Chavo dealt another whack on the thighs.

"Fuck me," Bob gasped. "Fuck my fuckin pig ass!"

As Chavo's friends joined in the taunts, the dude fucking me jabbed and drilled my asshole like a champion fucker. He dug his fingers deep into my pecs. He pinched and bruised my tender nipples and bit into my neck.

Just then, my macho dude roared and hurtled his load of cum up my ass. Chavo yelled a huge macho groan and slammed his cock all the way up Bob's ass.

"Take my load you fuckin' pig pussy!" Chavo yelled. Bob howled in agony when Chavo shot several loads of hot spunky jizz up the cop's hole. The rest of the gang yelled lustily as they unloaded their bloated ball sacs full of hot Hispanic jizz onto the cop's prone and unconscious body.

From afar, I heard the sudden wail of sirens. Chavo and his gang broke up and jumped into their Chevy. An enraged Flaco took out a can of spray paint and prayed the words "Pigs Suck Dick" over the windshield and sides of Bob's squad car in huge black letters.

Then he went up and stood over Bob who was still lying unconscious on the ground. Flaco laughed as he kicked over the cop's body with his foot and sprayed the word "*Puto*" on Bob's back and ass, after which he joined the others, and the car roared off.

It was time for me to go, too, and pronto. I wasn't about to stick around to see which of Bob's cop buddies would show up. The hot stud that had just unloaded his balls up my ass had vanished. I quickly made my way out the back exit only to see my hot *hombre* sitting on a trash can while the once-scorned drag queen kneeled down to suck his dick.

With a powerful thunder crack, the storm broke loose in all its fury, loosening torrents of rain upon the ground. I scurried under the awning of a nearby taco stand. Within seconds, a bunch of squad cars pulled up in front of the *Jalisco*. The bar was soon surrounded by a swarm of evil-looking officers with their nightclubs out ready to crack heads.

I later heard through the grapevine that a reward had been offered for any information leading to the arrest of whoever had perpetrated the outrage against one of the El-Lay boys in blue.

Needless to say, there were no arrests. But there was no doubt in my mind that sooner or later, Officer Quinn would get around to dealing with Chavo and his gang.

Funny, but every time I smell some good weed, I always think of Chavo and half expect him to show up offering me his wares. If he were to invite me down some dark alley, do you think I'd hesitate?

THEIR BLOOD SHALL BE UPON THEM
Jamie Freeman

Beck always scared me. Maybe it was something about those blue eyes, ringed in bloodshot white and staring out from behind ȝry, oversized pupils; so intense you wanted to glance away just to stabilize yourself. His eyes could shove you backwards down a flight of stairs and then charm the police into looking the other way. From the first time I met him, years ago, before the wars; before he became a major player in the Bush Administration, those eyes had captured me, beating me bloody and leaving me for dead.

The first time I saw Beck, I was living in New York, writing for FOX News and earning my paycheck by wailing on the Democrats and the so-called mainstream press. I did this great piece on anti-Christian attitudes at Disney that got me a lot of blogtalk and a big raise, and I'd been celebrating at this little dive bar in the village where my cousin Peter worked. He always set me up with free drinks and would score me a couple of grams of coke if I was flush, and that night, I was fuckin' flush.

Peter and I crowded into the tiny men's room that opened onto the empty dance floor and did a couple of bumps just to get things going. In about a hour, we were both flying, Peter singing and pouring drinks like a fuckin' cartoon of Speedy Gonzalez and me sitting there talking to anyone who'd listen about how Glenn Greenwald and the fuckin' *Huffington Post* were trying to destroy America, you know, getting up a pretty good head of steam, hands flying and words tumbling out all over the bar. My teeth were chatting like a *flamenco* dancer's feet, and I was sailing so high I didn't really care who was listening; I was just talking and talking.

I remember looking up at the television because I heard some familiar turn of phrase, like a setter turning his ears to the wind to hear trace sounds of home. It was my Disney piece running again, loudly.

11

Homo Thugs

There were a bunch of guys standing around watchi. their heads as if they couldn't believe it. A tall redh and shaking jeans and a tight T-shirt stood on point, his white C with skinny straining as his toes took the full weight of his body. I re Taylors held a drink in his right hand, something clear like vodka or his left arm curved around in a broad arch, sorta graceful, but he place in this dump. He stood there for a moment like that, ele above the dinginess of the room, and then he bounced three times his toes and let his feet come down flat against the grimy woode planks of the flooring. And as he brought his arm in toward his body, I saw one of the guys who was standing with him turn from the television, look right at me, and shrug. Just that, just a simple gesture, like 'What the fuck ya gonna do?'

I stopped in mid-sentence, stared, and then shrugged back. The guy cracked a half-smile and eased down off his barstool. He ambled over to me. I use that word very specifically – I'm a fuckin' writer by trade, remember? – So, he ambled over to me like a Terminator on the make, slabs of muscle moving under his clothes like armored plating inside a flak jacket. His giant shoulders and V-shaped body slid down in distinctly angular lines to a thin waist and slim hips. His legs were strong and thick, aesthetically matched to his broad chest, but not too big. He was so fuckin' hot I could feel a hard-on worming its way up against the inside of my jeans despite the dampening effect of the drugs.

Up close, I could see those soon-to-be famous sky blue eyes, staring out at me from dilated pupils and eclipsed when he blinked by a seam of dark, almost feminine eyelashes. He squinted a little, a trio of age lines running prematurely from his eyes toward his ears. He had dark curly hair and this intense, almost angelic aura, even back then, that made me want to kneel down in front of him right there on the sticky floor of the bar.

He looked at me for a minute, then said, "You gonna share that candy, baby?" He slid his thumb under my nostril and then licked the tip of it, grinning and stepping closer, his huge, hard package sliding against my leg.

In about five minutes, we were back in the storeroom behind the old rumbling ice machine that buzzed and banged like a transformer ramping up to an explosion. He had the last half of one of the baggies and was digging around with a key doing bump after bump, and I was down on my knees, extracting the pendulous length of his slowly hardening cock from his jeans. I pushed his jeans all the way down to his ankles, exposing his perfectly formed legs to the dim light that trickled in from the overhead window, strained through the grime of a couple of decades of neglect. The hair on his thighs was thick but quickly tapered to nothing, his calves steely smooth and hairless. His cock shot out ramrod stiff from thick, loosely curled bush that was more silky than kinky, the hairs soft against my nose and cheeks when I went down on him.

I blew him until he pulled me up off the floor, wrenching my right shoulder so hard the joint ached for a week. He turned me around, lubed me up with spit-slicked fingers as thick as sausages, and then plowed into me so fast that all the air left my lungs in a gasp and tears squeezed out onto my cheeks. Blood rushed to my head, and I tried to pull away from him, but then I lost my balance and would have fallen if he hadn't grabbed me around the waist and shoved me back down onto his huge cock. The pain sliced through me as he started to fuck me again – hard, like a skinhead kicking his righteous anger into an immigrant's brown belly.

His arms were clamped around me, pinning my arms and positioning me, so he could get more penetration. It went on a long time, and I remember thinking it might never end, that he might actually fuck me to death. My heart was racing from the coke and the adrenaline, and I couldn't quite keep an erection going. I heard him grunt and felt a flood of semen curling into my guts, and I thought I might lose my balance again. Light flashed behind my eyes; out of control, my body threw itself at the side of the ice machine.

He grunted again, stumbled against me, his weight slamming me against the cold metal. He thrust a couple more times, holding me close and immobile with his giant arms. I felt a string of saliva fall from his mouth onto the back of my neck, and then finally felt his girth begin to eject itself slowly from my ass. I pushed him out and felt cavernous and hollow and exhausted. I leaned against the ice machine, my forehead burning hot against the cool metal. I reached out my arm to steady myself on a stack of liquor boxes. My pants were pushed down around my ankles, the back of my legs suddenly exposed, sweaty and cold. Come oozed down the inside of my right leg.

And when I turned around, he was gone.

Jesus Christ, he was hot.

I didn't see him again until the spring of 2004. I was living in DC then, covering the White House for FOX News, reporting on the political mêlée surrounding Patriot II and the first of the Executive Orders that became known collectively as the Levitican Code. Hindsight's 20/20, but back then we really didn't think anything much would come of all this. We figured the Democrats would weep and gnash, and some A.C.L.U. lawyers would maybe try to get things reversed, and the network would get an indignation-fueled ratings bump, and eventually people would get sick of it all, and they'd vote a Democrat into the White House who'd reverse everything Bush had done. The Secession Crisis was still about two years away, and none of us could see the storm clouds gathering on the horizon, much less the bloody turmoil of the coming Civil War.

I had this friend Danny who would sometimes meet me at the bathhouse over on 14th Street to hang out and cruise. One Saturday, we'd popped some Viagra and were hanging out in the sauna scouting possibilities when a corn-fed muscle cub from Wichita named Calvin stepped into the steam sporting a bulging towel and a toothy grin. Danny and I had fallen all over ourselves to get at the guy. We followed him out of the sauna and down the hall to a dingy cubicle where Danny sucked him off while I slid my slender cock inside his tight, hairy ass.

An hour and a half later, we were sitting in the Thai Palace restaurant on P Street with heaping plates of Pad Thai noodles and a couple of Singha beers, watching the weekend crowds rush past our window.

Danny was a crime reporter for *The Washington Post* who had a Dickensian knowledge of Washingtonian social circles, from the loose tribes of homeless who lived in the Metro tunnels to the Black and Latino street gangs to the staffers on the Hill to the members themselves, and all the way up to the Bush-Cheney inner sanctum.

14

He was telling me about this story he was writing about the growing presence of militant Christian groups in the capital. He rattled off a list of half a dozen organizations, mostly dominionists and endtimers, that had relocated from the hinterlands to take a more active role in the Last Government, as they'd come to refer to the Bush presidency. Last Government, as in the last government before Jesus comes back. The heavily-armed groups had names like Elijah's Commandos, Gabriel's Fist, Warriors in Christ, and the Crimson Trumpeters.

At first, most of the groups had been relatively quiet, settling into empty office spaces on K Street or up near Farragut West, sending angry letters, doing some light pamphleting, operating slick storefront recruiting centers, and steering clear of direct involvement with the government. But things were starting to change: more altercations, more violence, more police, and more blood on the streets of the capital.

"Jesus, Danny, they're like fuckin' street gangs for Christ."

"Yeah, that's exactly what they are. Matthew, Mark, and Luke with guns and attitude."

"Fuckin' crazy."

"Yeah and scary, 'cause they're more organized than the Crips or the Bloods. They've got complicated corporate structures like, say, the Black Gangster Disciples, but nobody's exactly sure what they're moving."

"Faith," I said, interrupting him. "They're moving faith."

"Maybe," he said, wary of committing to that idea.

"What else?"

"I dunno. I mean, it's not street drugs. This guy I know from the G.D.s confirms there's no change in the street market at all as far as they can tell, and the same with the Latinos in Columbia Heights. *Nada.* Nothing new is moving on the streets, no drugs, no guns, no people. So everyone's kinda running around worrying and fretting and nobody knows what to do. I talked to this girl from the A.T.F. and said there are literally hundreds of extra Feds from Homeland Security, A.T.F., F.B.I., D.E.A. Pretty much every agency with a domestic law enforcement mandate has people here on the streets watching for illegal activity, but so far the most they've come up with is some assaults and some misdemeanor B&E. It's weird, David. I don't quite know what to make of it." He sighed and looked at his plate, digging around with his chop sticks. "Okay, so here's my angle on all this," he said. "There's this guy Beck who's the leader of this group called the Christian Brotherhood – the Cee-Bees – and he went to see Bush yesterday."

"What?" I felt a chill run down my spine.

"Yep, he's got a fuckin' rap sheet goes back a decade, and yesterday he was in the lockup for beating the shit out of a couple of lesbians over near Logan Circle. So this uniform I talked to over there at the station said they got a call, and Bam! an armored SUV with government plates showed up and took him away. And suddenly, this Cee-Bee motherfucker has an audience with the Emperor."

"Well, fuck me Danny."

"Yeah, that's what I'm saying," he said, taking a swig of his beer.

"So what's that all about?" My head was spinning. I knew Bush was a religious wingnut, hell I'd waded through enough White House bullshit, from prayers at press conferences to revival-style sing-alongs on Air Force One, to know he was thumping the *Good Book* pretty hard, but this affiliation struck me as something new and sinister.

"I think Bush is looking for a little plausibly deniable political muscle."

"What? Like a goon squad? Come on, Danny, he's the fuckin' President of the United States, he's got Black ops coming out his sanctified ass."

"Yeah, but he can only go so far domestically; it's the Nixon dilemma."

I shook my head. "Huh-uh. No."

"Beck's kinda like Bush's Ernst Rohm. Only instead of publicly recognizing him, Bush brings him in on the sly, gives him a little quiet protection, keeps the police or the Feds at bay and suddenly Bush has a private army on the streets of DC."

I stared at him for a long time in silence. "That's fucked up," I said finally.

Of course, Danny was right about everything. Beck and the Cee-Bees did emerge as the most powerful force on the streets of DC. Within a year, they had effectively seized control of most of the smaller gangs, stifled trafficking in drugs, guns and humans, enlisted the Blacks and the Latinos as crimson-clad foot soldiers, and begun sporadic enforcement of the Levitican Code. Adulterers, gender traitors (homosexuals), life takers (users of contraception) and baby killers (anyone involved in an abortion) were suddenly being accused and sentenced in theatrical street courts that more often than not handed down sentences of death by stoning. By the time the Metro Police showed up, the Cee-Bees and crowds of the faithful had disappeared and the Office of the Chief Medical Examiner had to be called to clean up and catalog the mess.

By the beginning of the Secession Crisis of 2006, there were Cee-Bee chapters all over the South from Georgia to Texas and scattered across the Mid-West. And when the National Civilian Security Act of 2008 placed the Cee-Bees and half a dozen similar organizations under the direct control of the Executive Branch, there were over 85,000 uniformed members armed with sticks, stones, knives, guns, and Bibles.

Danny and I finished dinner, walked back to Connecticut Avenue, and parted ways on the platform at the DuPont Metro station. He gave me a quick, self-conscious hug and hurried off, running to catch his train. I watched him walk toward the back of the car, taking an aisle seat and pulling his Redskins ball cap down low over his eyes.

As the train picked up speed, my eyes slid along the outside of the car, the bright squares of the windows illuminated from within like a row of aquariums. A familiar face flashed into view, pale blue eyes and a big grin full of teeth that looked lupine in the yellowish light. His head was shaved, and his lip was split down the middle and crusted over with dried blood. His face looked older, but I knew him at once. I recognized him from that night in New York, but I still didn't know his name. He nodded at me, a casual but directed gesture that picked me out of the crowd and sent me a message I was not yet able to decode. He was there for an instant and then gone.

17

Homo Thugs

Later in the week, I texted Danny to confirm our plans to watch *Deadwood*, but the fuckin' cocksucka was nowhere to be found. I called him a couple of times, and then called his office. Courtnee, one of the interns, answered his phone and told me he was MIA; nobody'd seen him since last week.

"Well, is anybody out there looking for him?" I asked.

"Um, I dunno?" she said, her voice rising vacantly at the end of her sentence.

I hung up on her and threw my phone across the room, smashing it apart and poppin' the battery. Fuckin' thing's indestructible.

I called a couple of his friends, but nobody'd heard from him since the afternoon he and I had dinner at the Thai Palace.

I went over to his apartment and tried to get the doorman to let me in. He mumbled something about policies and pretended to read his *Cyrillic* magazine, pointedly ignoring me. I walked around back to the fire escape and took a couple of flying leaps before I finally connected with the ladder, sliding down with it as it crashed to street level. I tried six windows before I found one I could push open. I clambered across the wooden sill into a long carpeted hallway. I took the stairs two at a time to eight and ran down the hallway to Danny's apartment.

I tucked my fingers inside the cuff of my shirt sleeve and tried the knob.

The door was unlocked; my blood ran cold.

Inside the apartment, the normally tidy living room had been turned upside down. Papers were strewn everywhere; a filing cabinet had been overturned and emptied of its contents. The Polish movie posters that lined the wall above Danny's sofa had been thrown across the room with such force that the glass in their frames had exploded, covering half the room in shards of glass that glittered in the orange evening sun. In the blank space where the posters had hung there was a short message painted in precise, rusty letters: THOU SHALT NOT.

What the fuck?

I must have said the words aloud because the silence around me was broken by a response that slithered out of the kitchen like an alligator stalking a duckling.

"That's what I'd like to know."

I jumped at least two feet in the air.

He appeared in the kitchen doorway, leaning against the doorframe with a pint of Chubby Hubby in one hand and a spoon in the other. He licked the spoon and watched me with those cool blue eyes.

I stared at him. He was barefoot, wearing tight jeans but no shirt. His chest was smooth and vast and perfect.

"What are you doing here?" I asked

He spooned a hunk of ice cream into his mouth and chewed slowly, affecting a thoughtful pose. He leaned closer to the wall, his chest and arm muscles rippling in the orange light like a Dreamsicle melting on a sidewalk. My cock moved inside my jeans.

"I remember you," he said through a mouthful of peanut butter and vanilla malt.

"You didn't answer my question," I said.

"Nope," he agreed shoveling another spoonful of ice cream into his mouth. His lips were wet and sloppy and the grin he gave me was icy and electric.

"So you're not gonna tell me?" I asked.

"Why should I? You're the one who's trespassing."

This surprised me. "What about you?"

"Oh no," he said, scraping the bottom of the container and shoveling the last of the ice cream into his mouth. "Danny asked me to come here."

"Where is he?"

Beck looked at me with those piercing eyes, a momentary softness passing behind them. He tossed the empty ice cream carton and spoon onto the floor.

19

"Do you know who I am?" he asked.

"Yeah, you're the guy from the ice machine at Round Bar in New York."

He shook his head in mock pity.

"Fuck you, your condescension! What the fuck are you doing here?" I shouted suddenly, startling us both.

He laughed; I clenched my fist.

"I told you. Danny asked me to come over."

"So where the fuck is he?"

"Yeah, now you're catching up …"

"Fuck you!"

"I've already done that, haven't I?" he said, rubbing his fingers across the growing bulge in his jeans. "You want some more of this?"

I stepped back. "Where's Danny?"

"You are so fucking single-minded. Jesus, David ..."

"How do you know my name?"

He paused. "Here's the deal, David." His voice was hard now, the tone riding beneath the surface of his syllables violent enough to make me queasy with fear and desire. "Danny asked me over to talk about a story for *The Post*. When I got here, the door was unlocked and the place was a mess. No Danny. So I thought I better wait around for him, maybe have some ice cream, watch a little TV. That okay with you, David?"

Something finally clicked and I said, "You're Beck."

He grinned at that, a big carnivorous grin, and I imagined I could see his cock thumping under the close, gamey denim. He pushed off from the wall with his shoulder, sliding upright and watching me from beneath dark lashes. The muscles of his chest rose and fell slowly with his breathing, the nipples hard and bronze and angry in the fading glow from outside.

He shrugged, pulled a black T-shirt off a hook just inside the kitchen, and started stretching it across his hulking upper body. Stylized gothic lettering across the chest of the shirt read, 'Jesus Died for You, You Fucking Ingrate.' He looked up at me; pleased to see me watching him.

"I'm Beck," he said. "What do you know about Beck? I wonder. What has our Danny told you about this man, Beck?"

I took a step back and slipped on loose papers, my arms wind-milling in histrionic circles. "Goddammit!" I shouted, catching myself on a bookshelf and looking for a firm footing.

"Now, now, David. You mustn't use the Lord's name in vain. It's a new world out there. Tomorrow doesn't belong to the blasphemous."

I looked pointedly at his shirt, but remained silent.

"Think what you like, David. Makes me no nevermind."

He turned around, walked into the kitchen and returned with a pair of dingy socks and a scuffed pair of Timberland work boots. He knelt down, pulled on the socks and stepped into the boots, tying them in precise double knots.

"I'm outta here, David. You see Danny, tell him to come see me. He knows right where to find me."

He walked to the door and then stopped to look back over his shoulder. "You got any more candy to share, you call me, too, hear?"

And he was gone.

I stood staring at the closed door for a long time, wondering what to do next.

I found Danny's body in the kitchen, eviscerated in a lake of blood on the ceramic tile. A basting brush coated in drying blood lay on the floor beside his body.

The police took me in for questioning, and despite the conviction of the Russian doorman that I'd killed Danny, the M.E.'s preliminary timeline pretty much exonerated me. I told the cops about the story Danny was writing and about finding Beck in the apartment.

They asked me over and over if I there could have been someone else in the apartment with Beck. Then after a couple of hours, two guys in dark suits, probably Secret Service, came in to convince me I hadn't seen anyone in the apartment at all.

I eventually signed their statement, inadvertently dripping blood on the final page and causing the taller of the two suits to kick over the table and storm out the door to print another copy. According to the statement, I arrived, found Danny dead in the empty apartment, and called the police immediately.

About a week later I came home from work to find Beck waiting in the silent darkness of my living room. When I flipped on the light, I saw him sitting in a wingback chair facing me, one leg crossed over the other, ankle to knee, looking relaxed and calm. He was wearing jeans, boots, and a plain black T-shirt. He had on a red ball cap featuring a blue circular patch with a red cross and white stars. He eyed me calmly as I dropped my shoulder bag and tossed my keys on the table.

"Did you come here to kill me?" I asked, too tired to deal with his shit.

"Did the S.S. do that to your face?"

I touched the stitches self-consciously.

"Secret Service," I mumbled.

"That's what I said."

I looked at him and felt helpless and exhausted, like a doe stumbling blindly across the center lane of the Beltway during rush hour. "You want a beer?" I asked.

"Whatcha got?"

"Landshark?"

"Pussy."

"Fuck you, man. You want one or not?"

"Sure, I'll take your lager, David."

I got a couple of bottles out of the refrigerator and handed him one. I was close enough to him to smell cigarettes and Old Spice.

"Thanks." He took a long swig, never taking his eyes off me.

I sat opposite him on the couch, sinking low in the worn cushions and sipping my beer.

"You ever been to Canada?" he asked finally.

"Fuck you!" I shouted, jumping to my feet and slinging my bottle wildly in his direction. A whirl of frothy beer splashed across the coffee table and soaked one leg of his jeans.

Two figures came storming down the hallway from my bedroom. A black man with a gold tooth and a gun tucked in the waistband of his pants, and a short Mexican-looking guy, all muscle and macho swagger. They stopped when they saw Beck still sitting in his chair, taking another long gulp of his beer.

"These gentlemen are my associates." Beck waived his arm at them, but watched me; eyes seeking out the cracks beneath the veneer of my hard breathing silence. "T.N.T. here provides security for myself and my lieutenants." The black man nodded uncomfortably, flashing me a grin, but saying nothing. "And Pepe coordinates communications and transportation." Pepe flicked his head back in a quick jerking motion.

"They're good guys with a Biblical understanding of retribution. So as you can imagine, if I thought for one minute you'd thrown that bottle rather than accidentally dropping it on the table, I'd have to end your life. You can see that, can't you, David?"

I didn't answer him.

"You answer the man when he talks to you, Muthafucka," T.N.T said, leaning in low to look into my eyes with his own yellow-ringed orbs.

"Yes," I said, looking from T.N.T to Beck. "I can see that."

"I knew you could be reasonable," Beck said to me, then to the others, "Gentlemen, please wait for me outside the building. I think it's time Mr. Worthington and I had a discussion."

The two men grinned at this, gold teeth glinting in the fading light as they strutted out the front door of my apartment.

I heard the door slam and looked at Beck.

He was smiling, but his eyes were dark and dead.

My hands were shaking.

"Let me try this again," he said, looking down at his beer, slowly twirling the bottom edge of it against the leg of his jeans, the condensation leaving a twisting series of overlapping crescents. "You ever been to Canada?"

"Yeah, once."

"Whereabouts?"

"Toronto."

"Right," he said, nodding. "You should go back there."

"Are you threatening me?"

"Oh no, David, we're way beyond that. No, I'm not here to threaten you; I'm here to save your worthless, godless, fucking faggoty, heathen ass."

I stared at him blankly.

He glanced out the window at the dying day.

"It's a new day here in the old U.S. of A. The beginning of something most people will never really understand; something magnificent and sacred and important." He finished his beer and set the bottle carefully on the floor beside his chair. He stood up and stretched, his body sliding along the vertical plane, a long thick cord of muscle. His shirt rode up above the waistband of his jeans revealing a small tuft of hair that curled and captivated me.

"Here I am talking about destiny, about life and death, David, and you're fuckin' staring at me like a dachshund in a sausage factory. Don't you care about anything?"

"What, like God?" I asked.

"Fuck you, David. God's a red herring; he always has been. I'm talking about power." His eyes gleamed. He walked over to the window and paced back and forth. The lights of the city and the last moments of sunlight conspired to light him from behind, casting a saintly halo of pale light up behind his clean-shaven head.

"This is bigger than God. This is apotheosis, man, about men rising to the level of the gods, reaching out to take control of this sad, dying world of ours. Bush doesn't give a shit about God. Oh, he can wail and testify, but when push comes to shove, it's all about the power. He's gonna take a third term. Fuck the Constitution. Fuck the illiterate voters, too hopped up on fear and shopping and TV to know who they're voting for anyway. They'll hand him the country like they did last time, and when he seizes total control, all those Christian soldiers will march in his defense because they think it's the Will of God. They're gonna rip the republic apart, and we're gonna build a monolithic power out of the ashes of the retched refuse."

"Do you really believe that?"

"Of course. Christians are easy; they're primed for tyranny."

"And Dubble Yew can marshal those forces?"

Beck's eyes burned. "He's smarter than people think, and he's good at gathering the right people around him."

"Like you."

"Like me. I've already started the mission, fuckin' cleansing the country from street level. I've got soldiers in Atlanta, Birmingham, Jacksonville, Miami, Jackson, Houston, Dallas – fuckin' all over the place bringing the gangs and the street economies right into line. That's something nobody's been able to do before, and it'll make all the difference when the time comes. I've got rival street gangs working for me who were killing each other over fuckin' crack empires a year ago. And now they're part of a movement, full of purpose and faith and Biblical rage. They're finally becoming haves instead of have-nots and they're marching in time to my cadences like obedient Christian soldiers."

"What about people who don't fit into the new order?" I asked.

"Like the Levitican Offenders?" he asked.

"Yeah, like you and me?"

He turned slowly, eyes glinting murderously. "I'm not like you," he said, his raspy voice hovering just above a whisper. "Maybe those people ought to go to Canada."

"So what do you get out of this?"

"Are you interviewing me, David?" He grinned, crossing his mammoth arms across his chest.

"No, not really," I smiled.

"Old habits die hard, I guess."

"I guess they do," I said.

He moved over to stand in front of me; fists planted on his hips, and said, "Here's the deal, David. I'm gonna fuck you. Then you're gonna pack up your shit, rent a U-haul or whatever, and head north tomorrow. And if you stay here, I'll gut you like I did your friend Danny."

He grabbed my chin and pulled me roughly to my feet.

"Take off your clothes you piece of shit," he barked.

I kicked off my shoes and stripped, standing silently before him, my cock bobbing in front of me, my breathing heavy and labored.

He reached down with one hand, pulling the buttons of his fly open, his monster cock flopping out, swinging blindly. He shoved me down onto my knees and pushed his enormous cock into my mouth. He fucked my face like he would a ripe cantaloupe, twisting and shoving my head around sending flashes of pain up from the base of my skull. I moved with him, trying not to gag on the thickness of him, pushing down my throat and brutally gagging me.

When he decided he'd been serviced enough, he reeled in his enormous cock, drawing it out of my mouth like a man retrieving a fire hose. The tip of it glistened and dripped with saliva and mucous and precum.

"Get up," he said, grabbing my hair and pulling me to my feet again. He grabbed my cock, wrenching it hard and sending me tumbling past him toward the short hallway. "Get in there and find some fuckin' lube."

I stumbled into the bedroom, rifling through the bedside table. When I turned around he was standing in the doorway naked, the dim light from the open bedroom window casting his chest in patterns of light and shadow that made my cock jump.

"Don't just stand there, David. Lube yourself up before I take you dry."

I poured a glob of cold lube into my hands and slid my fingers in and out of my asshole while he watched with an ugly, amused look on his face.

"That's enough," he said grabbing my arms and throwing me face down on the bed. He was inside me before I could react, his enormous body supported by the thick columns of his stony forearms. He slid deep inside me, his length and girth pulling and stretching and prodding me in rippling waves of pain and pleasure.

I groaned and he pushed harder, each thrust slamming deeper inside me, pounding my prostate and splitting me apart. I was gasping and making this tense animal sound halfway between a sob and a growl. He grunted in my ear, his voice deep and guttural. When his pitch rose suddenly, and he broke his rhythm hosing down my insides with cum, my own body reacted by sending a stream of cum out onto the bedspread beneath me and sending a flash of light up my spinal column, like an EMP exploding and wiping consciousness from my brain.

When I awoke later, my body was smeared with dried sweat, lube, cum and blood. Beck was gone and the lights in the apartment were off. In the glow of a nightlight, I saw something scrawled on the wall opposite my bed. I reached for the bedside lamp.

'THEIR BLOOD SHALL BE UPON THEM'

I had my belongings packed in a rented U-haul and was on my way North before sunset the next day.

Epilogue

As I write these words it is March 22, 2011. I have been living in Toronto for seven years. From a distance, the Civil War is an incomprehensible monstrosity that plays out on television like an endless miniseries. Beck was right about almost everything. Fear moved the people to embrace the Will of God's President over the foundations of their liberty. The nation split apart like a jigsaw puzzle, fracturing along the hidden fault lines made deeper and more dangerous by decades of culture wars.

I talked about Beck with my therapist, and she urged me to look at childhood events that might have shaped my masochistic tendencies. I yelled at her and kicked over an end table.

Sometimes I dream about Beck. About the feeling of his monstrous cock boring into me and hollowing me out, coring me like an overripe apple. When I wake up in the middle of the night, my stomach sticky and smelling of his skin, I sometimes wonder how long it would have taken him to kill me if I'd stayed.

CLUB BUNNS
Logan Zachary

"Crap! I went the wrong way. What else was new?" The October night settled on Baltimore as a warm breeze blew through my blond hair. I turned around and headed back the way I came, six blocks up West Lexington Street and then six more blocks to the bar. Club Bunns, what kind of bar would be named Bunns? A rabbit bar? The *Damron* gay guide said it was a gay bar close to my hotel, and on Wednesday nights, they had male strippers. What more did I need to know?

The annual mystery convention was in Baltimore this year, and I was ready to party and have fun. As my footsteps echoed along the street, I passed the hotel where I started and continued through the mall area. On the next block, a business was boarded up. The store fronts along this block appeared run down, badly in need of a paint job.

Papers and garbage lined the street. Didn't anyone clean? How hard was it to walk a few steps and throw the litter into the cans? The sidewalk rose and fell, bricks uneven and broken. My foot caught an edge, and I tripped, catching myself. My footsteps echoed down the mall street and images of a movie set in a bad part of town came to mind.

The next block had more businesses boarded up and spray painted graffiti blazed across them. Where the hell was this place? I had watched *The Wire*. These streets could be very dangerous. I slowed; *maybe I should go back?* I looked at a store front – 413. I was only two blocks away. Besides, I really needed a beer.

Sweat dripped down my back and soaked into my underwear. I could feel the cotton stick to my ass. Humidity and exertion made me damp and sticky.

The mall of stores ended at the corner, and a dark alley loomed across the street.

I hadn't seen anyone in blocks. The hotel had activity, but this part of the city was dead.

Walking around the block looked better. More light along that way, but it also added three extra blocks. Two blocks to go, if I hurried. I peered down the alley. No movement and one dim light half way down. I doubled my pace and entered. My eyes scanned the walls, and every shadow that moved. The smell of rotting garbage hung in the air.

The alley widened and more light filtered in. A tree appeared and a small square of grass separated the street. I stepped out of the alley and cut across the boulevard to the odd side of the street. 608 stood in the middle of the block, and neon letters spelled out Club Bunns. A low constant thump, thump, thump emanated from the bar. Disco.

I quickened my steps and approached the heavy wooden door. The windows on either side of the front were covered with bamboo shades. As I stepped inside, a man sat on a high stool with a flashlight. "ID." He was a bald, lean man with the darkest skin I had ever seen.

I fumbled with my wallet and pulled out my Minnesota driver's license.

"Derek Armstrong," the man read, "welcome." He motioned for me to enter.

A small ramp lead from his seat to a brick wall. At the corner, the room opened to reveal a rectangular bar where two bartenders bounced from side to side like penned animals. Streamers hung from the rafters above the bar.

To the left, the room descended into a dance floor with a stage that dominated the wall by a DJ's booth. The walls were painted black with silver lightning bolts running around the area. Mirror balls hung from the ceiling, and light flashed and reflected from all the silver.

I walked along the brick wall to the back of the bar and rounded the end to find a stool with a view of the stage. A pool table, juke box, and dart board lined the hallway to the bathrooms. Black and white square tiles covered the floor like a chess board.

As I sat down, a bartender approached, "What'll you have?"

"Miller Chill."

"Don't have that one."

"Blue Moon."

"Nope."

"Bud Light Lime."

"We got Bud light, and I can put a lime in it."

I nodded. "Sure." I was always attracted to dark skinned men. Being blond with a fair Finlander complexion, my skin burned easily and tanning was next to impossible. Looking around the bar, I noticed only Latino and African American men surrounded the bar.

The bartender placed a bottle in front of me.

I set a twenty down.

He smiled and walked to the register.

I looked down the other side of the bar and realized that I was the only white person in the bar. Being from Minneapolis, I encountered a diverse community, but I was never in the minority. I felt out of place and wanted to apologize for being here.

A woman entered the bar and took the seat next to me. She had the smoothest skin, so soft and mocha rich. Her hair was pulled back, smoothed slick to her sides and carefully circled out into a frizzy bun.

She wore a vest that revealed deep cleavage and two well developed breasts.

She was beautiful. Even the gay man inside me could see that.

The bartender set a red drink in a tall frosted glass with a straw down in front of her. She nodded and gave him a husky, "Thanks." Her hand reached for her drink.

That's when I noticed how large they were, very masculine. Then the light went on. She was transgender. No drag queen looked like this, so graceful and fine featured with permanent breasts. Her vest showed all she had was real.

She turned to me. "How are you doing tonight?" Her voice was low and sexy.

"I'm doing well."

"Visiting?"

"I'm here for the weekend."

"My name is Kim."

"I'm Derek."

"Are you here for Pride?" She pointed to the Baltimore Black Pride signs that lined the bar.

"I'm here for a book conference."

She nodded. "You're a writer? A creative mind?"

"I'm working on a mystery, but I'm still looking for an agent and my big break."

"Honey, I am, too. I design clothes and do interior design." She pointed at the streamers. "I helped with all of this."

"It looks great."

"As long as the strippers don't pull them down, until after Pride."

As if on cue, two lean young men walked out of the bathroom in sneakers and underwear. Both were well muscled and beautiful. One guy walked up to Kim and kissed her. "Hey babe," he said.

"Hi, Dylan," she said.

He turned his back to me and hugged her. His back muscles rippled and his butt flexed. His black hairless body was flawless. Such a fine man.

I could feel my mouth start to water as a stirring occurred in my pants. I needed to adjust myself, but before I could, Kim spun him around. "I'd like you to meet Derek. He writes mysteries."

He extended his hand, which was almost twice the size of mine. His grasp was firm and warm, power flowed deep within this man. "I gotta get to work." He kissed Kim and walked to the other stripper.

She patted his ass as he left. A perfect bubble butt.

He reached back and pulled down the waistband a little, mooning a quarter ass to us.

I couldn't take my eyes off his deep crease, sculpted gluts. There was even a dimple.

"He's so fine," Kim said, "and wait until he takes those briefs off."

"They can get naked in Maryland?"

"Oh yes. These boys are very hot."

"In Minneapolis, the strippers can go nude, if they're in an enclosed shower stall."

"How do you tip them?"

"There is a slit where dollars can be passed to the dancers."

Kim grabbed my arm and laughed. "You should go down to the Eagle, just don't go under the stairs."

"At our Eagle, we have Bingo on Thursday nights and Showtune Sundays."

"How sad," she said finishing her drink.

I motioned for the bartender to get her another one.

The other stripper stepped up onto the bar and started to dance. His hand rose up and hit the streamers.

"Andre!" Kim stood up and glared at him.

He strutted down the bar and shook his ass in her face.

She slapped him hard. "I worked for hours putting them up, don't you dare knock any down."

The bartender laughed as he set our drinks down. I paid him and slipped a dollar into Andre's briefs.

"Thanks," he said, stuck his tongue out at Kim, and moved down the bar.

"I'm waiting to hear if I'll be on the next Project Runway."

"I love that show." We clinked drinks and laughed.

Andre approached and pulled on the streamers above Kim and winked at her. He knelt down in front of me and thrust his pelvis forward. He pulled his waistband forward and let me peek in. Nine inches of semi-erect uncut wood.

I slipped in a few more dollars. It looked hungry.

He moved on and Dylan came back. He lowered his narrow hips and rocked them back and forth. His balls and cock bounced inside his briefs.

I pulled out my wallet and only twenties were inside. I took one out and waved it at the bartender and then back to Kim and my drinks.

He nodded and returned with change.

Dylan pulled his undies open.

I had to hold myself back from taking his cock out. WOW!

He humped and waited for my money.

I stared, hypnotized by his dick.

Kim patted his ass. "Don't be greedy."

I laughed as he pulled his briefs up and danced down the bar. "Well, I think I should head back to the hotel."

"The night's not over yet, now is it?"

"It's getting late, and I need to get up early."

But before Kim could reply, three men pushed into the bar.

The bouncer yelled, "Hey," but they continued on.

Each man had on a pair of wrap around sunglasses, despite the late hour. All wore black tailor-made suits that molded to their bodies. Black jackets hugged their frames and revealed their muscles.

"You'd better wait a few," Kim's hand touched my arm. "Charles isn't one to tick off."

I sat back down and took a drag on my beer.

The trio walked around the bar and their leader motioned to the stage. "When does the entertainment start?" Charles motioned to his henchmen.

They approached the bar and motioned to the dancers. "Showtime, boys."

Kim looked into her drink, avoiding their stare.

Dylan and Andre slid off the bar and headed to the stage.

"Music," Charles called into the air.

The disco died, and hip hop started.

Andre and Dylan stepped on stage and swung their booties to the beat. Andre slipped his briefs down, showing a cresting moon and a plumber's crack. Their skin glowed in the light, deep rich and mocha sweet.

"We need a woman up there," Charles said, to no one in particular.

None appeared.

He turned to Kim. "Maybe you should get up there."

Kim smiled and shook her head.

He looked over at me and leaned forward. "You came here for something, didn't ya? What didja want?"

Kim turned to face him, as her hand touched my leg.

"I came to see male strippers. That's what the guide said was here on Wednesday nights."

"The finest ones in Baltimore. Come with me." He waited for me to slip off my stool and guided me to the stage. He rubbed his hand up the smooth ebony leg of Andre. "Feel this. See how smooth he is." He grabbed my hand and slapped it against his calf.

His skin was warm with a sheen of oil. So soft and warm, I caressed him even more.

"See, you like it. You can't let go yet." He pulled on the dancer's leg, forcing him to squat. His hand stroked up his thigh and ran over his black underwear. "Oh yes, you'll want to feel this." His hand rubbed over the bulge in front.

Slowly, it grew in length and thickened against the cotton.

"He's a big boy," I said.

"I think it's your turn." Charles turned to me.

"What?" I took my hand and rubbed up the length of Andre's shaft. It seemed to swell under my touch.

"No, I meant for you to join them up there." He pointed to the stage.

"Oh I don't work here. I'm here ..."

"You do now." He waved me to the stage.

"I was just leaving."

"Not until you get what you came for."

"Just let him ..." Kim started.

Charles snapped his fingers. One of his thugs stepped forward and grabbed me.

Kim stood up, "He has nothing to ..."

Pitt grabbed her and held her close.

Bull blocked my path and pointed to the stage.

Dylan and Andre continued to gyrate, concerned looks on their faces.

"He's here, he dances." Charles nodded to Bull.

Bull picked me up and placed me on stage. "Dance."

The opening riff of music for "Push It" came out of the speakers, and I started to stiffly shake my hips.

"Shirt," Charles said, waving his finger up and down my length.

I started to unbutton as my gaze went to Kim.

She mouthed, "Sorry."

My shirt was open halfway, as I pulled it wider to expose my hairy chest. Thick dark hair covered my body, unlike the blond on my head. I pulled the shirt out of my jeans and undid the cuffs.

A Latino man from the bar came over to the dance floor. He stood far away from the three, but watched us.

The rest of my shirt was open, showing my furry six pack. The shirt tales flapped as I moved.

"Push it, push it real good ..."

Charles motioned for me to take my shirt off.

I slipped it off and tossed it to the side.

Dylan moved closer and rubbed his bubble butt against me.

I swiveled and butted him back, sliding up as he squatted down.

Charles motioned for my pants.

Dylan tapped my shoe with his foot.

I knew what he meant. Kicking off my right shoe, I moved across the small stage and sent it flying to my shirt. The left one followed.

Andre danced over to me and leaned back so his pelvis bulged forward.

I mirrored his motion as Dylan came up behind me and reached around, unbuckling my belt.

He slipped the belt open and off before I knew what had happened.

Dylan took the belt and folded it over. He moved around Andre and slapped his booty with the leather. A loud crack against the flesh was heard over the music. He moved around to my ass and did the same thing.

SLAP!

A sharp sting warmed my cheek.

A few more men gathered around, and a dollar was thrown on stage.

Andre reached forward and unzipped my fly.

My cock suddenly swelled as the pressure was released. I didn't even know I was aroused until that happened. Sweat rolled down my back, the lights, the dance, and the nerves stressed my body.

I unbuttoned my waistband and my jeans popped open.

Dylan pulled the back end down and used the belt on my tighty whities. They glowed in the black light. My dick strained against the Egyptian cotton.

Andre slid up and pushed my jeans down one leg.

Dylan followed suit and pushed the other side down. He tapped my ass and held out both of his hands for me to sit down on.

As I sat, Andre pulled my pants off. All three of us danced in our underwear.

Dylan spooned me from behind as I spooned Andre's ass. Our bodies moved as one.

More dollars were thrown on stage. Crumbled balls of bills littered the dance area.

My hard-on sandwiched between Andre's cheeks, as Dylan's slipped along my crack. My cock tingled with each motion. I could feel wetness slip out of my tip and soak into my Calvins.

Dylan's hands reached around my hips and his fingertips explored under the elastic band. They combed through my curly hair and brushed alongside of my shaft. I thought I'd lose the load that boiled in my balls.

A wave of cold water splashed across us. Charles had thrown a drink on us.

My cotton undies turned semi-see through.

Another glass soaked us.

The wet material clung to my shaft, revealing all eight inches.

More money landed at our feet.

"Strip," Charles ordered, as the music morphed into Jermaine Stewart's "We Don't Have to Take Our Clothes Off."

Apparently, we did, to have a good time.

Dylan turned his ass to the crowd and bent over. He wiggled his butt back and forth as he slipped his wet shorts down his long legs. He stepped out and threw them to the side.

Andre did the same thing on the other side of me.

I stood in amazement as these young bucks bared all. Their hard cocks bounced in time with the music. They turned, and both dicks pointed at me as a spot light shown on my groin.

I covered myself as the two men approached. Dylan grabbed from the front as Andre grabbed from behind and ripped my briefs off. A cool breeze flowed through the hair on my balls as my cock slapped my belly.

Dylan dropped to his knees and spread his legs wide, so I could move closer. His tongue licked the tip of my cock, and my back bent, thrusting my ass up.

Andre leaned forward and licked down my open crack.

My spine straightened, and my cock slipped into Dylan's waiting mouth. Andre slipped his tongue into my ass, and they held me trapped between their hot mouths.

My legs couldn't hold me up from the sensory overload. They threatened to release as did my cock. I threw my head back and savored the pleasure.

"… to have a good time, no, no …"

Condoms rained on stage.

"Fuck 'um," Charles demanded.

Dylan tore open a packet and slipped one on my cock. He spit into his hand and quickly put one on his huge dick. He turned me around and nodded at Andre. "You're going to do him."

"What?"

"And I'm going to do you." Dylan slapped my ass.

"WHAT!"

"Just go with it, and no one gets hurt."

Except my ass.

He whispered in my ear. "Charles is dangerous. Don't piss him off."

Andre looked over his shoulder and nodded. He slapped his ass and leaned forward, spreading those muscular cheeks. His bubble butt flexed as his tight hole winked at me.

I stroked my cock and felt the lube on the condom. My finger trailed down his crease and circled his opening.

His ass bounced in time with the music.

Andre rocked back on my finger, and I felt the tip slide in.

"Yeah, stick it in, deeper."

Dylan rubbed his cock up my crack and encouraged me to move closer.

Andre bent forward and pushed back.

I pulled my finger out of him and guided my cock to his crack. I rubbed it up and down, as another downpour of dollars showered over us.

Dylan slapped my ass, and I jumped forward. My fat tip found his tight opening and pressed forward.

A thundering beat filled the room. "Rhythm is a dancer ..."

My pelvis rocked back and forth as did Andre. Our movement synchronized and pumped back and forth. I felt my cock enter him as my body slid forward.

40

The crowd cheered, and inch by inch I filled him.

Dylan's hands grabbed my shoulders as his massive meat slapped my cheeks. It bounced from right to left and finally aimed for the bull's eye. He pelvic thrusted as his feet shuffled across the stage closing the gap between us. I felt his girth explore me.

I felt myself clamp down.

"Relax," Dylan whispered in my ear, his tongue slipped out and entered. Shivers ran down my body, and I could feel warm radiate through me, and my muscles started to relax.

Dylan's dick found the spot and pressed in. He humped my rump as I pushed into Andre. I ping-ponged between them and felt him slip in a little further. His mushroom head was huge and hurt as it tried to pass through the tight opening. He pushed me forward, my cock slid into the hilt of Andre, as my balls bounced off his butt, Dylan slammed into me.

I felt myself stretch beyond where it had ever been before. Pain quickly turned into a warm sensation. His shaved balls bounced off my furry ass and the tiny prickles distracted me further.

The crowd yelled, "Oreo! Oreo!"

My mind flashed to the cookie and wondered why, and then the image of the three of us on stage. So I was the cream filling.

Andre stood up, and I grabbed his shoulders. I had more room to pull out and drive back in. My increased freedom allowed Dylan a larger arc to drill my ass.

The crowd chatted "Oreo!" as we kept in time with the music.

My balls no longer dangled low, slapping Andre's ass. They started to pull up along side of my shaft. I reached around and fondled Andre's huge cock. It was slippery and hot. As my fingers wrapped around it, Andre's whole body jerked.

I almost shot as his ass clamped down on my engorged flesh. I stroked him a few more times and felt him sink back into the beat.

"... feel it everywhere ..."

41

His balls swung and slapped the back of my hand as I jacked his cock. Warm precum oozed down his shaft, making my hand move faster.

Andre rocked his hips like I've never seen. Short, tight humps that intensified all that flowed through my body.

I no longer noticed the crowd, the lights, or the dollars at our feet. All that was left of me was pleasure. Entering and exiting, rolling across my body, through my body, into Andre, into Dylan and back into me.

"I'm going to come," I choked out.

"Wait," Andre said. He moved off my cock and lay on the floor. He spread his legs and started jacking his cock. "Take off the condom and shoot on me."

Dylan didn't wait for me. He pulled the rubber off and threw it over his shoulder. He continued to pound my ass, as his hand stroked my cock. His fingers pulsated and humped harder and faster. He kissed my neck.

As his wet tongue touched my skin, my balls released. A stream of white cum streaked across Andre's smooth chest. The pearly white cream shone against his black skin. As another hot wave shot out of me, rope after rope of cum splashed over him.

Andre's body jerked as his cock exploded. His streams of cum mixed with mine, making a lattice of criss-crossed frosting his torso.

Multiple orgasms washed over my body as Dylan continued to pound into me. My butt clamped down on him and I felt his body tense.

He pulled out of me and ripped off his condom. He jacked his dick, and it erupted like a fireman's hose. Wave after wave sprayed over Andre. Dylan leaned against me as his orgasm wracked his body. A sheen of sweat on his leg made us slip against each other.

The crowd roared and dollar bills rained down on us.

Charles nodded, and his thug released Kim.

Kim reached over the bar and pulled a towel out. She pushed through the crowd and handed it to me.

42

I wiped my cock and handed the towel to Andre.

He quickly cleaned up as I grabbed my clothes and his underwear.

Dylan slipped his shorts on and started to pick up the dollars.

As soon as Andre finished wiping off, he dressed and joined Dylan.

I stepped into my underwear and wrapped my shirt around my back. Despite the hot lights, a chill descended on me. I finished dressing as the last dollar was flattened and bundled.

"We'll give you your share," Dylan said.

"It's yours, keep it," I said.

Kim handed me my beer, and I chugged it down. I didn't realize how dry I was, and the cool, wetness refreshed me. I set the empty bottle on the bar and kissed Kim. "Thanks."

"I'm sorry," she said, as she held me in her embrace.

"Now, I really have to get back to the hotel." I stepped out of Kim's arms and walked down the side of the bar.

Andre and Dylan handed me a wad of bills.

I divided it in half and slid one into each of their briefs. I kissed each on the cheek and continued to the door.

"Wait," Charles said.

I paused at the door and turned to face him.

"We have strippers every night this week," he said.

The crowd cheered, and I left Club Bunns. As I walked back to the hotel, I hoped the next day would fly by, so I could return for round two.

DOOPER AND DANGLE
Mark Wildyr

I seen Dooper down at the old railroad roundhouse this morning. He ain't been around much since the Mayor Dude declared war on graffiti. I don't mind Slick Feathers bashing tag banger gangs or toys or even throw-up guys, but me, I'm a piece artist, and I ain't in no gang. Hell, I'm my own gang. I live for the art, man. The art! I got skill in my work. Damned near half that big mural on the concrete *arroyo* Mayor Dude promoted a few years back is my art. Earned me some fame; local papers run flicks of my stuff.

But that ain't the point. Art's what I do; who I am. I'm Up! I'm All City! Go anywhere in Albuquerque, and you'll see my tag. Even if Mayor Dude gets out an army of uptight volunteers to scrub every fucking neighborhood every fucking week, you'll catch my work if you look for it. Dangle's my sign, but I do it wild style, so nobody who don't read graffiti's got a clue. The handle comes from the way I write with lots of drips. Not the wacky, accidental dribbles a toy makes, but bold drips I draw on purpose.

Dooper's a black kid my own age, but he hangs with a crowd that calls themselves the Highsiders. APD calls them gangsters, but really they's just dudes that like to sling paint. Might be into boosting their spray cans, but who don't? Dooper's a fair writer, hisself, but he ain't as good as me. His real handle's Super Dooper, but it got shortened to Dooper real quick 'cause he ain't as fly as he claims. Before Slick Feathers got his ass reelected Mayor Dude by declaring war on graffiti, I used to trip over Dooper's raggedy ass all the time. We battled more'n once in hard get-up duels with some of the crews acting like judges. Coupla times they fucked up and said his work was better, but mostly they done it right and give me the burn. Got so intense there was some bad blood. We scrapped once, and I give him a mouse, but it looked more like a purple prune on his chocolate skin. Fucker split my lip and wrenched my arm, so I couldn't bomb for a week. I didn't mind that so much, but it put me wrong with the

Highsiders, and some of them dudes is dangerous. Had to watch my back after that.

This morning, he was hitting up a piece on an inside wall of the roundhouse. The big abandoned railroad engine turnaround is a cool place for taggers. Dooper's mural was pretty wild, if you go for old fashioned bubble letters and 3-D styles. Me, I like blockbuster with a little computer mixed in. I do fades and clouds and fly colors when I bomb. Still, old Dooper had technique, sort of.

He slunk out the door when I showed up, so I examined his piece real hard 'cause a couple of colors caught my eye. Like I said, the Highsiders usually racked their paint, but Dooper sure as shit didn't steal Icy Grape and Jungle Green 'cause Krylon don't make them no more. Blended them, likely. Done a good job, too.

I may be all about art, but a guy's got other needs, too ... know what I mean? Truth is I'd like to get together with Dooper. His long legs and bubble butt sorta get to me, and his trousers always looked packed and proud. I can't just come out and tell him that, so I laid a piece back-to-back with the work he done a few minutes ago. Right in the middle I painted this fancied up black butt with a big, white dong stuck up it. Wasn't pornographic or nothing ... at least not to nobody but another tagger. Just so there wasn't no mistake about it, I signed my tag, drips and all!

I'd come out of there peddling my bike funny, my prick riding high and getting in the way. Maybe I'd look up Juanito before heading home. I got in this young Mexican's pants a couple of years back, and him and me still get together every few weeks. First time I seen him, I thought he was a girl ... or a boy. Had this little bowed belly that coulda ended in a weenie or a gash. Turned out to be a sausage. He was a small, whip-thin, full-growed man that just looked like a pretty girl. Whenever we got together, he'd blow me, or I'd fuck his ass.

Sorta feel sorry for Juanito. His culture's got all that machismo bullshit, but that don't mean his buddies don't fuck him, they just mess him up some after they do. He come over a year back beat up so bad I asked why he didn't call the cops. He just grinned the best he could through split lips and told me he got the whole gang ... all eight of them. He fucked or blew every one before they started whaling on him.

After that, I took to wearing a rubber when I was with Juanito. His ass was cute and all that, but it wasn't worth getting AIDS over.

Guess I'm a rainbow sort of guy. Handsomest, buffest, manliest dude I ever seen was an Indian. Met him five years back when I was barely eighteen. Showed up one night when me'n some guys was sitting around a campfire down by the yards swigging beer and swapping lies. Just walked out of the night and plopped his ass down beside us. When the beer played out, we pooled our change and AmerInd, that's what I called him 'cause that's how them anthropolologists or whatever they is labeled his people, donated his last quarter. Before the night was out, everybody flaked out and headed home or to their spider-holes except me'n him. I hung around because I was in love; he probably stayed put because he didn't have nowhere to go.

When AmerInd got drunk enough, I talked him out of his britches and sucked his big, fat cock. Liked that dong better'n any I ever seen before or after. Now you'n me both know a man's jizz ain't sweet ... except AmerInd's was. It was thick and yeasty, and I gulped it down like a vanilla milkshake ... or maybe a strawberry since he was a red man. Afterward, he wouldn't do nothing but jack me off. Done a good job of it, though, except he kept muttering about what a fucking warrior he was. Fact is AmerInd was a mean drunk. I figured he's moved on. Went back to wherever he come from, likely. He wasn't no New Mexico tribesman. Come from Montana or Wyoming or Oklahoma where they grow them big, tall, good-looking Plains Indians.

And now, I was hankering after old Dooper. Brown, red, black. Not bad for a white boy. Course, I hadn't landed the black guy yet, but I wanted him, and that's what counted.

# # # # #

I got me the sweetest setup in the State of New Mexico. A year back, I found this old, abandoned adobe sitting right in the middle of a fallow field in the South Valley and squatted in the dark for a couple of weeks before I fixed up the shack and moved in permanently. Now I had a safe place to stow my piece book and plan out my patterns without nobody bothering me or looking over my shoulder to bite my work before I hit it up someplace.

I slept like a baby that night after seeing Dooper, dreaming about how he was gonna react when he spotted his ass up on the wall with my cock stuck in it. Woke up bright and early, found enough scraps to make a breakfast, and then washed up in the old bathtub. I decided against shaving; hell, my beard was only three days old.

When I wheeled into the roundhouse that morning, Dooper was already there, looking up at my piece with balled fists planted on his hips. That butt I admired was sorta trembling, and I don't think it was from getting hot over my art; hot under the collar maybe. Some glass crunched beneath my boots, and he whirled like he was ready to get it on. I tried to make it casual.

"Lo, Dooper. Wha'cha doing?"

"Reading your filthy work," he snarled, white teeth gleaming. "You're a motherfucker, Dangle! A motherfucking motherfucker!"

"You know what they call that? Redundancy. I remember that from ..."

"Screw you'n your fancy words! What you mean putting that up there like that?"

"You don't like your ass plastered on the wall? Looks good with my cock up it."

I'm an artist and all that, but I never seen so many shades of black. One minute he was standing there, a black man with sort of a mahogany hue, and then he went shoe-polish black. Finally, he aped one a them East Indians that look like they dusted themselves with soot. He wasn't taking this too good.

"Your cock up my ass!" he roared. "Your cock up my ass!" He sputtered, spitting like a housecat caught in the rain. "Your cock up my ass!" He sounded like one of them actor fellas practicing to get a line right.

Don't know what woulda happened if we didn't hear tires scrunching on rocks right then. Cops and Mayor Dude's men make the rounds now and then in a losing battle to keep bums outta the old roundhouse. I still had my bike in my hands, so I high-tailed it out a far door. I don't know what the hell Dooper done, but I didn't really give a rat's ass, neither.

# # # # #

For the next few days I had a weird feeling up and down my bony spine. Got the idea somebody was watching me. Seen a few of Mayor Dude's cars with that city triangle on the side, but it wasn't no authorities making me goosey, so it had to be Dooper or his gang. You'd think a black dude would stand out something fierce, but I never caught sight of hide nor hair. Musta been another Highsider.

Juanito come by one afternoon, so I let him lay me out on the bed. Never quite figured how such a little mouth could swallow so much cock, but he sure done it good. He was kinda hot hisself, and we rested a while, so I could fuck him before he left. Did a bang up job, he claimed. Probably did, too, 'cause I always try my best for a guy.

A couple of mornings after that, a noise outside my door woke me up. I always sleep buff, so I was as naked as the day I squeezed out between my mama's thighs. Old Dooper stood there with a spray can in his right hand, his mouth open in surprise. His eyes had white showing all round them deep brown pupils.

I glanced over my shoulder and seen what he was up to. He'd been bombing. This long, black cock arched up outta a pair of dangling balls and disappeared in some guy's mouth ... a white mouth. My mouth. He hadn't fancied it up or nothing. Anybody, but anybody who seen it would know what it was. Shit, I done him the courtesy of camouflaging it with graffiti. Course, maybe he would've, too, if I hadn't caught him in the middle of it.

I come to my senses in time to dodge the paint he sprayed at me. Knocking the can from his hand, I grabbed his ratty shirt and jerked him inside. When the door slammed shut, I whirled to ask him what in the hell he thought he was doing? I guess he figured I was coming for him 'cause he lit into me, arms, knees, and elbows churning!

I act tough, but I ain't no street fighter. Can't keep from closing my eyes when I see something coming! Old Dooper was a battler, and

49

he give me everything he had, and then some. I knew I was in trouble in thirty seconds flat. He was mad and wasn't gonna give me no break. One set of bony knuckles caught me on the chin and another whopped me up side the head. He musta grown another arm, 'cause a third set slugged me right in the belly. I went down for real.

I couldn't a been out more'n a minute or so, but when I got SOS I knew where I was again, my naked ass was tied to the bed, belly down. I shook the cobwebs outta my eyes and fixed on my right arm. He'd lashed me to the bed frame with my clothesline. My clothesline! He cut up my freaking clothesline! Then I figured out my legs was spread real wide, lashed to opposite sides of the bed. Didn't take a Wall Street lawyer to figure out what was going down.

"Now wait a minute, bro! You can't do this! I never done nothing to you!"

He shifted to where I could see him, and I took in a long expanse of gleaming black flesh. Shit, his butt wasn't the only thing sexy about him. He had a good chest. Something on him moved. Oh, shit! It looked like a fucking black Mamba rising up out of a nest of kinky curls to point a big, blind eye right at me. Motherfucker kept on growing. Sheeeit!

"You put my butt right up on the wall with your skinny dick fucking it," he snarled. "I figure you get the chance, you gonna leave your puny, white skag up there. 'Sides, I ain't your bro. I'm your worst nightmare, motherfucker!"

"Dooper, you can't ..."

The shit he couldn't! He crawled between my legs, and I let out a squall that lifted the tin roof. He didn't do no foreplay or nothing; he just parted my cheeks with his big hands and lunged. My butt was on fire! My bowels was probed, man! Fucked! Violated! Plumbed by a big rod of red-hot steel. He shoved again, and the rest of it went up my ass. I couldn't help it, I wiggled my body out of sheer pain, but all it done was get his mind offa hurting and onto fucking. He settled down to rocking and rolling. And that dude could do both. He pulled it all the way out, parted my ass cheeks, and sent it home again with a loud grunt.

You know what? It didn't hurt so bad no more. Can't say I liked it, but it sure felt strange ... strange good, sorta. About three seconds later, I changed my mind. Fuck your Aunt Millie, I did like it! He rubbed something mighty sensitive up inside me every time he done the rumba on my backside. The fucking bastard knew how to do it! Pretty soon, I started raising up my butt to meet him.

"You like it? You like a cock up your ass? Din' never have one so good before did you?"

"N ... never had any!" I grunted, trying to put some anger in it.

"Don't give me that shit!" he gasped. His voice took on a labored quality. "You been prissing 'round trying to hook me for a long time now."

"Trying ... fuck ... your ... ass!" I groaned my words between his strokes. Man, something was happening down there. My balls was zinging! My ass was singing! And my cock was playing fiddle on the blanket. Shit! I was gonna come! Come while this wild dude fucked my ass!

Didn't happen. Dooper let out a whoop, and black snake grew a half inch as he unloaded in my ass. Then he fell over on top of me, his cum shooting up my shit hole while he laid dead still across my back. It squirted and squirted and then settled down to oozing. He didn't move a muscle, but the Mamba started crawling outa my channel. Dooper might fuck good, but when it was over, it was over!

After my breathing got easier, I started to get mad. Maybe it was 'cause I'd been cheated out of my own gasm ... and it felt like it was gonna be a nut cracker. Or maybe it was 'cause sure as shit he'd brag up what he done. All the fucking Highsiders'd know about it. Hell, they might even come looking for some of the same. Or maybe it was just 'cause I didn't like being assfucked after all, but my blood started rising.

"Get off me, you motherfucker," I said in a low voice, butting his groin with my ass. "You get the fuck out of here. I get loose, I'm gonna kill you!"

"Don't see how," he said lazily. "I took you fair and square."

51

"Took me by surprise," I said, bumping his groin again. "Fair fight, I'd take you clean."

"You ain't no fighter, Dangle. I din't even work up a sweat ... 'cept on your ass."

Suddenly angry, I twisted my whole body, dumping him on the floor. Mistake. He got up and started slapping at me.

"You son of a bitch!" I yelped. "I'll tell everybody you like to fuck man-ass! I'll ..."

I don't know what else I was gonna do, 'cause he whopped me a good one right on the temple and night time come crashing down in the middle of the morning.

#####

It musta been some time before I come to. When I opened my eyes, the sun was coming in the west window right square in my face. I moved ... and groaned. My muscles was sore, and my bung hole hurt. Rats! Dooper had fucked me! Still flat on my belly, I rolled over and set up. At least the fucker untied me before he left. I'd kill the son-a-bitch when I seen him again. I started to get up, but fell back on the bed when a shadow moved.

The motherfucker was still here! Naked and black as a raven, he leaned against the wall in the corner of the room, looking down his nose at me. My adrenalin started flowing. I come offa the bed and took him by surprise. Guess he figured I was still groggy or weak or something. Barreling into him, I mashed him flat against the wall. Don't know why his spine didn't break, but it didn't. He got his wind back fast and started whupping on me. He backed me clear across the room. I might be a better tagger, but he sure as shit was the better fighter. I got downright scared. He beat me so easy before, wasn't no doubt what was gonna happen this time. He was hurting me with them bony knuckles.

Desperately, I sacrificed an old kitchen chair I'd bought for two dollars at a yard sale, splintering it to smithereens right over the top of his head. Son of a bitch staggered, shook his head, and started for me again. But he was hurt, so I had time to take a chair leg, only piece I

52

still held in my hands, and slam it across his ribs. Something popped real loud, and he reeled back onto the bed. I run for the door, but hesitated when he didn't get up and take after my butt. Besides, I was buck naked! He'd flopped belly down on the mattress, black ass shining at me. I shrugged off enough of my terror to edge over to him, careful to keep outta range of them long, ropy arms.

"Dooper?"

"Uhhh," he groaned. He made like he was gonna move, but that petered out, so I got braver. I poked him with a finger. He mumbled something. Figuring it was payback time, I used them same binds he'd made me helpless with to lash him to the bed. He didn't even try to fight me off.

"Dooper, you son of a bitch, you gonna get yours! I whupped your ass, now I'm gonna fuck it like you done mine. You gonna get fucked!"

He tried to struggle, but didn't put much into it, so I walked around to where he could see me and played with myself till I was hot and hard. It felt good when I crawled between his knees. I rubbed my throbbing cock all up and down that long satiny crack till I thought I was gonna come before I ever got it in. Had to rest a minute to cool off, so I took to swatting at his head and calling him names. He took it. Didn't put up no fuss at all. Figured he was beat fair and square, I guess.

Dooper let out a strangled yelp when I pulled his ass cheeks apart and laid my dick to his pucker string. Tried to wiggle out of it, but I shoved again, and just like that, his muscle parted. I slid right up that dark channel. Don't know if it was 'cause I had to fight so hard to get at it or what, but that was the best silk purse I ever stuck it in. When I was buried to the hilt, I laid down over his back and rested to keep from losing it too soon like I done the first time I fucked a gal when I was fifteen. She never even talked to me again.

But old Dooper was gonna get a royal fucking from the best damned tagger in the county! I started out slow. Real slow. Then I built up a head of steam and plowed his ass good. He must shit king-sized turds, cause that hole was plenty big. Slick. Slippery. Hot, hot, hot! Whenever I was about to lose it, I'd stop and drape over him like a bedspread to cool my nuts. Then I'd take after it again. Dooper never did get into it, never butted me with his ass like I done him. He just let out a groan now and then. When I got so close I couldn't stop, I really laid into him. This was one fucking the dude wasn't never gonna forget.

And then I shot my balls. I knew it was coming, but it was so good it still caught me by surprise. My nuts drew up like they was climbing inside me. My toes curled. My fingers bit into his arms. I spread my legs wide so they was riding the inside of his. I was in contact, man! A close encounter of another kind! It went on so long I was trembling like a man with Parkinson's or whatever that shimmy shit is called. I stopped being mad and figured Dooper was the best pal I had in the universe … if he didn't get up and kill my ass when I turned him loose. With that sobering thought, I figured I'd better mend some fences.

"Dooper, that was some ride, man. We cool now? You know … even Steven?"

He went stubborn and wouldn't talk. I butted him with my half-shriveled cock. He just laid there. Plotting his revenge, probably. I raised up and looked over his shoulder. His eyes was half closed. His mouth was open, and there was blood trickling out of it.

What the shit? I come off him like a shot, my old cock slick and slippery and hanging at half-mast. But I wasn't worried about it right then. I took a closer look. Dooper was out of it … bad. He was breathing all right, but he was gone somewhere in la-la-land. When I bent over to take closer look, a gout of blood gushed out of his mouth. I stumbled backwards, jabbing my ass on the corner of the kitchen table.

Man, the fucker was hurt! I remembered the snap when I waylaid him with the chair leg. A rib! Bet I busted a rib! Then I bounced up and down on top of him for twenty fucking minutes … or twenty minutes fucking. Damn, old Dooper was in a bad way!

I tore around the place getting my clothes on and yelling I'd get him some help. But I come to a dead halt at the door. What the fuck would the cops think? Shit! The dude had my cum up his ass. The place was a wreck from where we'd been fighting. We was both beat black and blue and bloody. And this fucking, fat, black cock was painted right smack on the door. Not only that, but I had all my paints and supplies in the house. They was gonna bag the two biggest taggers in the state and a couple of assfucking perverts all in the same haul.

What was I gonna do? Dooper needed help bad! After about fifteen seconds, I hit that room like a tornado ripping through it. My best paints, the piece book with my plans and designs in it, and a few clothes was all I could salvage. Stowing them in my bike's saddlebags, I tore off down the road for the nearest pay phone.

I blurted out that somebody needed help and told them where before slamming down the receiver and racing back to watch from an apple orchard across from my place. Seemed like it took forever, but after a while, a black-and-white crawled down the driveway and drifted to a stop. Two cops, one thin with a doughnut of spare flesh around his beltline, the other with a respectable beer-belly, got out and approached the place with hands on their pieces. They jabbered over the prick painted on my door before finally going inside. Shit! I'd forgot to untie Dooper; his ass'd be staring them right in the face.

A little later, an ambulance come down the drive at a snail's pace like it had all the time in the world, and that worried me some. Maybe old Dooper was dead meat. But when they hauled him out on that stretcher thing they use, he was covered with a sheet except for his head, so he was still breathing. As soon as they took off with the siren wailing, I headed out.

Albuquerque was done for me now; I was in big trouble. Mayor Dude had my fingerprints from when I was busted for tagging four years ago. They had Dooper's ass to show I raped him. And they had lots of my paints and custom tips. Not only that, but I'd forgot my stash of weed and the meth tabs I keep for when I need a lift. I was baked chicken around here, and that didn't even take the Highsiders into consideration. They'd beat a war drum before they come hunting me.

I pedaled my bike through the unlighted back alleys until I got out of the south valley. They wasn't so many lanes behind the houses on the east side, so I had to take to the roads. Ever time a car come up behind me, my skin crawled like it was a cop riding my ass. Yeah, I was burned in Albuquerque … probably in the whole damned state.

Too bad. I liked it here. Got hot, but like they say, it's a dry heat. Didn't bother me none. And the winters was good. But the cops here ain't queer-friendly, and that's what they'd figure I was. Shit, guess I am, come to think on it. Been three years since I diddled a gal. Man, I sure hoped old Dooper come outta this all right. I sorta liked his black ass. But that's the way it goes, I guess. Wonder where I'll end up, and what adventures I'll find when I get there.

One thing about it. I got my art to live for wherever the fuck I end up.

GANG SLAVE
Christopher Pierce

Anyone who thinks men aren't animals hasn't been the sex slave of a gang before. I had degrees in anthropology and sociology and actually believed that men were noble creatures, more advanced and evolved than lowly animals.

I was wrong, and I learned my lesson well.

It all started when I moved into an overlap zone without knowing it. Everyone knew that gangs controlled most of the areas in the city. I knew it better than most, because I had been on the city's negotiating team and had dealt with the gangs close up. After lengthy talks with us, the urban warriors had agreed not to hurt citizens, as long as the different gangs' territories were clearly marked. When the gangs stayed out of each other's way and in their own areas, everything was fine, and the city went on like normal.

It was the overlap zones that were a problem. Overlap zones were the areas where gang ownership was still in dispute, and the different groups would fight to establish dominance in those parts of the city. The overlap wars were fast and brutal, over before law enforcement could stop them.

Citizens were still safe, as long as they stayed out of the overlap zones. But everything that was caught in a zone became gang property including people.

I was out of town when the warnings hit. I didn't have a phone in my car, so there was no way any of my friends could tell me. While I was on my way home from a business trip, my neighborhood had been declared an overlap zone. So anxious to get home, I barely noticed that my building seemed deserted. I wanted to drop off my stuff and hit the gym. Proud of my body, I wanted to keep it in shape.

When I got into my condo, I opened the window and then pulled my e-mail up on my computer. I saw the flashing urgent message instantly. The e-mail warned me that I was now in an overlap zone. My blood froze, and I knew I had to get out of there right then. But before I reached the door it slammed open and what I saw framed in the doorway caused me to stumble backwards and fall on my ass.

A man stood there, with another one on either side. He was not tall, but had a bare built-up chest that made him look like a bodybuilder. Between his pectorals was tattooed the interlocking circle symbol of the Centurion gang.

The two men at his side were taller and looked sub-human. Their chests were also tattooed with the symbol. Even without the guns hanging from their belts, these three men would have terrified me. I knew them, and they knew me.

They walked in like they owned the place, slamming and locking the door behind them. Their eyes were predatory as they looked at me.

"We've been waiting for you." The leader in the middle said. "Is there anyone else here, boy?"

For a second I thought about saying there was someone else there. But I didn't know how bad this was going to be, and lying to them could only make it worse.

"No." I said quietly, as I started to stand up. Instantly one of the men rushed forward and smacked me across the face, hurling me back down onto the floor. I guessed I was staying there for the time being.

"'No, sir!'" he hissed like a snake. The leader regarded me impassively, the slightest flicker of his eyebrow his only expression. My cheek was throbbing where I had been hit.

"Yes, sir," I said submissively. I didn't try to stand up again.

"You have a new name now, boy. It's Hole. You got that?"

"Yes, sir." I said, my mind reeling with the fact that I had been trapped by the Centurions and was bound to being their property unless I could find some way out of this.

"Hole needs to be broken in, guys," the leader said. The two men with him grinned and walked forward, unlocking their belts and dropping their pants to the floor. My eyes darted down to where the clothing fell, guns fastened to their belts. The weapons were only a feet away from me. I could have grabbed them if ...

"Lock him." the Centurion leader said. One of the guys yanked a pair of handcuffs off his belt.

"Get your hands behind your back, Hole," he said. I must have hesitated too long, because the other man kicked me in the stomach. All the air rushed out of me in a whoosh, and I staggered forward onto my chest.

"Yes, sir ..." I said helplessly as I put my hands behind me. Planting one boot between my shoulder-blades, the guy with the cuffs snapped them around my wrists and locked them together. Then he grabbed my hair and yanked me back up to my knees. I let out a yelp of pain and fear, and the gang members laughed.

"Don't worry, Hole," the leader said. "You'll get used to it. You're Centurion property now."

Then one of the guys stepped forward towards me. He had ratty blond hair that was pulled back in a pony-tail. His eyes were dark and mean. He turned around and thrust his ass in my face. I started to back up when I heard the leader's voice.

"Take care of my man, Hole. Clean his ass."

"Yes, sir," I said helplessly. Closing my eyes, I plunged my face towards the guy's butt. It was rank and nasty, but I had my orders – everyone knew the Centurions were not to be argued with. I stuck my tongue out and started working him, licking up and down the inner sides of his buttcheeks. I stroked them up and down, leaving trails of moist slimy spit. Bits of his ass hair worked loose into my mouth, gagging me. I couldn't believe it, but my dick was getting hard. Could it be that I liked what was happening? Was it possible? I could feel the warm bulge in my pants getting bigger and bigger. Something in me was responding to this crude, rough treatment.

But it was crazy. A few minutes ago I had a normal life, a good job ... and now I was the sex slave of an urban gang. My life was going to be utterly changed. If I wasn't killed by the gang members, I would become their permanent possession, used and abused by them until the end of my days.

None of it mattered. My cock was hard and wanting attention. I could feel my responsibilities and troubles falling away from me as I rimmed the man's ass, running my tongue around the edge of his asshole. Everything about my life that I couldn't stand, none of it mattered any more. No more taxes, no more long hours at work, no more empty condo with no boyfriend ... now all there was were the Centurions, and my only task was to be their slave.

Was this what I wanted? Was it possible? How could these men treat me so brutally? Didn't they know that intellect and reason were what separated us from the animals? Didn't they know that years of study and research and history had proven that violence and war didn't solve problems that they only made them worse?

But none of that mattered. These angry dangerous men were the ones in power, not me. I, with my college degrees and my intellect and my three-piece business suit, was the one on the floor with my hands cuffed together and my face in a guy's ass.

I stuck my tongue into his asshole, and he grunted in pleasure.

"Yeah, that's it, Hole, you're doing good. You're a born slave ..."

Sticking my tongue in further and massaging his tunnel with it was my answer. I could feel his body start to twitch and shiver. I knew he was jerking his cock off and that he was almost ready to come.

Then his ass pulled away from me, and he whipped his body around to face me.

"Open up, Hole, time for your first load." Precum was leaking out of his shaft as he pumped it. I knew it was going to explode any second. The other gang member grabbed the back of my head and forced me forward, my mouth taking in the blond one's big cock.

Thick torrents of sticky jizz spurted from him and shot down my throat. I gagged and swallowed, trying to get it all down. Before he was even done the other one pulled me towards him.

He had dark short hair and scrapes and bruises all over his face. He must have been in a fight earlier.

"My turn to use you, Hole," he said, and forced his uncut pecker between my lips. "Suck me good or we'll waste your ass."

I didn't have any choice, but I would have done it even if I hadn't been their prisoner. It was like I had found my calling in life. I knew what I wanted to do now, for the first time in my life. I wanted to serve these men, to take care of them in any way they wanted.

That dick worked its way into me like a snake sliding into a hole in the ground. The dark haired guy started reaming my mouth really hard, as if he was fucking my ass, sliding in and out with ferocious energy. He mumbled under his breath as he did it.

"Yeah, Hole, that's all you are, just a hole for us to fuck, all your holes are ours, your mouth and your ass, they're the same thing to us, you're just a hole for us to use ..."

My cock was straining against my pants. It was so totally hot to get used this way, like a piece of meat by these hot horny men. But my hands were securely bound behind my back. The metal cuffs were starting to cut the skin of my wrists.

I swallowed the precum of the dark-haired guy. I choked and gagged, trying to keep his cock in my mouth and still breathe. If he hadn't been holding my head in place, I would've fallen backwards from the force of his assault. He had to be getting close, he had stopped muttering and now was grunting and groaning like a bull in heat.

Then it happened, and he squirted his load deep into me. It was different from the first guys cum that had been thick and sticky. This man's cum was thin and liquidy, pouring out like water from a faucet. I gulped and swallowed, knowing there'd be hell to pay if I spilled any of it. Swallowing the delicious jizz down was fucking hot, and I loved it.

Suddenly there was a loud noise from the hallway outside my front door. Instantly the gang members crouched low on the floor. I imitated them, dropping down and lying on my stomach.

"It's the fucking Dragons," the leader said, speaking of their rival gang. "They're here already. Killing time, guys."

The men that had used me yanked their pants up and pulled their guns off their belts. All of their attention was on the door.

"They're right outside," the leader whispered. "They're going to try to jump us. Get ready ..."

Suddenly there was a deafening roar from the other side of the room. There were flashes of bright light, and suddenly the three Centurions slumped forward onto the floor – with gaping bullet holes in their backs.

I wanted to stay silent, but couldn't help letting out a moan of fear and alarm. They were dead, I knew instantly. I turned to look in the direction the noise and light came from.

Climbing in through the window came three men. They were similar to the Centurions, but these men had dragon-like serpents tattooed on their bare chests.

The first one into the room was short and beefy. His smoking gun raised, he ran over to the fallen warriors and checked them out.

"History," he said, and the other two climbed in. In this crew, it was a tall man that was the leader. Skinny and pale, with short buzz-cut red hair, he grinned at me. I must have been quite a sight ... a terrified young man with dark blond hair in a business suit with his hands cuffed behind his back.

"Looks like the Centurions didn't waste any time," one of the other guys said.

"No," said the leader. "And neither will we. Come here, boy ..."

So scared I almost pissed my pants, I couldn't because my dick was so hard. I wanted to resist but knew it was impossible, especially after seeing what these men were capable of. Struggling to my knees, I bowed my head submissively and started to move towards the grinning man.

He put his gun back in its place on his belt and loosened his buckle. A second later his fly fell open and a monster cock shot out. It looked primed and ready for action, as if killing the Centurions had aroused him.

"That's it, good boy ..." he said, sneering. His other men were taking the dead Centurions' guns and searching through their clothes.

With one hand the Dragon leader grabbed me by my cuffed wrists and yanked me to my feet and I cried out in pain. He hit me across the face, and I shut up. Unfastening my belt and ripping my pants open, he tore them down to expose my naked butt.

I started groaning then, a low guttural cry of fear and humiliation. The leader just grinned and spit on his dick, getting it nice and greased up. Then he went behind me and stuck his cock up my ass. I cried out, and he covered my mouth with one hand.

The other Dragons turned to watch, pulling out their dicks and starting to jack themselves off. The organ in my hole felt like it was on fire, pulsing and thrusting inside me.

"You'll get used to it, slave," the leader said. "You're Dragon property now. We've been planning this for a long time, and now you're finally mine, Mr. Negotiator."

He started pumping me really hard then, and I felt my heart sink as I realized I had been set up from the beginning. The gangs were never serious about the negotiations; they just wanted to get their hands on me.

Soon enough I felt his cock shoot off inside, pummeling my glutes with cum. The other men shot off, too, spilling their cum all over the floor as they howled at the ceiling. The sound was primitive, savage, and brutal. That was when I realized that these men were animals.

And when the Dragon leader grabbed my own throbbing cock and jerked me off so hard that my spunk shot out of me, I knew that I was, too.

HOUSE CALL
H.L. Champa

I walked through the automatic doors of the hospital, enjoying the feeling of being out of my scrubs. Reaching into my pocket, I pulled my last cigarette out of the pack, lighting it with my worn-out book of matches. I exhaled smoke into the night sky and rubbed the bridge of my nose roughly between my fingers. It was so quiet outside the hospital; a far cry from the insanity that was just behind the doors. But, the booming bass of an approaching Cadillac Escalade interrupted my peace. The full tinted glass didn't let me see inside, but I had a good idea who it was. The front window descended, and I saw his face appear from the darkness.

"You know, those things will kill ya, Doc."

"So, I've heard. Thanks for the tip. What do you want, Vince?"

"What, I can't come and visit an old friend?"

"No. What do you want?"

I took a deep drag from my cigarette and deliberately blew it his way. He still looked so good. It had been over a year since he had last made an appearance in my life, but my stomach flipped over at his dimpled grin.

"We need a favor, Paulie."

"Really, what could the DeMarco family possibly need from me?"

"Nicky needs a doctor right away."

I tamped out the butt of my smoke against the dirty concrete. Vince stared at me, his fingers drumming quickly on the steering wheel. His impatience should have made me move faster, but it didn't.

"Gosh, Vin, if only there was a place you could take Nicky to get him some medical attention."

I pointed to the doors with my thumb, eliciting a laugh from inside the car. He pointed at me, snapped his fingers and winked. It was a gesture I'd seen many times before; usually after I told a particularly bad joke.

"We need it to be a bit more discreet than that, if you know what I mean. Like last time. We can make it worth your while."

"I'm sure you can. But, that's hardly the point."

"Sure. I forgot. The great doctor doesn't care about money. You're a saint, is that it?"

I sighed and looked at the ground, my mind conflicted. After the last house call Vince had coerced me into, I wasn't too keen to get involved with that side of his "family business" again. But, that night had reinforced one thing. I never could say no to him.

"Give me a minute, to get a few things. I'll be right back."

"Thanks, Paulie. We won't forget this, I promise."

# # # # #

I sat in the back seat of the SUV, between two huge men in black suits. If they hadn't been so scary looking, it would have been funny as hell. They were all something out of a movie, a long-held stereotype that was alive and well in my hometown. Vince and I had grown up together, our lives intertwined for years and years. Everyone knew who his father was, and what the "family business" really meant. No restaurants, clubs, or bars they fronted hid what was really going on. While I went off to medical school and my real life, he became exactly what we all knew he would, right down to the pinkie ring and black suit. I glanced up and caught his eyes in the rearview mirror, staring back at me in the dark.

"Don't worry, Doc. We'll have you back in no time."

"That's very kind of you, Vin. So, now can you tell me what's wrong with Nicky?"

I was shocked when he laughed, his head shaking as he filled the car with his powerful voice.

"Dumb ass shot himself in the leg."

"Jesus. Are you serious, Vin? He could be bleeding to death right now and you're laughing."

"That's why I came to you. I knew you were the guy to fix him up. You took care of me, and my bullet hole was way worse. This should be easy for ya."

I didn't bother to push him for further details about how Nicky was, knowing it wouldn't do any good. He pulled into the parking lot of a warehouse, the only building around for miles. I had driven past it before, but barely noticed it. In other words, the perfect location for Vince's business. He pulled the car up to the door with a screech and his entourage got out. I followed, not knowing what else to do, trailing behind Vince into the wide-open space. There, in the corner on a couch, was Nicky. He looked pale, and one leg of his pants was soaked with blood.

I started to move towards him, until I was stopped by another huge mountain of a man that appeared from nowhere. He grabbed my bag and turned me around, pressing me against a pillar with his forearm. Vince stopped walking long enough to notice and run back to save me.

"Jesus, Dom. Calm the fuck down. He's the doctor, you moron."

"Sorry, boss. Force of habit. Besides, he don't look like a doctor."

He let me free, picking up my bag and straightening out my clothes with his huge, meat hook hands. I looked around and saw all eyes on me, everyone glaring at me as Vince worked to defuse the situation.

"Careful, Dom. You keep that up, and the Doc just might ask you for your number."

Dom's hands disappeared from the collar of my shirt after the taunt, clearly more fearful of my preference for men than any wire I may be wearing. He recoiled as if I was on fire, his eyes moving over me with disbelief.

"Christ, Vin. You had to bring Nicky a queer doctor. You sure do keep some interesting company."

"Relax, Dom. Paulie would never be into you. You're not his type. Besides, he's a friend. Someone we can trust, if you catch my drift?"

Dom didn't say another word and let me past to get a better look at Nicky and his gunshot wound. He looked limp on the couch, but I could see his chest moving slowly as he labored to breathe. Vince hovered over me as I opened my bag and retrieved some gloves and a scissors. Cutting away the grey wool of his pants, I came to the wound, a small trickle of blood running down his leg before I could cover it with gauze. Vince paced, trying to put on an air of calm for his crew, but it wasn't really working.

"So, Paulie, what's the verdict?"

I continued to examine Nicky, trying to ignore the prying eyes and the stares of half the DeMarco family muscle that filled the warehouse.

"Vin, get over here and hold this gauze while I get my supplies ready."

"You want me to do what?"

"You heard me. Just hold this gauze tight to the wound. You want me to help him, don't you?"

He dropped his suit jacket, rolled up his sleeves and gingerly put his hand over mine, pressing down on the bloody cloth. As I tried to pull my hand away, Vince held me still, his fingers curling around mine for just a second's worth of contact. Our eyes met, but when one of the flunkies behind us cleared his throat, Vince let go and pushed my hand away. The tingles that ran down my spine caught me off guard, my reaction out of proportion to what had really happened. I dug into my bag, finding the syringe of antibiotics I had "borrowed" from the hospital. Jamming it into his good leg, Nicky finally stirred as his face registered the pain. He looked down at me and Vince, his eyes still half-closed and glassy.

"Paulie, is that you?"

"Yup, it is. Well, Nicky, you are a lucky guy. Looks like the bullet went clean through, so once we sew you up, you should be fine. Next time, aim a little better, okay? Vince, I want you to ease off the wound, slowly."

I nodded at him, and he moved his hand back, revealing the hole in Nicky's leg. There was no time for anesthetic, but somehow I didn't think he would mind too much. Vince, however, had to turn his eyes away as I did my best patch-up job I could on Nicky's shredded wound. I knew I shouldn't say a word, but I couldn't resist having a little fun with him.

"You gonna be okay, big guy? What's the matter, you don't like blood?"

"Shut the fuck up, Paulie. I'm fine. Just finish what you're doing, and we can get you out of here. And, get this dumb ass home."

As I wrapped Nicky's stitches in fresh gauze, Vince walked a few steps away and conferred with one of his henchmen. I couldn't hear what they were saying, but their faces were serious as hell. For the first time, I noticed the gun tucked into Vince's waistband, and the holsters on all his compatriots. His head snapped back towards me, his expression angry and impatient.

"You about done, Doc?"

"I'm finished. Just make sure he takes one of these pills twice a day until they are gone. If he gets a fever or the wound isn't healing, let me know."

I handed Vince the orange bottle who in turn handed it to the huge guy waiting next to him. I tried not to watch as two huge guys gathered Nicky up and dragged him past us and out the door.

"Come on; let me get you back to your car."

Vince seemed to be in a hurry to get rid of me, not even giving me a chance to clean up the mess Nicky's injuries had left behind. He slammed the metal door shut, locking the padlock that kept the contents secure. We got going without a word, the SUV rumbled over the rough gravel parking lot until we hit the deserted road. Looking down at my hands in the dark, I finally noticed they were shaking. I reached into my pocket, searching for a cigarette to calm my frayed nerves.

"Can I smoke in here?"

"No you can't. I told you already, that shit is bad for you."

"Forgive me if I don't want to take advice on how to stay healthy from you."

"What the hell is that supposed to mean?"

Without thinking, I reached over towards him and put my hand on the gun in his pants. Then, before he could stop me, I moved my hand over the place I had stitched up over a year ago. The scar it left on my mind was just as profound as the one I left on his stomach. I could still see the look on his face when he showed up on my doorstep, bloody and scared out of his mind. I had barely managed to save him that night.

He grabbed my wrist, pulling the SUV to the side of the road without letting me go. We sat in the dark, his fingers hurting me, but I didn't try to pull away.

"You think getting shot is good for you or Nicky?"

"Hazard of the job. You know that."

"Then, maybe you need a new job."

"Very funny, Doc. This isn't a job, it's my life. There's no changing that."

He looked down, his eyes avoiding mine for the first time all night. They came to rest on our hands, still locked together by his iron grip. Before I could stop it, another smart remark came to my lips.

"You might want to let go of my hand. I mean, what would Dom say?"

He laughed, but didn't let go, his fingers moving to lace through mine instead of retreating all together.

"Sorry about that. He's not very enlightened, as you can imagine. Did I offend you, Paulie?"

"No. But, how do you know he's not my type?"

"I'm pretty sure you told me many years ago that you weren't into wiseguys."

"I'm not. That's why I like you so much."

He yanked me closer, his hand leaving mine to grab a handful of my T-shirt. His eyes bore into me, his piercing stare no longer scary or ominous. It was the Vince that no one else saw; the Vince that only I got to be with. The one I thought was long gone.

"So, you still have a little thing for me, huh Doc?"

"Damn it, Vin. You know I do."

His kiss was whisper soft, the heat of his mouth bringing back the welcome memories of our misspent youth. In some ways, it was just as thrilling to taste his mouth in that moment, as it was when we were fifteen. Our secret had lived for years, until his "family" obligations made it too risky. It was obvious from the time we were kids that guys like Dom wouldn't be the only one who had a problem with us being together. He pulled back, his forehead resting on mine for a moment before looking at me again.

"Paulie, thanks for helping us out tonight. I really appreciate it."

"Oh, God. Is this the part where you tell me the 'family' owes me?"

"No. I owe you. And, I think I know how I can repay you."

Vince kissed me hard, removing his gun from his waistband and placing it in the console before opening the door and getting into the backseat.

"Are you going to stay up there all by yourself, Doc?"

I got out into the night, taking a few deep breaths of moist air before joining him. The door closed with a thud, the backseat so much more spacious without two huge Italian guys in it. This time, there was just one, and I didn't mind being close to him. Our mouths met, our tongues mingling and blending in a deeply familiar way.

He made quick work of the button-fly of my jeans. Putting his hand in my boxers, he wrapped his fist gently around my cock, which was already half hard. I groaned at the contact, my eyes locked with Vince's. He jerked me slowly while his other hand massaged my thigh, my hips rising and falling without conscious thought. I leaned forward, stealing another deep kiss before falling back against the leather seats. When he dragged his thumb over my weeping slit, I bit my lip harder than I needed to.

Vince smiled and winked at me, before leaning over to wrap his lips around the head of my cock. I stared in silence as he moved his mouth up and down over my cock. It had been so long since I had seen him that way; felt him that way. His eyes were closed; his stifled moans caused his lips to vibrate, sending shock waves through my body. As much as I wanted to keep looking at Vince and his mouth moving over me, I let my eyes fall closed and my head hit the back of the seat. My hands fisted his hair, the dark brown strands wrapping easily around my fingers. I was surprised when he let me push him down; control him for just a few moments. In typical Vince fashion, I didn't last long. Despite my insistent hands, he started setting his own agenda, ignoring my silent pleas for more.

After just a few strokes, he had me right on the edge, teetering on the brink of coming right in his mouth. His slow, deliberate pace inched me closer, each sweeping pass of his tongue was a new slice of exquisite torture. Part of me wanted to try to stop him, to hold onto the feeling for a little while longer, but it was beyond me at that point.

"Vince, I'm going to come."

He didn't speed up, just kept sucking me maddeningly slow, tightening a fist around the base of my cock, jerking in time with his pulling mouth. I moaned in the quiet of the car, my own voice sounding foreign to my ears. My cock jumped and trembled uncontrollably, my muscles all tensing and shifting at once. I felt my hot come fill his mouth, his tongue lapping up every last drop. Finally, my body calmed, Vince's mouth slowing until it was barely moving at all. His lips left me spent, my heart no longer trying to leap out of my chest.

He leaned back, but didn't stay still for long. He practically tore his shirt open, his old wound staring me right in the face. This time, I touched his bare skin, my fingers trailing over the thick stitch marks, my sloppy work leaving him more mangled than I should have.

"I really made a mess out of you, didn't I?"

"Nah, it's fine. Besides, scars are sexy, aren't they, Doc?"

"I might be a little biased towards yours. I don't think Nicky's will have the same affect."

He kissed me, his hands on his belt buckle. I held my breath as he pulled his pants and boxers down, his cock springing forward. It was beautiful, thick and darker than the rest of his olive skin. Just as perfect as I remembered. The flared tip begged to be licked, and I was unable to stop myself any longer.

I cast one last look up into his eyes, now glazed with desire. My tongue ran along the ridge of his cock head, softly teasing until I closed my mouth around him. His loud gasp startled me. He had always been so quiet with me before, for fear of being caught. As I moved his cock deeper into my throat, moan after moan rang out around us. I heard his ragged breath, his pleasure clearly overwhelming him. Vince wrapped a strong hand around my neck, pushing himself deeper still, until he bumped the back of my throat.

"Don't stop, Paulie. God, please don't stop."

I had no intention of stopping, not until I got to taste him the way he tasted me. His grip loosened, but his hips continued thrusting forward, fucking my face more than I was sucking him off. I didn't care, I like him controlling me. Taking every inch of him, swirling my tongue around his thick head each time he pulled out. He was babbling, words falling from his mouth so fast I couldn't understand them. But, I knew he was close. With a near scream, Vince pushed forward again, his hot come shooting out of him in long spurts. As I swallowed, I heard his hand hit the window, his fist pounding as he struggled to regain his composure. He let me go, his hand sliding down my back before it was gone completely.

We sat next to each other for a few minutes, our hands touching once more. He looked at me, his eyes softer than I had seen them in years. With all the energy I could muster, I leaned forward and kissed him. I knew it would be my last chance for a long while. But, as much as I wanted to make it last, reality got back in. His cell phone rang out in the quiet, his world clearly never very far away.

As the phone clicked shut, I knew the moment had passed. Vince returned to his usual self, closing his pants quickly and running businesslike hands through his hair. By the time he threw the door open to return to the driver's seat, it was as if it had never happened. As I pulled up my own pants, I took one last look at Vince's scar before his shirt covered it. Once he was put back together, his gun returned to its normal place.

We started driving towards the hospital, civilization coming back into view. Despite his earlier objections, I grabbed a cigarette from my pocket and pressed the lighter button down. He looked over at me, grabbing the stick from between my lips.

"Not worried about dying anymore?"

He grabbed the glowing coil and lit up. Blowing his smoke at me, he laughed as I waved my hand in front of my face to dissipate the cloud.

"If a bullet can't get me, cigarettes don't stand a chance."

We were back at the hospital faster than I anticipated. I hesitated before opening my door, not wanting to see him go just yet. I knew what I was waiting for, but I also knew I wasn't going to get it. Cutting my losses, I got out of the car, looking back over my shoulder at his huge SUV. His window went down, his cigarette butt landing next to my old one on the ground.

"Thanks, Paulie. I'll see you around, okay?"

"Unless it's under different circumstances, I sure hope not, Vince."

Just like when he first pulled up, he pointed at me, his fingers snapping in time to his wink.

"Good one, Doc."

SQUEEZE MY GRAPES
Peter Eros

Out of the Northwest, a summer squall raced through the Sonoma Valley. The light changed to sapphire, then a kind of gray-green. The atmosphere, already thick with humicity, turned aqueous, making the air so heavy it seemed as though I was moving underwater as I ran from the upper ridge of the vineyard down to the verandah of my daddy the Jefe's house as the downpour hit. It rattled windows and shuddered the wisteria against the corner posts. Daddy Kai stood in the doorway of his bedroom, wearing a pair of shorts. He beckoned, and I followed.

His right hand grabbed my shoulder and pulled me into the room. His shorts were already on the floor. I slipped out of my sandals and tore off my tank top and shorts, my prick already dribbling precum. Kai lay back on the bed as I crouched between his thighs. My hair brushed his belly as I worked over him. Sweat lay on us like seawater. We seemed oiled with it. He groaned out loud, feeling his cock swell beyond its natural girth, quivering for release, as I slowly, delicately, used my nails, fingertips, lips, tongue, and hot breath to excite him.

I savored each moment, reaching out to feel his heart pounding against his ribs, his breath short and hot at the back of his throat, gasping intermittently as I added a delectable nip here and there, tweaking his distended nipples. His eyes were closed. He was immersed in the heat of his own desire. He groaned. He reached down and gently drew me away from his engorged cock. He opened his eyes and drank in my slick nakedness, my swollen prick, my carved thighs, so strong, my narrow waist, the flare of my rib cage and my pumped pectorals riding atop.

Daddy Kai's eyes smoldered, heavy-lidded with lust. They inflamed me. With his strong arms, he brought me upward like a doll, until I straddled his chest, and he could slurp my bobbing prick. I cried out at the contact, my fingers entwining in his hair as I pressed my hips forward and back, establishing a rhythm. It was slow at first as I savored the hot lick of his tongue, the nibbling of his lips. I was dripping with need, my upper body shaking in anticipation as he sucked me deep into his throat. He pulled groans of ecstasy from me as he extracted my precum.

I held my pelvis immobile, feeling the pleasure dancing through me, rippling my musculature in uncontrollable waves. I felt the tide pulling me onward and at last gave myself over to it completely, bucking my hips against his mouth with frenzied need, my hair flying around my head as if I was in the midst of the storm raging outside. It was what Daddy Kai was waiting for. He pushed me away from his mouth, down his torso and onto his swollen, spit-slicked prick. I gave a wail of delight as, with one long, ecstatic thrust, he plumbed me to my depths. The heated contact was all I needed in my aroused state to push me up the last several notches. Kai convulsed inside me, he drew my torso down to him, enjoying the scrape of my nipples against his, feeling it all the way down into his explosive scrotum. My fingers stroked his cheek while our tongues dueled wetly, my cock jetting cum between our heaving bodies.

At length, we did nothing but listen to the rain drumming on the metal roof. It diminished with the same slowness our pulses took to return to normal. He lit a joint and took a deep drag before handing it to me.

"How long has it been now, Pedro?"

"Three months."

"Thank God you found me. You make me very happy. Are you happy?"

"*Si, Si!* I like it here very much. You know I love you, Daddy. You have given me a home in this lovely place, and money, good food and clothing, your loving companionship, and the best sex I have ever known. Why wouldn't I be happy?"

It was true. Five months before I had left Acapulco. I headed north to find my *El Dorado*. I am twenty-two years old. My mother raised her five children all alone. Somehow she earned the money to buy her two boys a good education with the Jesuits, and unlike my brother, I was sensible enough to concentrate on learning English. But it isn't much use in Mexico unless you have contacts among wealthy and influential people. I had work, but only menial. I'd been an agricultural worker in the vineyards and a busboy in restaurants. But my only chance at a life was to head north.

I had been a diver off the cliffs at Acapulco, thrilling the tourists, but gaining little for myself except the adrenaline rush of the moment, and an introduction to wealthy men who were willing to pay for some time enjoying my well-formed and agile body. Most of them were married men, affluent enough to afford a double life. I didn't mind. I enjoyed their mature company, and their practiced certainty about what they wanted from me, so much more satisfying than the fumbling, embarrassed and inexperienced boys my own age. Those randy Papa's taught me a lot about how to pleasure a man as well as financing my journey to *al norte*. I fucked with tourists also, brushing up my English as I pleasured them for profit, learning the necessary words and phrases that the Jesuits never taught me.

I took the usual route north, through Tijuana. In that ramshackle town I made contact with the coyotes who arrange passage for us illegal immigrants. They aren't hard to track down. I found a cell phone toting coyote right at the bus station, next to a police wagon, loudly quoting prices of $400 to $800 for transportation to Los Angeles, with custom trips available to anywhere in the U.S. for a negotiable, higher fee.

We traveled at night. I don't know where we crossed the border, I only know it was somewhere in the desert. Unaware just when we crossed the border, we walked for four hours until we struck a dirt road, and a cell phone call prompted the appearance of a van with no headlights. There were ten of us crammed into the back of the van. Somewhere in Southern California on the third day, we were hijacked by rival gun-toting coyotes. The hijackers set up a buy-back meeting in the parking lot of an auto parts store. But when the two smuggling teams met in the night, gunfire was exchanged instead of money. Three people died – one smuggler from each side and an eighteen-year-old boy (treated by all the smugglers as stolen property) who was shot by accident as he waited in the truck. I felt really bad. Emilio was a sweet kid. He and I had been pals on the journey. I had cuddled him and wiped his tears when he wept in the night, and sucked his sweet cock to pacify him. Now he was dead.

I fled in the confusion. Near the on ramp to a highway I hitched a ride with a Mexican trailer truck headed north. The driver was *simpatico*. He was headed for Sacramento and was glad of the company, especially when he found I gave such good head. I didn't know where Sacramento was, but I didn't care, just glad of the opportunity to sleep at the back of the cabin and to eat at the truck stops. Carlos, the driver took an inland route, heading up through San Bernadino, so I never saw Los Angeles or San Francisco. I was amazed by the flatness of the agricultural terrain as we neared the end of the journey.

By the time we got to Sacramento, I'd sucked the driver's big cock at every stop, and he'd fucked me several times, so he was grateful. He called a friend who was a farm worker organizer. He found me a room with a fruit-picking family, and I was soon picking berries and mucking out stables for minimum wage, until I found a job where the farmer paid me a little better and treated me well. I shoveled shit or hacked weeds out of a drainage ditch, my muscles pumping up and feeling good in the glow of the sun. I sometimes stopped to watch the hunky studs in the fields bucking bales of hay into a wagon, stacking them to teetering heights.

I was still poor, but I felt delivered from poverty. I had hope and ambition, and was away from the scrutiny of family and friends. I was free among strangers in the eventful world where I could practice being someone else until I was someone else.

When word came of an expected weather change, I was added to the hay-gathering team. There were four of us: the farmer's nephew Clete, a naïve boy who was tall and ruggedly handsome, and two Mexican brothers, Miguel and Aurelio. Miguel, short and stolid and solitary, spoke very little English, and rakish Aurelio did the talking for both of them and then some. While the rest of us did the heavy work, Aurelio gave us advice about girls, larcenous border guards, clod-brained farmers, bumbling cops and the whores who supposedly loved him. He made us laugh.

The farmer had a lot of hay to bring in and should have hired more hands. He pushed us hard and made us work long hours. During the last week or so, I spent the nights at the farmhouse, sharing a room with Clete, so I could get to the farm with the others at sun-up and work until dusk. Clete showered then went to bed naked, making sure I saw what he'd got, a huge, cut veiny prick. But I ignored him. I heard him gasping as he jacked himself off in the night, but I was too tired to offer any encouragement. The bales were heavy with dew when we started bringing them in at dawn. The air in the loft turned steamy from fermentation. I was sunburned, covered with scratches. I could hardly get out of bed in the morning.

Aurelio's beat-up old car broke down toward the end of the week, and Clete started driving him and Miguel to and from the decrepit motel where they lived. The final night, when we took them home, Aurelio asked us in for a drink. Clete tried to beg off, but I wouldn't let him. We drank tequila and beer, smoked pot, and listened to Aurelio. Within an hour, we were lying on the beds and fumbling with each other's clothes, Clete acting like an offended virgin at first. But once I'd exposed his prick and went down on him, he soon acquiesced. A wild spark in his eyes, a voice thick with lust, he moaned,

"Oh fuck yeah! Oh man! You suck good."

My fellow peons dragged off his gaping clothes and quickly stripped themselves. I pulled my clothes off as I sucked and turned myself around, so we could sixty-nine, but the other two were pressing Clete from either side. With my eyes, I traced the clean lines of Clete's chest, free of hair. His belly was flat and lean: I could see the outline of every muscle there. His groin was rampant, like something chiseled in granite. He had very muscular legs, wiry like a runner's. I felt myself growing, the breath quickening in my throat, as little twinges of regret that I'd not taken advantage sooner niggled with my brain.

Clete finished the roach, turning it under his tongue and swallowing it. He reached out and twisted one of my tits. I lay on top of him the heel of my hands on his pectorals, my fingers tweaking his nubs. I loved the feel of him, the resilience and the hardness. Aroused, he had become hard all over. I leaned down and bit the side of his neck. He took hold of my hair and pulled me prone atop him. His knee began to part my thighs. My juicing prick ground against his leg. My heart was hammering hard.

Aurelio and Miguel each took one of his wrists and quickly, before he could protest, handcuffed him to the headboard. Miguel produced some Vaseline and I primed my crack and sheathed Clete's long shaft.

"I need your mouth," he groaned. His face was contorted with desire.

"Fuck that. I want you in me," I replied.

I straddled him and buried him with one downward thrust of my buttocks. He was deep inside me. We groaned simultaneously. My inner muscles massaged until I felt the fluttering of his lower belly.

"Oh!" he gasped. "More!"

I gave him more, in tiny increments, increasing the friction from moment to moment. I thought he was going to have a heart attack. Aurelio sat on his face, pushing his dick between the gasping lips, leaning across Clete's spasming body to eat my mouth. Miguel was behind me, reaching beneath my humping butt to lube Clete's virgin crack with insistent fingers. Clete convulsed beneath me, the force inside him gathering and releasing, gathering and releasing. I had never been with a man who came so long and deeply. I gasped and whimpered my nether lips spasming as I suctioned him to explosive conclusion. My heart was hammering hard. My hot, greased penis seemed to have grown to four times its size. My back arched, and I cried out my ecstasy as Aurelio jacked my prick, and my jizz shot in explosive pearlescent bullets, coating Clete's bouncing torso. They oozed down his sweaty skin in pungent rivulets.

I slid from anchor, reeling and at the edge of sleep. But Aurelio and Miguel were just getting started. Miguel sat on Clete's face and pulled the big boy's legs back toward him, exposing the *Americano* butt for Aurelio to plow with his thick prick. Clete, still shackled, suddenly became aware of what he intended to do a moment before it happened. He cried out at the invasion by the hot, greased penis. Miguel, ignoring his protests, thrust his butt back on the open mouth as he leaned forward and sucked in Clete's now flaccid cock, pushing the boys flailing legs forward, so they settled on Aurelio's shoulders. Carnal heat was on Clete like a blanket. He felt as if he was being penetrated by a horse. Shame and sickly fear expelled his previous euphoria. He began to cry. I leaned over and caressed his head, brushing the hair from his eyes. I kissed his eyelids. He made a deep sound in his throat as he felt the embedded cock thickening in his colon.

"Leave me alone," he panted.

Aurelio laughed.

"Do you really hate it?"

"Yes!"

My mouth enclosed Clete's, and when our tongues twined, a great shudder rippled through his entire frame. My fingers were busy tweaking his tits. His pelvis squirmed as Miguel enthusiastically sucked his newly burgeoning cock, and Aurelio plunged into his molten core, rearing and thrusting all the way up. Clete, gasping, felt the air rush from his lungs. He panted against the side of my neck. Tears filled his eyes but for a different reason. The pain in his butt had subsided, to be replaced by indescribable spasms of joy. His prostate rejoiced. The feeling of Aurelio deep inside him, massaging his most intimate flesh engendered a completeness he had never before experienced. He thrust his hips back against his impaler, exulting in the filaments of feeling, the heat of Aurelio spurting into the rubber deep within him. As his orgasm exploded into Miguel's gobbling mouth and throat, the palpitations of his body radiated all the way to the top of his head, triggering Miguel's release, his cock spontaneously shooting a viscous flood that pooled in the hollow of Clete's belly.

We groggily showered together trying to regain some equilibrium. Clete, more or less sobered up, kissed me goodbye. The work was finished. He was going back to the farm; I needed a new gig. I briefly worked at Taco Bell, my job basically to make the tacos. But I ended up doing more work than I think I was paid for, and I reeked of tacos. My skin reeked of it, my hair smelled of it, and the little hat stank of it.

I signed on to work as a dishwasher at a college dining hall. The job consisted of dumping food-soiled plates and trays into a vat of rushing water. My partner was an eighteen-year-old, with sandy blond hair and blue-gray doe eyes, a Bosnian refugee, with gleaming skin stretched over lovely bones. He didn't speak very much English, but he did tell me he used to be a ballet dancer. Boris was his name.

The dishwashers always closed down the dining hall. One night, after everyone else had punched out, Boris and I took a break. I'd brought a joint from home, and we set two milk crates up on the floor and smoked. The dishwashing machines were off, but steam still rose from them like jungle mist. As I handed him the toke, I stripped off my stained apron, sweaty T-shirt and baggy kitchen trousers and Boris' blue eyes blinked. I hadn't been wearing anything underneath. My dick was slick and sweaty, and began to expand, enjoying its release.

Boris sucked the aromatic smoke into his lungs and gave me a salacious smirk, both depraved and innocent. As he handed back the toke, I held his fingers and pulled him into an embrace. His right hand grasped my dangling jewels and our mouths joined, tongues probing. He didn't have to be asked to strip. He flung down the apron, squirming out of his T-shirt, revealing his beautiful white torso and pert rosy nipples. His only blemish was a prominent vaccination dimple on his shoulder. He slid down his trousers, then his skimpy briefs. He stood naked, his ample uncut cock stiff, straining up and out from his muscular thighs and ripped abs.

He knelt and spread the garments on the floor, both his and mines, so we could lie down on them and spread-eagled with his arms wide open in invitation. He pulled me down on top of him. We inhaled more dope and breathed it into each other. My mouth was against his in a very tender kiss that grew warmer, more desperate, wide-open, tongue hard and probing. He tilted his head back offering his throat. His breathing quickened as I licked and nibbled. We writhed against each other, his hands between my legs, pushing the loose flesh up and down over my veiny stiffness, and I felt a trickle burning towards his fingers.

He pulled his legs back, bent against his chest, and I went down on his winking anus, sucking and reaming as he groaned his delight. I spat in my hand and slicked up my throbbing prick then pushed into his hot, slippery anal mouth, till I was deep inside his hungry warmth. Fully engaged, he bounced his butt against my pelvis, moving with accelerating vigor until he was slapping his ass against my hips with each thrust. His feet drumming on my back holding me to him. Boris was shouting words I didn't understand. The shouts soon became unintelligible grunts and moans. As I shot my wad deep inside him, Boris' equipment swelled even bigger and let fly right over his head. He giggled with satisfaction, hugging and kissing me and murmuring his thanks.

We showered together in the locker room and dressed slowly, unable to stop touching, embracing and kissing. Boris asked me if I'd like to move in with him. I told him I'd think about it. The next day he sported a hickey on his neck the size of a crabapple. He burst into tears when I told him I'd decided to head for the wine country around Santa Rosa. It wasn't that I didn't like him. He was beautiful and loving and very sexy, but I had ambitions and wasn't ready to settle down with anyone just yet, no matter how gorgeous.

I'd been chatting to one of the food delivery guys, and he offered to transport me across country to the wine capital. I accepted. I wore my best jeans and a tight T-shirt. He gave me a Santa Rosa newspaper, and I perused the classifieds, hoping that someone on a vineyard wanted staff. The Ratzinger Winery was the only one advertising. My delivery guy dropped me at the gate though it was several miles out of town, in a really hilly area.

I had all my possessions packed in a duffel bag. It was a weekday, and regular tours were being conducted, a sort of tram being pulled behind a tractor. The wine shop was open and the staff was friendly, but they said the boss was away till later in the day. He'd only recently inherited the place following the death of his father. When I explained that I had no transport, they said I could take a tour and then wait in the shade on the seat by the side gate to his residence, and they gave me a sandwich and a soda.

When I first saw Kai Ratzinger, he was piloting his Harley Soft Tail Classic down the steep canyon road and into the ranch house front yard. He had silver rimmed riding goggles clamped tight over his eyes. He was wearing threadbare and skintight 501s, scuffed work boots, and a dark blue silk bomber jacket over a tight white Lycra T-shirt. I saw him before he saw me. His head was held high as he captained the behemoth cycle around a corner. He looked hellbent and happy. He noticed me standing in front of his house, and the motorcycle dove to a stop. He slid the driving goggles up onto his forehead and looked me over, revealing his unusual, almond shaped, and sapphire blue eyes under hooded lids. There was a questioning glimmer in his eyes. Then, above the roar of the motorcycle echoing through the valley, something clicked. His full, moist lips spread into a smile. It said many things. It said, "I like what I see. We can get along. I think I'd like to screw you."

Then he did something totally unexpected.

"Push the code!" he yelled above the roar of the cycle. The code? He told me the code. I entered it into the call box and the electric gate opened across his driveway. I'd known him exactly fifteen seconds, and he'd given me the keys to his house.

He propped the bike in the open garage next to his Lancia then came to join me. He had the tall, broad-shouldered bearing of an airline pilot. The bulge of his crotch was prominent and a full, firm ass gently stretched the denim of his jeans. He was forty-five but looked ten years younger. He gestured for me to go ahead of him to the entrance.

"Do the honors, kid. Can you remember the combination?"

Again I pressed the buttons, and he pushed open the ornate, paneled door. He grasped my shoulder with a muscular hand and thrust me ahead of him. As the door slammed behind him he spun me around and into his arms, pressing me to him, and engulfing my mouth with his own. Startled, but happy I relaxed in his embrace and enthusiastically responded with my agile tongue. He drew his head back and held my shoulders firmly, gazing into my amazed but excited face.

"Son, I guess you need love as much as a job, and this Daddy sure as hell does."

I'd later learn that he'd called the office on his cell phone and knew that I was waiting. He thrust me ahead of him into his bedroom, both of us stripping our clothes off as we went, my eyes quickly taking in my surroundings. The bed was huge and covered with a paisley patterned quilt. The headboard was mirrored and a built in wardrobe with mirrored doors ran the entire length of the left-hand side of the room. I didn't at first notice the mirror on the ceiling above the bed. Another large mirror adorned the right-hand wall, next to the French windows that opened onto the verandah, and a large TV with a VCR stood against the other wall, so that it could be viewed from the bed. He popped in an XXX-rated tape and a bunch of hot, dark, muscular guys with huge cocks flickered to life on the screen, sucking and fucking and groping each other.

Kai held me at arms length, appraising my body. I gazed at his pumped, smooth pecs, his large dark-brown nipples standing proud of his chest. His skin color was like milk chocolate. He was totally hairless, including his groin. Totally smooth, like a prepubescent child, but much bigger, the largest cock I had ever seen. Like mine his was uncut, and hung neatly over his balls that were also hairless and pulled in tight against his body. His prick was dribbling freely, throbbing and impatient to release its simmering juices, bouncing up to greet me.

He reached out and took hold of my hand, guiding it to the smooth skin of his belly. My hand traveled right to the base of his prick, now hard and stiff. I made a fist around his cock and moved it all the way along its silky length. I wiped his liquid onto one of my fingers and moved it to each of my nipples, gently rubbing the moisture into them, heightening the erotic sensations that were flowing through my body. I left one hand on his prick, not wanting to let go of this new toy, and stroked his balls with the other, fondling each one under their hairless, smooth sac.

"Oh yes, sweetheart!" he murmured, "squeeze my grapes!"

I looked up at Kai's face and smiled at him, nervously, as I obeyed his instruction, marveling at the size of the huge nuts moving beneath my fingers. We looked into each other's eyes and stared for what seemed like an eternity. Then I felt his fingertips lightly brushing my ass. My manhood tingled with delight. I could smell a mixture of cologne and perspiration on him. We could feel each other rising in response. Our lips made contact; our bellies crushed together, our hands grappling each other's buttocks.

I got down on my knees and stroked his silky smooth cock with my tongue, and then took as much of it as I could into my mouth. My tongue traced its length, slipping under the foreskin and against the sensitive tip. He squirmed and thrust, pushing my tongue further under his foreskin. Then I went down on him. I somehow swallowed it all without gagging. His naked glans was all the way down my throat. I pumped and slurped, rubbing my wet lips along his warm length, as my hands continued to fondle and squeeze his balls.

He quivered with delight, and tilted his head back, licking his lips. His deep breathing soon became moans of pleasure and excitement, as he took over and started fucking my face. He pumped his pelvis forward, making me gag occasionally. I gripped his smooth ass cheeks tight, helping, pushing him in and out of my mouth. Each time he pushed in, I held my tongue just at the tip of his prick, catching his foreskin and rolling it all the way down his shaft, massaging the sensitive head with every inch of my throat as I swallowed him down. I wanted him to come in my mouth. I started to squeeze his prick between my lips, as my tongue furled around him tightly. My right hand massaged and squeezed his balls, while the other hand probed his asshole. He shot a huge load within seconds. I gulped and swallowed, hardly losing a drop, exulting at the feel of his milky ooze in my throat and gullet.

He withdrew from my mouth out of breath. He fell onto the bed, dragging me with him. I lay beside him, my heart still pounding hard and fast in my chest. I still couldn't believe I was doing this with one of the most gorgeous guys I'd ever seen. I snuggled close to him, and his hand caressed the back of my neck. The video was still grinding out erotic images. We watched distractedly. I was so horny I couldn't concentrate.

He asked me about myself, and I blurted a brief synopsis of my life. Then he explained his own heritage. His mother was part Hawaiian, part Japanese, while his father, despite the Germanic name, was an expatriate Frenchman, a strong-willed man that, like his father before him, had traveled extensively throughout the world. Forty years ago his father had taken over a run-down bankrupt vineyard and had reestablished it. It was now one of the finest vineyards in the district.

Kai had grown up in Sonoma, attended the local university, then worked and studied at leading vineyards in France and Australia. His mother died when he was a boy and his father had been a hard taskmaster. But the old boy, who hated hypocrites and religion, accepted his son's gayness with equanimity, admitting that he'd had many pleasurable encounters with his fellow man during his own travels. Now Kai was adjusting to being in charge. He intimated that he was looking for a compatible companion. a loving son who would pleasure his Daddy, so he didn't have to hunt for friendship and sex. I slipped into his embrace and kissed him tenderly on his forehead, eyelids and nose. Our lips met, and my tongue forced an entry. He responded avidly, chewing on my lips as his tongue dueled mine, thrusting to the back of my throat.

He slipped from my embrace and opened one of the mirrored doors. It was his bathroom. He took a piss, then went to the VCR, popping in another tape. I went to the bathroom and when I returned he was on the bed, squeezing some lubricant onto his hand, and poking two fingers up his own ass. He knelt on the bed on all fours, facing the screen, waving his gorgeous buttocks in my face.

"Fuck my big Daddy ass, Pedro. Show me what you can do."

He took one of his hands off the bed and spread his ass cheeks for me, giving me my first glimpse of his smooth ass crack and his puffy rosebud puckered hole. I shoved my face right into his crack. I tantalized it with the tip of my nose and my tongue. I pressed his cheeks together, inhaling, licking and sucking on his beautiful buns. I licked around the edges of his tunnel of bliss. I probed deeper, opening my mouth wide, pushing against and stretching the skin of his anal wall. He groaned and grunted, and I could feel him jerking with delight as I thrust my tongue into his asshole. It tasted wonderful. Then I took my seven inches and tickled his buns with it. My prick was so hard and full that I could have come just from that minor friction. But I held it in.

I took one of his hands and placed it on my slippery dick so that he could guide me into his ass. I pushed in and he sighed with pleasure. I pumped in and out. His breathing increased sharply as my thrusts accelerated. He pushed back when I pushed forward. I moved harder, faster, exultant at the feel of my foreskin rolling back along my shaft as it slid against the lubricated walls of Kai's tight hole. I reached beneath him and stroked his wet and bobbing cock. Just then, I felt a tightening in my balls, and I grabbed his hips and pounded into him the most powerful orgasm I had ever had. I emptied my load of spunk into his ass, as he shot his load just from the feeling of me inside him. He tumbled onto his side with my cock still embedded. His arms thrust behind him grasping my buttocks, holding me in.

When my cock had recovered, deflating till I had no control, it slid out of him. Our respiration had returned to normal. After a short respite, fondling and kissing, Kai pulled my ass onto his mouth, reaming me fiercely as I gasped and squirmed with glee. He lay on his back and pointed to his cock, gesturing for me to ride it. It had expanded once more to a daunting length and girth. I took the lube and slathered him liberally. Then I straddled him and settled my ass down, peeling back the foreskin with my fingers as I slid the massive head between my ass lips.

He pushed his pelvis upward as nine inches of his thick, smooth weapon dredged through my colon, stretching my inner muscles beyond anything they'd previously experienced. His cock was so big and thick that it truly felt like it was splitting my ass open. I settled with my butt against his groin, his probe completely contained, and rested for a moment while I got my breath. My shit chute gradually adjusted to the unaccustomed girth of the intruder. As I began to relax my ass muscles and his shaft became further lubricated with my ass juices, it became tolerable. Then I moved up and down slowly, gradually picking up speed, enjoying the feeling of his balls slapping against my ass cheeks every time he pushed in down to the base of his cock. My ass was comfortably opening, taking it all, pulling him in as he pushed. With each downbeat my ass grabbed and clung to his shaft like a glove, and each time on the upbeat, it felt like my colon was being pulled inside out. He looked up at me humping on his belly and grinned.

"I'm your Daddy and you're my cock-sucker and my butt-fuck now, Pedro, my son, mine and mine alone. Do you think you can handle that?"

"Ooooh yes! *Si! Si, Padre!* Oh please yes! Ooooh! Fuck my ass!"

If he'd wanted me to be his slave, I'd have said yes at that moment. Waves of ecstasy were flooding through my body, emanating from my assaulted prostate, and the turn-on glimpses I was catching of our activity in the surrounding mirrors. He breathed in and out deeply as he pumped up into me. I lost all control, bucking on his groin like a wild animal. And I felt the pulses shooting throughout his whole body. My ring of ass muscle clenched tightly around him and he gasped. His body began heaving; releasing cannonades of cum so fast that I could feel the individual jets splashing up deep inside me. His orgasm became mine as he took my cock in his hands and wanked me so energetically, I instantly shot my wad all over his stomach and in his hands. He laughed breathily and sucked my discharge from his dripping fingers. I lay on top of him; his huge pole still embedded, our bodies vibrating with the electricity of our combined sexual energy. Our warm, sweat-slicked chests pressed together, our cum-glued bellies palpitating against each other. I rested my face in the hollow of his neck, feeling the pulse against my cheek. We both fell asleep. We awoke three hours later to the sound of thunder.

It has been three months now, and Kai has taught me a lot about the running of the vineyard. He bought me a wardrobe full of stylish clothes and a lightweight motorbike, so I can get around and has initiated an adoption process through his lawyers. But principally he has taught me things about my body and its sexual possibilities that would never have occurred to me. I feel as if I belong to him, that his flesh and my flesh are one and the same. I have become that someone else I always wanted to be. Daddy Kai can squeeze my grapes any time, and *Deo gracias*, he does.

BIG DOG, LAP DOG
Landon Dixon

Thug Sorrell shoved the little blond up against the dirty grey metal warehouse wall. "Mr. Ice wants his money," the big man gritted.

Stick Hansen's bright blue eyes darted left, right. But there was no one else around, the late-night hour, the rolling fog and the biting chill, leaving this particularly dilapidated section of the Montreal docks empty, abandoned. "Sure, sure – Mr. Iciano'll get his money," Stick soothed, spreading his arms in supplication. "I just need a few more days is all. The interest is kind of ..."

"His interest is your interest," Thug cut in, deadpanning his boss's mantra, his brown eyes dull, dead. He placed a large, black hand on Stick's shallow chest, pinning the man up against the wall, leaning his whole 260 pounds in. "You owe $400 – you pay it now."

Stick gasped for air, his options fast disappearing like his breath. A medium-bad pool and card hustler, he had twenty bucks in his pocket, and little prospect of getting anymore in a hurry. But he'd heard rumors – about Thug Sorrell. And so he took a gamble, the only one left to him.

"I-I just need some more time," he gulped, fluttering his long eyelashes, writhing his young, lean body against the big man's suffocatingly pressing hand. Then playing his hole card, his trick shot, slipping a pale hand in between Thug's tree-trunk legs and brushing his fingers up and along the front of Thug's black pants; long, delicate card sharp fingers tipped by well-groomed pool player nails caressing the man's crotch, lightly and tantalizingly stroking the man's cock behind the thin material of his pants.

"What the fuck!?" Thug grunted.

The two men stared at one another in the fog and the cold. Stick darting the pink tip of his tongue out to bathe his plush, red lips, sensitive fingers searching, swirling, scrambling between the other man's legs. Thug's shaved head gleaming dangerously in the dim light

91

thrown off by the lone bulb at the top of the warehouse, his black leather jacket shining dully, long arm out and rigid and unyielding.

And just when Stick thought for sure his desperate bank shot had bounced back at him, his bluff had been called with deadly consequences, he caught a flicker of life in the big man's loan shark enforcer eyes. And the ultra-pink tip of Thug's tongue snuck out and bathed his thick, black lips.

For a guy versed in reading suckers and sharks, that was all the communication Stick needed. His lips curtained a bright, white grin, and he rubbed the front of Thug's pants more forcefully, feeling a certain something stir to life between the man's legs. Thug feeling the slick little man's soothing, sensual fingers all through his big body. Knowing the guy was playing him, but cock tingling and engorging deliciously nonetheless, the sensation exquisite and expert, surreal in their surroundings.

Stick gazed into Thug's liquid eyes and let his fingers do the talking, the promising, trailing up and down the swelling length of Thug's cock. Then reaching further down and under, briefly cupping balls, before coming up again, stroking again. Making Thug clench his fencepost teeth and suck in his breath, his extended arm shaking a little now, palm dampening the front of Stick's hipster shirt.

To anyone foolish enough, or drunk or high enough, to be out on the docks at that time of night, in that kind of weather, it would've looked like the shakedown it was supposed to be – goon pressing mark for the Man's cash. But up close, it had taken on a whole new dimension – mark pressing goon for the man's capitulation.

Stick lightly and assuredly gripped Thug's cock through the big man's pants and moved his warm hand up and down the blood and lust-swollen length of dong, cradling and pumping. Thug's labored breath puffing out of his mouth in white clouds, planted legs quivering now like his arm, sweat sheening his broad forehead, body gone as hot as his demeanor had been cool before; cock a shimmering piece of meat between his legs.

Stick's mouth broke petulantly open to expose his long, lush tongue, as he pressed his advantage, eyes shining and fingers and hand quick-stroking. He could feel the heat from the big man's trembling body, feel the fire from the big man's pulsating dong. He gripped harder, hotter, pumped faster.

Thug's balls tingled and tightened, boiled, his cock surging, shooting. He jerked, spurting semen. Coming with a suddenness and intensity that surprised both men, cock-teased to passionate and uncontrollable orgasm; dark stain on his dark pants growing and spreading.

"Fuck!" was all Thug muttered, blazing and blasting and melting away under the Stickman's preciously pumping and controlling hand.

# # # # #

Thug paid off Stick's $400 debt to Mr. Ice.

The smalltime gangster peeled off a fifty and handed it back to the big man. Along with the patronizing words, "Good boy."

And when Thug got back to his crummy one bedroom in the Cote des Neiges District, Stick was there. Stretched out on his stomach on the Murphy bed reading a comic book, naked, his white, peach-fuzzed buttcheeks glowing round and soft and luscious under the single-bulb overhead light; except for the raised, ridged three-inch knife scar on his right buttock.

Thug closed the battered door and licked his lips, said, "Don't waste any time, do you?"

Stick laughed and rolled over on his side, stacking his slender legs, giving Thug a shadowed look at the semi-erect five inches dangling from his nest of blond pubes. "Well, we are partners now, aren't we?" he said.

"Yeah, I guess so," Thug agreed. He walked over and sat down on the bed, the springs groaning with his weight. He placed a large, black hand on Stick's lean, pale thigh. And Stick smiled, covered the big man's paw with his own slender hand.

Thug flushed with heat. He flipped Stick over onto his back and tried to climb on top of the naked blond. But Stick wriggled away, slippery as a fish and quick as a cat. He propped himself up on the pillows at the head of the bed and drew up his knees, grabbed onto his thighs. Legs open, cock swelling longer and harder against his flat stomach.

"How much you figure Mr. Ice takes in in a week?" he asked.

Thug stared at Stick's smooth, pink, cut cock, and swallowed. "Huh?"

Stick wagged his legs, making his cock jump, fanning the flames of the big man's desire. "I figure around ten grand – from the hookers and the bookies and the borrowers. I've been watching his operation pretty close for the past couple of months."

"You have, huh?" Thug murmured, watching the other's man's cock grow still longer and harder, rise up seductively off his little body. "Yeah, somewhere around that, I guess. Why?"

Stick wagged his legs faster, face shining and eyes calculating. Excited as Thug, but for other reasons.

Then his legs stopped, and he reached out and picked up Thug's hand and placed it on his now fully-erect nine-inch cock. He shuddered slightly, as the huge hand gripped his thick shaft. "Because we're gonna put the bite on Mr. Ice," he said, "like he puts the bite on everyone else. It's not much, but it's enough to blow this dead-end town and go somewhere where there's real action – like Atlantic City!"

Thug moved closer, heavy-handedly pumping Stick's cock, pulling the stiff pole towards himself, reveling in the hot, pulsing feel of the enormous appendage. "Uh-huh. And just how do we get the money from Mr. Ice?"

"You get it," Stick said, slowly wagging his legs again. He leaned back against the pillows and directed hooded eyes at Thug, offering up his cock and body. "You're the last guy to pay his collections to Mr. Ice at his office Sunday night, right? By then, the cash is bulging out of his safe. So, you just … take what's on hand."

"Simple as that, huh?" Thug breathed, hard-stroking Stick's cock from fuzzy base to purple crown, sweat on his palm greasing the action. His own dong rigid and yearning in his pants.

Stick sighed, rubbed his blond-downed chest with his hands, strummed his hard, pink nipples with his fingers. "Yeah, simple as that," he said languidly, curling a finger at the big man, then pointing down at his towering cock.

Thug instantly went to his belly in between Stick's legs, latching onto the little man's thin thighs with his hands, the blond's meaty hood with his lips. He hungrily gobbled up Stick's cap and consumed his shaft, roughly sucking Stick's cock almost right down to the perfectly-formed, tightly packaged balls. Before pulling back up again.

He repeated the process, over and over, sucking hard and heavy and long on Stick's jutting prick. Thick lips sealed tight to the clean-cut shaft, stretching the skin, pulling on the mushroomed knob at the end before diving back down again. Bobbing his big, bald head up and down, excitedly filling his hot, wet mouth and throat with throbbing cock.

Stick idly played with his nipples, Thug's sucking mouth on his dick, the pressure of the man's sweaty hands on his legs, warming him; the thought of $10,000 warming him much more. He brought his thighs together on either side of Thug's head and squeezed, getting the guy to suck even harder and faster, more fiercely and frantically. Ten thousand would be just the stake Stick needed to get in on some card and cue games he'd heard about in Atlantic City.

Thug dug his dirty fingernails into the blond's clean, white thighs and sucked urgently on the man's beating pink cock, staring earnestly up into Stick's dreamy blue eyes. Grinding his own erection into the bed. He inhaled the tangy-sweet scent of Stick's lithe body and mouthful balls, inhaling pipe so hard that he wet-vacced a drip of salty precum from the man's slit.

Stick shook his head, frowning. He abruptly pulled his dong out of Thug's mouth with a wet pop and said, "Let's see what you got, big man." Already knowing the answer from the jack-session last night.

Thug rolled off the bed and quickly stripped out of his jacket, T-shirt and pants. He stood naked before Stick lounging on the bed, his huge, barrel-chested, muscle-corded body gleaming, ridged stomach bulging only slightly; cock a blue-black, seven-inch licorice stick.

The little blond regarded the big man, the veined nightstick with the beefy knob. Stroking his own larger, longer, wider cock. "I don't know if my pretty little ass can take all that meat," he said coyly.

Then he stepped off the bed and ran a hand over Thug's bristling chest, skirting the teddy bear tattoo on Thug's muscled left pec and grinning, lightly fingering the man's jutting nipples. Ran the hand down over Thug's hard stomach and grasped his twitching cock.

Thug jerked, and grunted.

Stick kissed him lightly on the lips. And Thug tried to kiss back, hard and open-mouthed. But Stick danced just out of range, holding onto Thug's cock like it was a leash, a big dog on the end of it. Then he darted in and flicked one of Thug's nipples with his tongue.

The big man groaned, nipple swelling even higher, shiny with Stick's hot spit. The little man deftly and quickly sucked on it, the other, momentarily sinking his sharp, white teeth into the rubbery protuberances and almost tugging them right off the bucking man's chest. Before teasingly trailing his tongue down in between Thug's pecs and onto the rippling muscles of his stomach, sticking the wet tip into the big man's deep belly button and swirling it around, hand still hotly gripping the veiny leash.

Stick ran his tongue back up Thug's stomach and chest and licked the man's lips, then pointed at the bed.

"But … I thought you were going to let me …" Thug began.

"Maybe when the job's done, hardman," Stick said, shaking his ass.

Thug obediently crawled onto the bed and set himself up doggy-style, big butt thrust out, waiting. But Stick shoved him down, sprawling the man out on top of the bed. And then he climbed onto the back of Thug's quad-heavy legs, dug his fingers into the man's mounded butt.

Thug grunted, chewing on a pillow. As the blond worked the thick, rich flesh of his buttcheeks; then slapped one, the other one, spanking the pliable meat to gyrating. Stick briskly beat Thug's ass, leaving the huge buttocks shimmering and shimmying. Before pulling a tube out of his discarded jeans lying on the bed and roughly greasing up

Thug's crack, jamming his slickened fingers in between the heavy cheeks and scrubbing. Then greasing up his own cock, slick and shiny, hand swirling, Thug straining his neck to see.

And without asking permission to bareback, Stick mounted Thug's ass and speared his cock in between the man's cheeks. Bursting through pucker and plunging deep into his asshole.

"Fuck!" Thug growled, Stick's cock stretching and filling his bung, sinking full-length into his ass.

Stick lay over top of the groaning man, gripping the sheet on either side, loins pressing into buttocks, cock plumbing the depths of Thug's anus. "You like it up the ass, don't you, bitch?" he hissed into the man's ear, moving his hips, his long, hard cock back and forth in Thug's hot, gripping chute.

"Fuck, yeah!" Thug rasped. Surging with the wicked heat of the little man's body riding his, the blond's big, strong cock churning his ass.

Stick bit into the thick muscles shielding Thug's bulging neck, pistoning his hips, plowing Thug's asshole. Pulling almost all the way out – the man's ring clinging to his cap, ass rising to beg for more – then plummeting all the way back in again, pounding Thug into the bed. Over and over, faster and faster, slamming the man's ass with lightning speed and thunderbolt intensity, torquing up the heat and pressure full-blast.

"You gonna get the money from Mr. Ice, like I asked!?" Stick snarled.

Thug spat out pillowcase and groaned, "Yeah, yeah! I'll get the money, and we'll get the hell out of here – the two of us!"

The bedsprings howled, the bed jumping, the hot, wet cracking of Stick's driving thighs against Thug's shivering buttcheeks resounding like gunshots in the stifling apartment.

The big man gasped, "Oh … fuck!" His body convulsing, his surging, mattress-thumping cock exploding under the relentless pressure of Stick pile-driving his ass – shooting semen into the bed.

Stick fucked anus in a frenzy. He tilted his head up, shutting his eyes, face twisting with orgasm, cock blasting sperm into sucking ass. "I'm gonna be fucking rich!" he wailed.

# # # # #

"Mr. Ice wants his money," the big man gritted.

Three men out on a dark, lonely, fog-shrouded pier. One man with his back to the dirty grey metal wall of a warehouse, other two men crowding close.

"I don't got it!" Thug pleaded, everything so different on the other end of a strongarm. "It's gone!"

The muscled slab of meat with the twisted nose and cauliflowered ears slammed a cement hand into Thug's chest, crushing the man up against the wall. The other goon, a double-wide fireplug with a ridge of scar tissue beetling his one eyebrow, calmly jammed a gun into Thug's crotch and rasped, "Yeah, we know – you stole it!"

# # # # #

While in a darkened, trash-strewn alley off Ventnor, not far removed from the glitter and glitz of the boardwalk, another big man had a little man pushed up against a grimy brick wall, beefy hand pressing suffocatingly into shallow chest. "You owe Mr. Kreuter twenty Gs from the game last night," the crewcut redhead lisped. "And he wants it – now!"

Stick smiled softly, writhing against the big guy's manicured hand, bright blue eyes gazing into the beefcake's pretty face. Because he didn't know this town or this man quite well enough, he had to go with his instincts, roll Lady Luck's unfamiliar dice.

He gambled, slipping a pale hand in between Big Red's legs. And coming up … empty.

The war vet's freckled face went white, the little blond prick touching him in the most sensitive of places. He angrily jerked out the only rod he had now, and used it.

STREET LOVE
Garland Cheffield

It was like something right out of a porno! I couldn't believe this wasn't part of some elaborate wet dream. A part of me worried I would wake up, safe and sound in my own bed without experiencing the monstrous climax that was my due.

A slight cool breeze blew, but our bodies still glistened with sweat. It was an unusually hot night. The sounds of LA nightlife buzzed all around us. It excited me that dozens of people had no idea what was going on in the dark alley they passed on their way to their extravagant parties. Just the idea that someone could walk down that alley and catch us in all of our depraved orgasmic games nearly made me come.

Hood was balls deep inside my ass. He was pounding into me ruthlessly, stretching my asshole almost to the point of breaking. He was breathin' hard. Moanin.' Groanin.' Grunts low and husky. His sweat was dripping onto my skin, making it glisten.

Dozens of big muscular brothers, all different shades of yummy chocolate, stood around us in a circle, pants and boxers down around their ankles. Fists closed around their hard cocks, savagely beatin' their meats and watchin' as Hood fucked me.

He had me bent over a metal trashcan. I held onto the handles and screamed out in pleasure. Slapping my ass, Hood laughed and pulled my hair.

"You like that?" He asked, barely able to grunt out the words as he bit my earlobe.

I couldn't answer him. I wanted to. God knows I wanted to scream out, "Yes! I love it! No one's ever fucked me this good!" All I could do was moan.

"Answer me," Hood ordered slappin' my ass harder. "Answer me. You like bein' fucked over a trashcan? Huh? You like me fuckin' you in an alley? You like my boys watchin' you take a big cock up yo ass?"

Biting my lips I finally found that one magical word like Aladdin finding that precious lamp. "YESSS!" I screamed out.

Hood threw back his head and laughed. He plowed me harder making my small body shake.

"Yeah, take it all, boy," he commanded grindin' himself against me. "Take my big thug cock. You my little bitch boy. You my little white trash whore."

He was drivin' me crazy. I love it when guys degrade me while they fuck me.

"Oh my God," I moaned. "I'm such a dirty slut."

This elicited large chuckles from the group around us. It made me smile with pride to hear some of them whisper to each other, "Man, homeboy's nasty, bro." Little did they know just how nasty this little homeboy could be.

Looking at the bangers standing around, my eyes grew greedy, and I licked my lips as I imagined all of them taking their turns with me. Doin' things to me. Showin' my ass no mercy.

It was then that I noticed a very hot white guy standin' with them. He was tall as a giant, skinny as a beanpole. He looked like a bird. A bandanna and hat was perched on his head. He wore a T-shirt that was about ten sizes too big. His face was scruffy and both ears were pierced with diamonds that sparkled in the moonlight. Boy was fine, and he had one of the biggest cocks I had ever seen! No wonder he was a member of the gang. From the waist down, he was pure black. I wondered how he could walk without trippin' over the damn thing. This thought made me giggle.

"What you laughin' at man-ho?" Hood demanded hitting my ass once again. "Is there somethin' funny 'bout the way I fuck?"

I shook my head no. "You hit a ticklish spot," I lied.

This made all the brothers around us laugh. The white boy turned to his homies and whispered, "Just wait 'till I tickle him."

Hood's balls tightened against me. His moans got caught in his throat. Pressing against my back he increased his thrusting.

"Oh fuck!" He cried exploding inside me.

My eyes rolled back in my head and my mouth opened in a silent orgasmic "O!" as he shot load after load of his fiery cum inside me.

"There's more in there," he said holding my hips in place.

He gave a couple more thrusts, and sure enough I felt more cum enter me.

Pulling out of me he kneeled behind me and sucked his cum out of me! My ass puckered and my legs shook like jelly. His tongue was deep inside me, searching every crevice for any traces of rogue cum. If it wasn't for the handles of the garbage can, I would have collapsed.

When he was satisfied that he had gotten every last drop out of me, he turned me over and kissed me. My eyes closed in bliss as I felt his cum slowly slide into my mouth. His tongue was in my mouth swirling his salty-sweet go around, mixing it like one mixes a fine cocktail.

"Swallow it," he whispered.

His boys watched me and then cheered when I happily obliged his request. "Fuck man. He just swallowed that shit!" They exclaimed in amazement.

"So you wanna party with me and my boys?" Hood asked, grabbin' my cock and tuggin' it.

"Uh-huh," I answered pulling my pants up.

"You think you can handle my boys?" He asked.

"If he can I can," I said pointing to the only other white guy around.

"Milkshake's different than you," the leader said.

"The big question is can your boys handle me?" I asked looking at each of them.

They opened their mouths in amused surprise. I guess they thought just because I was a white guy who barely cracked five feet I would be scared of them. Or maybe I was the only white kid besides Milkshake who wasn't scared of them. The truth was I really wanted to be a part of their gang. I loved bangers. Tough guys who could pass for straight, guys who were big. Tatted up. Scary. Femme's didn't do it for me. There ain't nothin' wrong with girly guys, don't get me wrong, most of them are smokin' hot, but if I wanted to be with a girl I'd be with a girl. I want to be with a man. Dominated by a man. Roughed up by a man. I want a man's cock shoved up my ass.

"I think you gonna fit in just fine with us," Hood said putting his python like arm around me and drawing me close. "My lil' Short Stack."

He had called me that since I met him two nights ago. I work as a dancer at this club in Downtown LA that caters to closeted dudes and dudes on the down low. We get a lot of gay bangers who know they've found sanctuary. It's not like a normal gay club or bathhouse. Most people can't even tell what type of place it is from the outside. And the bouncers don't allow just anybody in. Discretion is of the utmost importance to our patrons. We do everything to protect them from anybody knowing they're there.

Hood immediately caught my eye. He was everything I look for in a guy. Big. Muscular. Not regular gym muscles, but muscles you only get in prison; he later confessed that he had done hard time. Shaved head. Every inch of his body covered with tats. I gave him a blow job in the back, and he started telling me 'bout his boys. He brought me to the alley and the rest, as they say, is history.

"Kris, you better be careful," my friend Peter warned me the next day when I told him what had happened.

"You worry too much," I answered.

"And you don't worry at all. These guys could be dangerous. They are in a gang. What if you get shot?"

"Pete, don't worry. They just want me for sex," I said, convinced nothing bad would ever happen to me.

"Well what if they rape you? Those street gangs do that you know. Haven't you ever heard of gang rape?" He tried to instill the evils of street gangs into what he called my 'fool head,' but I wouldn't listen.

"Look up your definitions. It's only rape if you don't want it. I want it. Besides I love rough sex. You know that. The rougher the sex the better the orgasm."

"Just be careful," he said taking my hands in his and reminding me of an old maid. "I don't want anything to happen to my best friend."

"Nothing is going to happen. I am a fine-ass boy in LA. I should be flattered that so many people want me. Besides we're young. We're supposed to do this shit when we're young. You're acting like a dried up old queen," I said with a giggle.

"But aren't you worried about getting an STD? I know you don't use protection."

"Would you relax about that shit! I get tested regularly."

"Yeah, but you don't know if your partners do. And you don't know who they screw besides you. Especially these thugs you're hanging with now. You know the type of trash street gang's have sex with. Who knows what kind of diseases they have."

"Would you shut up about the stupid STDS!" I shouted. "Fuck. I know you're an actor, but we're not shooting an after school special. Besides, condoms spoil it."

"Not as much as boils on your dick and pissing fire," he muttered.

"Pete, seriously," I said no longer playing. "If I want to be preached at I'll call my mother."

"Okay," he said. "I'll never bring it up again." Though I knew he would in a few days.

"Don't worry so much. I know what I'm doing."

He merely rolled his eyes. I knew he was just concerned that I was in over my head, and I appreciated his concern. He was the best friend I ever had but damn! He could be a real fag nag. That last thought made me laugh.

"What's so funny?" Peter asked.

"Nothing," I said in between laughs.

"You thought it, didn't you?" He asked. "You just called me that awful nickname in your mind!"

Peter thought fag nag was the worst thing I could have ever come up with. I had told him he should take it as a compliment, but he was having none of it.

"You'll go down in history," I had told him. "Soon everyone will want one. Stags never quite took off and hags are going out of style you know."

"It's insulting!" He shrieked causing several people on the street to stop and stare at him. "It's because of people like you that keep the world from taking us serious. People like you are the reason we're regarded as some sort of carnival folk."

You don't know how hard it had been to keep a straight face. Peter is a major drama queen. Guess that explains why he was in LA trying to create an acting career. He had stormed off. We didn't speak for a week. He made me promise never to call him that again. I did. Though I still thought it.

"What you need to do," he said once he had regained his composure, "is find a nice guy and settle down with him."

I rolled my eyes. "Spend the rest of my life with one guy? I'd die. A boy as fine as me was not created to be some suit's old maid or play the role of the diminutive little hausfrau."

"I am not Alexander's old maid or his hausfrau. I am his life partner," he said with an uppity air. "And Alexander is not a suit. He's an entertainment lawyer."

"Whatever. All I'm saying is guys our age are not supposed to have 'life partners.' We're supposed to be living life. I mean you're an actor, Pete. And you're actually pretty cute. Do you know how much dick you could get just based off those two factors!"

"There are more important things in life than sex," Peter said sounding like my mother.

"If that's true, may I die before the week is out!" I declared melodramatically sounding like an actress from the golden age of Hollywood.

"Don't say that!" Peter ejaculated quickly. "It might come true."

"Petey. Join the twenty-first century," I responded with a laugh.

Peter was one of the most superstitious people I knew. A devoted follower of every new age healer and spiritualist around he believed fully in positive thinking, karma and visualization. I choose to live with the attitude of if I can see it and touch it, it's real. If I can't then it isn't important to me.

Later that afternoon, I decided to go for a walk. It was an uncharacteristically mild day, low 70s. A calm refreshing breeze made me forget it was summer. It felt more like fall. The sun's warm rays felt good against my skin. I walked slowly steering clear of any shade, never wanting to lose the sun's gentle caress.

"'Sup, Short Stack?" A voice brought me out of my thoughts.

Turning around, I saw Milkshake. He was leaning casually against the wall in an alley. He had been so quiet. So still. I had walked past him without even seeing him. Talk about a chameleon effect.

"You always blend into walls, Milkshake?" I asked head tilted to one side, smiling slightly.

"I like it in here," he said. "It's the perfect place to grab unsuspecting white boys as they walk past."

Quick as a rattlesnake, his arm shot out and was around mine. He pulled me roughly into the alley and pinned me against the wall. His hips were against mine. Looking down he smiled at my growing bulge.

"Happy to see me, Short Stack?" He whispered huskily, making my cock grow to the point of bursting.

He was so close I could smell him, that masculine musk of a real man. It drifted into my nose and drove me wild. Even though we were cloaked in shadows, the tiny diamonds in his ears still sparkled. Almost hypnotizing me.

"Are you afraid of me?" He asked grinding his hips against mine. He was as hard as me. "Are you afraid of Hood? Of the other boys?"

"Why should I be afraid of you guys?" I asked. My heart was racing enjoying the game. "You can't hurt me."

His laugh was husky and whiskey stained. "We can hurt you bad boy," he promised. He had an accent. Some kind of southern. Maybe Louisiana?

My stomach knotted, and I just about came. Good God he was so hot! I wanted to fuck him right there in the alley.

"Is that right?" I asked.

Smiling, never taking my eyes off him, I slinked to the ground until I was face to face with his bulge. Slowly I unzipped his jeans and pulled them and his boxers down to his ankles. His monstrous cock sprang to life, hitting me in the face. Looking up at him, I squeezed his balls, making him rise up like a ballet dancer.

"Now how can you hurt me when it looks like I'm the one with all the power?" I asked stroking his length with my fingertip.

He chuckled. "Hood was right. You are bad."

"Bad to the bone," I said emphasizing the last word, squeezing his cock before licking it.

I was all set to deep throat that monster when a gruff voice yelled, "Hey! What are you two doin' down there!"

Turning, we saw a cop staring at us. Several bystanders were standing there, mouths opened in a mixture of shock and erotic amusement. A few people whipped out their cell phones and snapped a few pictures.

"Oh shit," Milkshake groaned pulling up his pants.

Taking my hand, we ran down the alley not stopping until we were several blocks away. Leaning against the wall of an ice cream shop we were doubled over, panting and laughing.

"You're okay, Short Stack," he said. "Come on. Let Milkshake buy you a milkshake."

He led me into the ice cream shop as I silently wished that I would be lucky enough to get a taste of his milkshake. We sat there in the sparsely populated ice cream store sipping our shakes in silence. We never took our eyes off each other. Clutching the straw in my fist, I slowly ran my hand up and down the plastic as I slurped the shake. I imagined the straw was Milkshake's cock and the cold shake his hot semen. Damn! Who knew ice cream could be so friggin' sexual?

"Mmmm ..." I moaned closing my eyes in bliss. "Good. I love vanilla milkshakes with a hint of chocolate in him. I mean it," I added quickly with a giggle.

Choking on his strawberry-banana milkshake, his face burned bright burgundy. Smiling I stuck my finger in my vanilla-fudge shake.

"Wanna taste?" I asked, voice barely a whisper.

"Sure."

Slowly I ran my fingers over his lips before I penetrated him.

"How is it?"

"Good," he said licking my finger clean.

"You got some on your mouth," I said.

His tongue poked out and began blindly searching for the rogue drops.

"Let me," I offered.

Leaning across the table, I roughly pulled his head to mine. Our lips locked for eons. Our tongues flicked against each other. When we parted, his eyes were wide and his breathing heavy.

"We can't do this," he said.

"What?" That wasn't the reaction I was used to.

"You're Hood's boy. You're off limits."

"Get this straight, buddy," I said dead serious. "I ain't no one's boy."

He chuckled as if I were a stupid naïve child. "You got a lot to learn about how gangs work. We may fuck you, but only as a gangbang and only with Hood's permission. You're his. There's now only one way out, and I don't think you wanna take that way."

"That's about to change," I responded definitely. "I fuck who I want. When I want."

"You just don't get it do you?" He was getting annoyed. "You're in a different world now little boy. We have rules. A code. You disrespect the code, you disrespect the rules, you disrespect Hood, you end up dead."

Milkshake finished drinking before me. Without saying a word, he walked out. Staring after him I knew what I had to do. I wanted him. Even though I should have listened to him but what can I say? I'm a fool.

Never did I think I would really be in a real gangbang. It was even better than I had fantasized! All those fine, muscular tatted up brothers who could easily crush me like a bug sticking their cocks in my ass, in my mouth. They were in the middle of playing how many cocks Short Stack can take. At the moment, I had three in my ass and two in my mouth. A personal best. My ass was stretched to capacity. My jaws unhinged like a snake swallowing its pray. Hood was stroking my hair as if I was a puppy.

"Good boy," he said pushing my face deeper into the cocks. "You like bein' my bros' slut?"

All I could do was nod. They all took turns fucking me. Pounding me. I loved it!

"You ready to become one of us?" Hood asked.

Eagerly I nodded.

Hood ordered me to sit down on the ground and open my mouth. I obliged. His boys all stood around me jerking off. One by one they came in my mouth in a glorious bukkake scene. Hood was the last.

Pumping his fist enthusiastically, it wasn't long before his jizz joined his boys' in my mouth.

"Swallow," he ordered. I did. "Good boy. Protein's good for you. Maybe you'll break one hundred," he laughed jovially.

Later, when we were alone his demeanor changed drastically.

"Remember," he said eyes burning, hands around my neck. "You're mine now. You belong to me. Don't fuck anyone to try and get me jealous," he warned his dick pounded into my ass so hard it hurt. "We ain't in high school. Betray me, and I'll fuckin' kill you."

Seconds later he came inside me and kissed me. His full pouty lips were soft as angel's wings against mine. All I could do was tremble.

Hood's words were engrained in my mind. I spent the night tossing and turning. When I did manage to catch sleep my dreams were filled with grisly images of Hood butchering me and hiding the body parts. When I awoke my sheets were drenched and clung to me like a second skin.

"I'm in way over my head," I confessed to Peter. He had come over as soon as I called.

"I warned you," he replied not trying to hide the judgmental uppity tone. "Those types of people don't fool around."

"You're not helping."

I didn't want a lecture from a self-righteous prude. I wanted some stroking. I wanted Peter to make everything magically better.

"Kris, you live your life a certain way and now you're paying for it."

As much as I wanted to argue and play the helpless, victim I knew he was right. This was my own fault. My own doing.

"So what do I do? How do I get out of this?" I begged desperately.

"Kris, you don't. You just can't leave a gang. You're a part of them. The only way out is death."

His last phrase sent chills down my spine. This was serious. I wondered how a naïve farm boy from Kentucky knew so much about LA street gangs.

Needing to get out of my apartment, I went for a walk. My heart was racing. I was sweating from places I didn't even know could sweat. Despite the warmth my body was covered with goose-bumps. Every noise made me jump. Hoping I was just paranoid, I still couldn't shake the feeling that I was being followed.

"Short Stack," a voice whispered making me jump.

Turning around, I saw Milkshake leaning against the wall.

"Sorry. Didn't mean to scare you."

Staring at him, my heart raced and broke simultaneously. I wondered if he knew how much I wanted him. Especially after last night when I found out just how good he was.

"Come here," he said taking my arm and pulling me into the alley.

Being so close to him my fear melted. It must have been him who was following me.

"I can't stop thinking about you," he confessed making my heart jump for joy. "Ever since last night. I want you so bad Short Stack. I need you. I wanna fuck you. Without the other bros watchin'."

It took all my willpower not to do cartwheels. Slowly, I leaned in and kissed him. His rough sandpapery stubble tickled.

"My name's Kris," I said when we parted. Short Stack was Hood's name for me. I didn't want any ties to the OG. Not when I was with him.

"Houston," he smiled.

Houston and I wanted each other. We both felt it. I'm surprised we didn't rip each other's clothes off and start fucking right there on the street. But we couldn't. I begged him to take me back to his place. I promised I would let him do whatever he wanted to me. Nothing was off limits. I wouldn't say no. He could make his most taboo fantasies reality but he refused.

"I'm sorry, Kris," he whispered in a tear-stained voice. "I can't put you in danger. I can't risk your life like that."

"I won't tell. Hood will never find out. I promise," I tried to persuade him.

"Hood has eyes and ears all over this 'hood. You can't do nothin' with him findin' out. This is his hood. He'd kill us."

"At least we'd die happy," I offered with a melancholy chuckle.

His smile was forced as he lightly stroked my cheek. "You're cute, Kris. Real cute. I wish it could be different, but it can't. I ... I don't know why I even sought you out. It was stupid. I never should have done it. I gotta go."

He vanished down the alley. I stood there in shock. Totally confused. Not knowing what the hell I was going to do. I had never wanted anyone as badly as Houston. This was totally foreign to me. This was love and lust all rolled into one.

"Fuck me," I said aloud causing people to turn and a few mothers to glare at me as they covered their kid's ears.

Instinct took over, and I ran for all I was worth. My tennis shoes pounded the pavement. My side hurt. I didn't even know where the hell I was going.

I had lost sight of Houston long ago.

Please let me find him, I begged. Please. Please. Please.

Finally it was too much. I couldn't run anymore. Defeated, I skidded to a halt and, leaning against a brick wall, tried to slow my heart back to its normal pace. Grimacing, I held my side and coughed. My chest rose and fell, heavy with exhaustion.

Damn it!

Wiping the sweat from my brow I gulped and, wishing I had some water, started to walk back towards my neighborhood. My legs were heavy as lead. My head hung, defeated.

"Persistent lil' fucker. I like it," an amused voice made me have a heart attack.

Turning, I saw Houston casually leaning against the alley wall. He flashed a grin.

"You into alleys?" I asked.

"Lots of fun things can happen in alleys," he winked.

A slow, mischievous smile spread over my lips. My heart continued to race.

"I must be crazy," he laughed. "So," he continued after an eternity of us just staring at each other, "you caught me. Now what?"

"I thought you said we couldn't do anything because of Hood," I said slinking slowly towards him like a panther.

"Fuck Hood," he said wrapping his arms tightly around me, taking my breath away. Drawing me tight against his body he kissed me.

"I already have," I giggled.

"So what do you want to do?"

"You," I stated, grateful I was tenacious when it came to cock.

Houston smiled up at me as I enthusiastically bounced up and down on his thick cock. Holding my hips in place he thrust in and out of me like a jackhammer that's short circuited. Throwing my head back I screamed with pleasure as he gave me the fucking of my life.

His radio was turned on full blast. I rode him in time to the music.

Slapping my cock, he clutched it tightly in his fist and jerked me off as he sang along to the music.

"Milkshake knows how to make Short Stack come and that's why he's better then Hood. Damn right, he's better than Hood. Watch me, pound his little ass hard."

Laughing, I kissed him. "You didn't strike me as a Kellis fan." He merely smirked and smacked my ass.

Bending me over the bed, he fucked me doggy style. His balls slapped against my ass. He kissed my neck as his hips thrust into me. I felt his low hangers tighten. Gripping my hips he pounded into me

112

harder, placed his hands around my neck and gently squeezed. With one good hard thrust I felt his hot jizz explode inside my ass. I felt his dick throb as load after load erupted from him like lava from a volcano.

"Stay there," he said out of breath.

Kneeling behind me I felt him spread my ass. My body trembled at the touch of his lips against my asshole. Sucking all of his cum out of my ass he turned me around and kissed me. My mind flashed back to when Hood had done this to me the first night I had seen Houston. But this time was different.

Our kisses were fiery as we swapped his cum back and forth between us. Our tongues flicked against each other, stirring his cum. Slowly we swallowed every last drop.

"So, what now?" I asked the question I had been dreading as I lay comfortably in his arms, finger lightly playing with his pink nipple.

"Make sure Hood never finds out."

"We could leave LA," I suggested totally serious.

"No way. This is my home. I can't leave it for no one. Not even you. But ..."

"What?" I asked looking into his deep emerald green eyes.

"Nothing," he said.

"Tell me," I whispered stroking his cheek.

"I think I love you," he confessed.

Nodding I kissed him and held onto him tight. "I think I love you, too."

"This is so fucked up," he sighed.

Once again I nodded and kissed his nipple. I didn't want to think about our future. At that moment, I just wanted to enjoy the present.

PIMPED IN CHINA TOWN
Jay Starre

It was 1927 and the height of Prohibition. Alan Wong and Johnny Li were young and ambitious – a little too ambitious.

Hustling a potent brand of smuggled Canadian whiskey, the young thugs had caught the attention of the notorious Bamboo Tong. Deep in the bowels of San Francisco's bustling Chinatown, the pair found themselves in a seedy warehouse with their pants down and unceremoniously draped over a barrel.

"This will teach you a lesson you will not forget."

The immaculately dressed leader of the dozen Tong members who'd confronted Alan and Johnny spoke with perfect diction. Very tall for a Chinaman, he easily dominated the more brutish members of the gang who surrounded the pair and held them in place atop the barrel they were draped over.

"Behold your own product, one which you will cease to market from this day on."

With that, two bottles of whiskey were produced. Greased liberally by smirking Tong crooks, the glistening objects were crammed between Alan and Johnny's naked brown butt-cheeks. With a little probing, the bottles were centered on two quivering assholes.

Alan glanced over at his partner. The look in his golden eyes could almost be called feverish. Alan knew him well; they'd been friends since childhood. That look was not exactly fear. It was excitement, nasty excitement.

As he felt the narrow neck of the whiskey bottle slide around in his crack, and then find his nervous butt-hole, he used all his willpower to open up that tender orifice. The brutes with their hands all over him weren't going to be merciful.

He focused his gaze on his partner in crime, as much to give himself comfort as anything else. Pinned over the barrel, his cock

115

rubbed against the smooth wood, growing stiff despite the dangerous situation – or perhaps because of it!

Guns were aimed at them. Rough hands gripped them. A slippery glass bottle was shoved between their round asscheeks and beginning to push beyond their crinkled butt-lips.

"OH MY GOD! PLEASE STOP! YOU'RE KILLING ME!"

That was Johnny, who was definitely not being killed. He'd always been the one to play it up, the center of attention and the life of the party. Now, he squirmed mightily, his amber butt rising to meet that probing neck and in the process, forcing all of it into his greased hole.

Hoots and laughter greeted the shouted plea, but mercy wasn't forthcoming. The neck of the bottle had driven deep into Alan's gut, and the larger part was pressing against his sphincter. He could see an identical bottle rearing up out of Johnny's butt, two rough hands coated in grease shoving it deeper.

He managed to relax enough, so the slippery bulk eased its way into him. Fuck! It was huge and it was stretching him wide open! Then, all at once, hands released him and the hovering crooks stepped back and away.

"Now, my young friends, if you wish to continue on in the same profession, namely crime, you will do your best to provide my superiors with an exciting demonstration of your willingness to obey them."

The bottle up Alan's ass was beginning to slide outward. He clamped his asshole around it; fearful it would shoot out and smash against one of the Tong and further anger them – not what he wanted at all! Regardless, he listened carefully to the tall leader's next words.

"You are to report tomorrow night promptly at the midnight hour to the Den of the Flaming Lotus. One of you will be the pimp and the other the whore. Prove yourselves and you will be admitted to the illustrious membership of the Bamboo Tong. Fail and you will suffer the consequences."

Like smoke in a stiff wind, the Tong thugs disappeared. The pair was left with their pants around their ankles and greased whisky bottles corking their tender bungholes.

"Can you shove mine in a little deeper? I'm just about to blow!"

Alan rolled his eyes and shook his head. He squatted back and released his anal grip on the bulk of the bottle shoved up his ass. He groaned as the object shot out into his hands.

"You fucking fool! This is serious. But at least there's no question of who's going to be the whore tomorrow night."

Johnny snickered as he used his own hands to shove the bottle another few inches up his straining asshole. With a loud grunt, he arched his back, drove into the barrel with his crotch, and shot.

The following evening was balmy, and the streets of Chinatown were crowded. Horses pulled market wagons and vied with honking Ford Model Ts while pedestrians darted in and out, and bicycles wove their way amongst all that chaos.

Most of the denizens were Chinese. Some dressed traditionally in their silk robes, while others were garbed in fine suits and others in woolen pants and cotton shirts. Nonetheless, there were plenty of white men, Americans or foreigners daring the dangerous night life in their search for pleasure.

Most of the Chinese were male, since the immigration of females was restricted. On the Street of the Gamblers, this was all the more evident. Alan and Johnny passed pagodas, restaurants, myriad herbal and vegetable shops, fish and meat markets, and all manner of other tiny stores dealing in gold, Chinese imports and of course illegal goods.

The Den of the Flaming Lotus naturally had a completely innocuous entrance. An alley off an alley terminated in a dead-end and a wooden doorway with only a small sign tacked above.

Within, everything changed. Two burly Chinese door-keepers patted them down and pointed upwards, indicating a narrow stairway to the left. Straight ahead, the hallway opened up to a main floor decorated in gaudy crimsons and populated by a seething mass of revelers enjoying the illegal liquor served up to one and all.

The sounds of their drunken merry-making were muffled by the dark walls of the stairway and then silenced as they came out on the second floor. Bamboo, lilies in fine Chinese vases, and tasteful carpets decorated the waiting room, along with an elderly Chinaman with an inscrutable expression.

"Come," he practically spit out, waving a ruby-robed arm at the pair.

They were ushered into one of the nearby rooms and the door slammed behind them. Sparsely decorated with more Chinese bamboo and art work, a single large bed dominated the room while an over-stuffed chair occupied a corner.

"You have five minutes to prepare." The voice from above startled the young thugs. Looking up, they realized the unusually high ceiling served a purpose. Along the right wall about eight feet up, a bamboo lattice served as a balcony balustrade. Behind it, stood the immaculately dressed Tong leader they'd met only the day before. He smiled beautiful white teeth in a feral grin. It was frightening.

On either side of him sat another half dozen Chinamen of various ages, all offering the same evil grin. A lamp behind them was extinguished, and they disappeared into darkness. Now, any new arrivals in the room would be unaware they hovered above and watched.

Alan's heart pounded in his chest. He was terrified, while his partner grinned with foolish anticipation as he plopped down on the bright red silk that draped the single bed. Johnny had chosen to dress in a cream suit that suited his light brown complexion but now clashed violently with the crimson of the bed silks.

Alan was dressed in a suit as well, although less flamboyantly than his partner in crime. His suit was a conservative dark-grey with a green vest and matching bow tie and bowler. His eyes, an unusual hazel, sparkled with a hint of that green.

"Get undressed, you fool! Now! Quickly. Display yourself for our soon-to-be arriving guest."

Johnny pouted his lower lip in a false display of hurt feelings, but did as he was told. He tossed aside his matching cream hat and tore off his black bow-tie before discarding the rest of his suit. Alan quickly rounded up the discarded articles and hid them under the skirts of the bed.

"How's this, Alan? Tempting enough?"

The young Chinaman was entirely nude. He crouched atop the crimson silks at the foot of the bed so that his bare backside would be the first thing an entering guest would see. He knelt with slim legs spread wide apart and leaned forward on his hands, arching his back.

Alan came around to inspect. Although extremely nervous about their chances of pleasing the guest they expected, and the watching Tong above, he couldn't help but feel his cock stir at the sexy sight of his pal on display.

Although his upper body was slender, his shoulders were unexpectedly broad. Supple muscle writhed under amber flesh along his back down to his slim waist and butt.

Between those parted cheeks, his asshole was plainly visible. It pouted outwards as he grinned and winked at his partner. "You know what I can do with this hole. Don't worry!"

A discreet cough from above alerted Alan to what he must do. Quickly, he reached out and grasped his partner by those perky buttcheeks and spun him sideways, pushing down on his head at the same time with an elbow.

Now, he faced the hidden Tong above, his fine bottom in the air. Alan spread the cheeks wider apart, which made the hole wink open for those above to peruse. There was more required, he sensed. One hand dropped between Johnny's splayed thighs and grasped his dangling cock. Thankfully it was suitably stiff. For such a small man, he owned a substantial cock and a pair of hefty balls.

Alan pulled it back and down so the Tong above got a good look at the fat thing, pumping it with his hand a few times as he slid his other hand into his buddy's parted crack and tickled the hairless asshole nastily.

He imagined he heard some muffled gasps of appreciation, but then the door behind them creaked out a warning. He barely had time to spin his partner back around to face their visitor.

"Welcome, Fine Sir! You like? All for you. Fine bottom to fucky-fuck. All for you, Sir!"

He faced the newcomer with his hands on Johnny's butt and his best smile in place. He spoke in the Pidgin English most Whites expected of the Chinese, even though he'd been born and raised in San Francisco and spoke American like a native.

The man was big. An Englishman from his looks, with a sun-burned face and bushy blond eyebrows. His pale blue eyes inspected the offering with what looked like approval while his plump lips curled into a small semblance of a smile.

He took off his own coat and tossed it over the stuffed chair behind him. Suspenders were snug across a barrel chest as he plopped down in the chair and faced the pair. So far, he'd said nothing and remained quiet as he used hairy-knuckled hands to unbutton his trousers and fish out an incredibly fat prick. He pumped it to full erection in seconds, all the while staring fixedly at the ass in front of him with those pale blue orbs.

Johnny couldn't see him with his head down, but he got into his role with his usual fervor anyway. He wriggled his sweet can in sexy circles and willed his asshole to clamp and pout as he arched his back and spread his knees even farther apart.

The Englishman spoke. "I'll be watching your bloke get his arse focked first, then I'll be focking his used arsehole afterwards. Sloppy seconds is my game, gentlemen."

Alan's hazel eyes blinked rapidly as he attempted to understand what was wanted. Did the big Englishman want him to fuck Johnny first? He didn't know! He could only stall for time and hope it would be clear soon enough.

"Very good, Sir. Yes, my friend gets ass fucked while you watch, then you fuck sloppy hole after! Very sexy, Sir. Very good Sir!" He was careful to roll his R's into L's as would have been expected.

He was saved by a second arrival. Another big man practically stormed into the room, so suddenly and quickly, Alan scrambled backwards in a hasty effort to bow and cringe with proper servility.

"Welcome, Sir. Welcome. This fine ass belongs to you, and this fine Gentleman watches. Is OK? Is fine, Sir?"

The second man was a Negro. Dressed in a dark woolen suit that looked as if it was about to rip at the seams, he filled the space between the seated Englishman and Johnny crouched on the bed with his bulk. His dark eyes nearly bulged out of his large head and his big mouth split into a toothy grin.

"Yep. Sounds damn good. Ya' Chinymen can take a good fuck, I reckon, from personal experience in the past. And ya' squeal like little piglets while you do. The English can watch me gut that snug hole with my big sausage, no damn sweat off'n my back."

With that, he began to tear his clothes off and toss them in all directions.

Alan bowed and whimpered as he hastily scampered around to fetch the clothing and pile it up on the single little table beside the bed. At the same time, he snatched a glance at the black tool bouncing between those immense black thighs.

It was enormous! He quailed as he thought of Johnny taking that massive sausage up his tender asshole. Almost frantically, he searched through the drawer in the night stand for what he hoped was there.

"Sir! Just for you! Best oil. Best for slippery ride. I pour for you, Sir!"

The Negro was already poised at the edge of the bed; giant prick bobbing in the air between Alan's spread thighs. The young thug had lifted his head enough to crane it around and get a look at what was in store for him. His almond orbs grew huge, and his dimpled chin quivered as he bit his lower lip and emitted a little shriek.

"Please, Sir! Give me big cock! I like fucky-fuck with big cock!"

Alan was already there and pouring the oil over that bobbing monster as it approached its destination. Big knees dropped onto the edge of the bed and the crimson silk bed covering. They drove slender brown ones farther apart as that rearing cock plunged into the waiting asscrack.

Smooth honey-brown flesh welcomed the black knob that slithered along it. Alan kept busy squirting a stream of the lily-scented oil all over that crack while Johnny did more than just submit to the inevitable. He reached back and spread open his crack with splayed fingers, displaying a winking hole that now drooled oil.

The black man laughed out loud as he planted his engorged member right on target. There were no preliminaries. He thrust with his powerful hips and rammed that slippery knob deep into the small brown slot.

The men who came to the Den of the Flaming Lotus were not looking for tender kisses and gentle embraces. No, not at all. They were looking for a nasty time. The Negro's big eyes focused with a luminous gleam on that quivering hole as it clamped around his buried cock-head. He licked huge lips and let out another booming laugh.

"Good fuck, lads! Damn good and tight! Now ya' open up for all Daddy's got to give!"

Johnny's entire body bucked as that gigantic black snake burrowed deeper, impaling him in a series of rapid thrusts that had him flopping and squirming and crying out.

The young thug was not asking for mercy. "Cock! Yes, Sir! More damn cock, please!"

His impaler laughed heartily, luminous eyes intent on the squirming body in front of him. He reached out and gripped the slender waist to hold it in place as he continued to feed his black cock to the quivering hole. It was a wonder to witness.

Alan's mouth was agape as he, too, watched the amazing display. He tore his eyes from that gut-goring to look at their other guest. Soft blue eyes were alight with pleasure and big pink tongue licked plump red lips. A hairy hand slowly pumped a satisfying stiff cock.

Their eyes met, and the Englishman nodded. Alan exhaled a sigh of relief. He only hoped the silent watchers above were getting what they wanted!

On the bed, his crime partner obviously was getting what he wanted. He screamed and begged and slammed his jiggling round ass back against the massive black pole drilling his poor asshole. He wasn't merely submitting. His hands were busy in his own crack, pulling open the hole with his fingers, or stroking the giant cock gutting him. When that black snake was yanked out momentarily, he dug his own fingers into his gooey, stretched hole in a nasty probe.

"Look what you do to me, Sir! A big damn sloppy hole for you! A big sloppy hole for big damn cock!"

That tiny orifice was not exactly a big sloppy hole, at least not yet, but it had been stretched. Now, the Negro's black knob slammed back home with a slurping squish. Both men yelled out their pleasure.

Alan had to admire his buddy. Johnny performed supremely. He shrieked and wriggled and humped. His lithe brown body was quickly bathed in a sheen of sweat, while his round buttocks glistened with oil. His asshole was a puckered brown sump that squished and spurted as that black pole drove in and out with hip-slamming ferocity.

The Negro reached ahead to grip Johnny's shoulders and hold him in place as he pummeled that honey-brown butt. It was amazing to see that huge black body bent over the slender brown one as cock reamed hole in a continual slithering slide.

For his part he kept busy pouring more oil into the nasty juncture of hole and cock, then hastened to their other guest to pour some of the same oil over his rearing pink prick. He even took it in hand and helped pump it, which had the seated Englishman grunting and lifting his big hips up off the sofa.

His pale eyes remained focused though on the nasty sight in front of him, namely the Negro's big black buttocks pumping against the Chinaman's lush brown ass. He licked his lips and grinned, no doubt imagining how juicy and sloppy poor Johnny's asshole would be once the Negro was finished with him.

That came relatively quickly. The man fucked so industriously he managed to push himself to a climax after barely ten minutes of kneeling on the bed behind his flopping victim and pounding his black cock home. With a roar, he yanked out his oily prick and took it in one of his dark paws. He pumped out an astounding geyser of nut cream. Cum ran down Johnny's sweaty back and jiggling buttocks.

"A damn fine fuck, gents. Damn fine. I ain't gonna be stingy with the tip, neither. Where's my duds?"

Alan scurried to help the Negro dress as his partner gasped and snorted for air on the bed, coated in cum. Their other guest remained seated, although his eyes were riveted on Alan's oiled ass and dripping, stretched hole.

The thug on the bed, playing the whore to his best ability, recuperated quickly. Both his hands were on his ass already and it was easy enough for him to spread the hole wide open with his fingers and offer their seated guest a good view of the flushed butt entrance.

"All for you, Sir! Damn sloppy hole for you. Very damn sloppy!"

He probed the gooey slot with a pair of fingers, making loud squishes as he dug around and pushed in and out. Alan had ushered the Negro out and shut the door, turning just in time to witness the provocative display. He was quick to follow it up.

"Yes, Sir! Damn good sloppy seconds ready for you! I take your clothes? You go for sloppy seconds?"

With an ingratiating smile, he helped the Englishman to his feet and took his clothes as he silently stripped, without taking his eyes off the crouching Chinese thug on the bed.

Johnny played it up. He continued stretching open his dripping hole, fingering it deep while moaning and wriggling.

The Englishman was naked in no time, his large body pink and surprisingly smooth. Blond fur coated his forearms and surrounded the base of his rearing pink prong, but the rest of him was smooth and ivory-pale. Although a muscular man, he was slightly overweight with a big butt and a round smooth belly. It was a total contrast to the giant Negro who'd just been working over the slender Alan.

He stepped forward, pale blue orbs on target. To Johnny's surprise, his hand flew forward and three fingers rammed into the hole Johnny stretched open. Hairy knuckles twisted savagely, then hooked and lifted. Johnny was raised right off the bed by the three fingers hooked in his asshole.

124

"Excellent. Sloppy enough, chaps. Now for a hearty ride. Sit on my prick and show me what you've got!"

The growl in that demand was plain enough. Johnny, grunting from the strain of those three big digits hooked up his asshole, still managed to rear upright onto his feet in a half-stand while spreading him even wider apart.

"Damn good, Sir. Please lay on bed for ride! Damn sloppy hole all for you!"

The Englishman grinned outright as he yanked his fingers from the slippery hole and dove between those spread thighs. Laughing now, he rolled over onto his back and sprawled out between Johnny's slender legs.

The thug-turned-whore was quick. He squatted directly over the rearing English prick and with a bright grin of his own, swooped down to envelop it in a squishy anal embrace.

Alan let out a gasp of amazement. Standing at the foot of the bed, he was treated to the sight of that puckered brown asshole swallowing up the entire length of the thick pink cock in a magnificent plunge.

And as if that wasn't nasty enough, the slim Chinaman at once began to ride it, rising up and dropping down with enthusiastic glee. Alan moved in to squirt more oil over the cock and hole to lubricate the action.

His own cock throbbed in his slacks as he watched that amazing impalement. The fat pink pole appeared and disappeared, coated in a slick gleam of oil, while the puckered brown asslips clung to it as they stretched and strained to swallow and expel it.

Perky, honey-brown butt-cheeks slammed up and down over the ivory-pale crotch. Johnny continued to use his hands to stretch open his own asscrack, and when he rose up enough to pull off that fat cock entirely, he would probe his own gooey hole with a pair of fingers and cry out, "Damn sloppy hole! All for you, Sir!"

The Englishman lay back with his muscular arms folded behind his neck and smiled. Alan kept an eye on his face to gauge his expression. His mouth was especially interesting to watch, with big, bright-red, plump lips slick with drool and spittle as he licked them with a very large tongue.

The Englishman must have noted Alan's gaze on his mouth. With a smirk, he swiped his fat tongue over those fat lips and called out to him. "Be a good bloke and drop your drawers for me. A sloppy hole isn't my only game. Eating out a snug bum is next on my list."

The thug-turned-pimp realized he had no choice in the matter. They had to please the big Englishman! He quickly kicked off his fancy dress shoes and unbuttoned his suspenders where they held up his slacks. They flew off, followed by his cotton underwear. Still wearing his coat, vest, bow-tie and bowler and dress socks, he scurried to the head of the bed and hopped up to straddle the Englishman's flushed face.

Massive hands seized his round ass and pulled downward. Gasping, he felt his asshole clench and pout in anticipation, but was hardly prepared for the slick, wet sensation of fat lips and slippery tongue suddenly glued to his asscrack.

Those giant paws held him in place as tongue went to work on his pouting hole. He groaned and bit his lip as that fat appendage burrowed between his nervous butt-lips and dove deep into him.

At the same time, Johnny chose to spin around, cock still inside his talented asshole, and now faced the foot of the bed as he continued to rise and fall over their guest's huge pink pole.

"Damn sloppy hole for you! All for you! Eat Chinaman hole at same time. Damn tasty that Chinaman hole. All for you, Sir!"

Alan leaned forward, his hazel eyes staring down at the perky ass slamming down over that English pole. The sight made him dizzy with nasty lust. Especially since that huge English mouth was busy on his hole and crack with loud, slurping greed.

The Englishman's fat lips clamped over his asshole and sucked it inside out. Then, they moved down to engulf his balls in one wet gulp. Then, they burrowed farther between his splayed thighs and captured his stiff cock, swallowing it to the root.

Alan was not at all slender like his buddy. He was stocky and muscular, and his strong thighs bulged around the Englishman's head.

His ass, equally smooth and golden, was much larger and rounder than his slim partner's. The Englishman seized it in his giant hands and squeezed as he attacked the crack with his big mouth.

The greedy lips smacked lewdly as they sucked on hole, swallowed balls, and engulfed cock. The fat tongue lapped all along the ass divide then settled on the tender hole and dug deep into it. The big hands held the pimp-thug in place.

Meanwhile, Johnny remained busy riding that fat cock while making sure to shout out as much nastiness as possible. Alan was reassured that his partner managed to keep his head and play it up for their unseen audience above. He only hoped they were doing enough!

The Englishman, unaware of the hidden eyes on them, was concerned only with his own pleasure. He knew what he wanted, and by this time was convinced the pair of Chinamen was going to provide that nasty delight for him. He shoved Alan off of his face and barked out his demands.

"Time for me to fock that sloppy hole. On your back, bloke, with your legs in the air."

The pair scrambled to obey. Alan assumed it was Johnny's ass the Englishman referred to, and was quick to position himself appropriately. He bounded to the foot of the bed and helped his partner get set up.

Johnny lay on his back, his feet in the air and his hands clasped behind his knees. His perky butt was wide open. His asshole pouted into a pink rosebud, sufficiently stretched by the Negro and English cocks he'd had up there. Just to be safe, Alan reached down to stretch open that dripping hole with a pair of fingers on either side of the gaping asslips.

"All for you, Sir. Damn good sloppy hole to fucky-fuck!"

The Englishman reared up off the bed like a sleepy giant come to life. He threw his massive thighs across the side of the bed, staggered to his feet and stepped around to the foot of the bed. Alan moved aside just in time for the giant to plant himself between Johnny's raised legs.

"Excellent. Now, I will fock that sloppy hole good!"

He did. His rearing pink cock drove down into the amber gash, slamming home with a squish. Johnny's almond eyes bugged out and his pert little mouth gaped in a shriek of surprise. Alan's own asshole snapped in sympathy, all wet with the Englishman's spit and pleasantly throbbing. A small part of him envied his partner's position.

The Englishman fucked hard and furious. He gripped Johnny's slender feet in his big hands and split him in two, pounding into this squishy asshole as he drove him all over the crimson silk bed covers. Alan was hard-pressed to keep up, squirting oil down over his partner's upended ass and watching with amazement.

Johnny was no longer pretending anything. His slender body was a flopping toy shoved, lifted, thrown and gutted all over the bed. He emitted a constant stream of practically incoherent gibberish and squeals.

The Englishman seemed well-satisfied. "A fucking piglet! A focking squealing, sloppy-holed piglet," he crooned in his deep growl.

Alan was in awe as the fuck went on and on. Whenever the Englishman pulled out, Johnny's asshole bloomed, now a truly sloppy orifice that seemed to have totally capitulated. The young thug's body was a limp rag by this time, his cock still stiff but seemingly forgotten.

Finally, thankfully, the giant blond achieved his orgasm. With a roar, he yanked his cock out of his victim's tenderized asshole and let loose. He sprayed the blossoming asshole with his cream, gobs and gobs of the sticky pale stuff.

Johnny managed a weak grin, sweat dripping from every part of his well-used body. Alan was exhausted himself from merely watching. He kept his head though, and helped the Englishman dress while complimenting him on the fine fuck he'd thrown.

"Very impressive. Englishman fucky-fuck so fine. Make sloppy hole very happy!"

"I'll be back, chaps. And I'll be wanting some more sloppy seconds. Fine work. Fine work."

He was gone, and they were left alone, except of course for the silently menacing observers above. Alan strained his ears for some kind of signal from the Tong leaders watching on the balcony but heard nothing.

Desperate, he hit on one final ploy to demonstrate their willingness to go all out for their new Masters.

Earlier, when searching through the drawer of the night table, he'd noticed a couple of other objects there. With a bound, he returned to the table. Opening it up, he reached in and snatched them up.

"We are reformed, Masters! We are no longer selling these, but are now your proper pimp and whore."

With that, he crammed one of the whiskey bottles deep into Johnny's asshole as the young thug lay sprawled back on the crimson silks with his legs spread and his knees up. He squealed, but took the bottle nearly all the way.

At the same time, Alan hopped up on the bed and shoved the second whiskey bottle between his own spread thighs. He promptly sat down over it, swallowing up a substantial portion of the thing in a desperate bid to impress.

The gooey wetness left behind from the Englishman's tongue bath helped – and his own nasty glow from all that wild fucking. He sat down on the bottle and wriggled his own lush butt over it while driving the bottle up Johnny's well-lubed and well-fucked asshole nearly all the way home.

Above, finally, a disembodied voice called out.

"Very good, gentlemen. You are now members of the Bamboo Tong. Tomorrow night you will return and take up your new positions."

Johnny's flushed face broke out into a wide grin. And he shot. With that whiskey bottle sliding completely inside his blooming asshole with a loud squish, he arched his back and sprayed a geyser of cum.

Alan groaned around the bottle digging into his own asshole. The realization they'd succeeded, and the sight of that bottle disappearing into his buddy's amazing asshole, along with the spray of cum were enough to get him off.

Homo Thugs

He leaned over Johnny and shot.

His partner pulled him down for a sloppy kiss.

They were now members of the Bamboo Tong!

MIDNIGHT HOUR
Mark James

After the cold drizzle outside, Gridline Diner felt warm and smelled of greasy food and strong coffee. Two men in the corner booth looked up when I came in. I walked slow, forced myself not to rush, hoped I didn't look like what I was, a Meth on the run.

"Rafe meet Harlon," Leo said. "Deep sky Captain."

Pirate, I thought, sliding into the booth. Leo was a cop so crooked he made a coiled snake look straight. No real Captain would be hanging out with him. "What's your ship?"

"Midnight Hour," Harlon said.

I looked at Leo like he'd lost his mind. "The slimiest brothel riding the skies? No."

His windbreaker didn't hide Harlon's solid body. He looked like the name of his ship, his skin a cool dark cocoa. He folded his hands on the table. "I ain't buying you for the fuck cabins. You're gonna be mine."

I took in his brown eyes, his bald head. The tattoos etched into the back of his left hand weren't coffin nails with my name on them, but they were pretty damn close.

"He agreed to buy off your sentence," Leo said.

Most men bought only a two-year contract, then a Meth Transfer had to hope someone else picked it up before his sentence was reinstated. "How long?" I broke out in a light sweat. He was taking too long to answer.

Leo reached in his pocket, brought out a mini tablet. "Five years." The cop's voice took on the oily feel of a black market street dealer. "Your sentence gets erased. Your DNA signature is wiped from the crime scene record. It's a good deal."

At the top of the contract on the screen, I saw my name. Below that, RS874B. "RS?" I glanced at Harlon. "In a pirate brothel? Are you insane? No."

"You don't have a choice," Leo said. "I already took the Captain's credit."

The reality of what Harlon had done to earn his tattoos hit me hard. "Find a way to give it back."

Leo's voice turned low, vicious. "That fight you ran from, it was on my beat," he said. "I'm getting shit to bring you in. That would be a real pain. I'd have to find the Captain another boy. If you make me do that, I'll fucking guarantee you a cell in Blue Ice."

Jesus. Blue Ice Work Camp was in Alaska up on the Snow Plains. Maybe people made it back, but I never heard of any.

Leo rolled a stylus across the table.

My choice was easy: the fire or the frying pan, Hell or Purgatory, ten years in a Work Camp or five years on a pirate ship. I took one last look at Harlon's tattoos, then scrawled my name on the bottom line. The stylus shook in my grip, but only a little.

Leo took the tablet, keyed in a code, then spun it around. "DNA signature erasure."

Which meant my DNA scan would buy nothing for five years. I hesitated only a bare instant before I pressed my thumb to the screen.

He scooped up the electronic Write Pad, got to his feet, and shook Harlon's hand. "Ever need anything; you know how to find me."

Just like that, I'd become a black market Registered Slave, property of a man with confirmed kills inside Ferron City, the toughest prison in the country.

Harlon reached across the table, stroked my cheek. "Let's get a cab. I gotta get back to my ship."

# # # # #

The cab smelled of stale cigarettes and old sweat.

"You ever been on a barge?" Harlon said.

"No, sir."

"You ain't gotta call me that."

"Sorry."

Harlon slid his left hand between my legs. "Fuck, lighten up. You're gonna see the world, be my cabin Boy."

With all those bodies under your bunk, could be a tight fit. "Your ship pretty big?"

"Used to be a cruise barge." He rubbed my crotch. "I got a beach up there."

I'll be honest. How he touched me, that slick arrogance in his eyes, he could have had me on my knees eight days out of seven, all but begging for it. But between the cab flying through pouring rain at suicidal speed, and the four spikes on the back of his left hand, I couldn't have raised a hard-on with a power jack.

Harlon played with my hair, let the silky feel of it run through his thick fingers again and again. He took my face in one hand, rubbed his thumb over my dark pink lips. "Damn. You're real pretty. What you done that they wanna put a sweet looking thing like you in a Work Camp?"

"He didn't tell you?"

"Told me about the fight. But that ain't enough to get you in Blue Ice."

I stalled. "You were in Ferron City. How come?"

He sat back, folded his hands in his lap. When he spoke again, his voice was flat, almost detached. "You heard about anybody in there for anything but murder? Answer what I asked you."

All at once, the back seat felt cramped; Harlon's bulk towered over me. "I didn't register. Then I got in a fight. I hurt someone. I ran."

"How come you gotta register? What you know how to do?"

"PK Burn."

Harlon was silent long enough for me to think he would put me out in the rain, and go beat the crap out of Leo, get his credits back. I held my breath.

"Quit acting so scared. I ain't nothing but a pirate making a living in the sky. I do what I gotta do. Ain't no more to it than that."

# # # # #

The cab stopped on the rooftop long enough for us to get out, then took off.

Barges are too big to land in a city. We'd have to fly up to it, higher than a cab was geared to go.

A sky copter waited on a launch pad – that had to be illegal. No one would get clearance for takeoff in weather like this. A man jumped out, waved both hands at Harlon in a gesture that was unmistakable – hurry up.

One look at the tiny copter, buffeted by the wind, and I knew I couldn't do it.

"Come on." Harlon grabbed my arm. "Weather's going all to shit."

The thought of getting in that death machine made my belly drop all the way to my knees. "On the roof like this, I don't think ..."

Harlon made a low impatient sound. Before I could say more, he swung me over his shoulder and raced through the rain.

I squeezed my eyes shut, sure he'd delay take off long enough to toss me off the roof. The roar of the copter's motor got louder and louder till it filled my head. Strong hands from inside the murderous thing's insides grabbed me off Harlon's shoulder. "Got him, Penny?"

A man's voice shouted. "Yeah. Go."

By the time I wiped water from my eyes and smoothed my hair back, Harlon was inside next to the pilot.

"Strap him in," the pilot said. His voice barely competed with the copter's straining engines, struggling to lift us against the wind.

Penny, the man in the bucket seat across from me, grabbed loose straps and wove a criss-cross harness over me in about two seconds flat. He fastened the last buckle into the seat between my legs, pulled tight. "Sorry. We got rough skies. You all right?"

It hurt less than a kick in my balls, but not by much. "Yeah, I'm fine."

We bounced through the sky like a jeep on a rocky road. I was trapped tighter than any fly ever caught in a spider's web. It was a bad time to dredge up old pirate stories, but they paraded across my mind like I was making my own holo, Rafe and the Pirate Terrors of the Sky.

The worst rumor about brothels like Midnight Hour was how they dumped used-up Boys overboard. I didn't see why Harlon's ship would be any different. After all, with four spikes, one for each kill in Ferron City, how hard would it be for him to pitch a scared Boy over the rail? Probably wouldn't even hang around till the screams faded.

# # # # #

As soon as we landed on Midnight Hour, a man yanked open Harlon's door. He shouted over the driving wind and the copter's engine. "Need you in the Tower. We move now, we outrun the storm."

"Right behind you," Harlon said. He looked at me over his shoulder. "You do what he tells you."

"I got him," Penny said. He was already undoing my straps.

"Where's he going?"

"Command Tower. Navigate us past the storm."

"Get out," the pilot said. "I got to stow the chopper."

Penny leaned in close. "Wait for me to jump down, then follow me. Understand?"

I watched him land on the slippery deck. It was a long way down.

The pilot turned around, glared at me. "Get the fuck out."

We were hovering above the deck. Oh God.

I jumped.

And slipped and landed on my ass. Penny threw himself on top of me, held me down. We both squeezed our eyes shut against the warm spray of the copter lifting up fast.

Penny shook water off his face. "Fucking storm wasn't supposed to blow in till tomorrow. Goddamn weather heads." He pushed himself up, hauled me to my feet. "Come on."

I ran behind him to an overhang that hid the top of stairs steep enough to be a ladder. On the way down, I tried to ignore how the barge tilted like a ship sailing rough seas.

# # # # #

On the second deck, the only light came from holo-movies that disguised the metal doors, turning them into windows on mansion-sized bedrooms, complete with four-poster beds.

In some rooms, a sleek, smoothly muscled boy was on his back, looking up at the man fucking him, writhing in ecstasy. In other rooms, a boy was on his knees, taking a man's cock impossibly deep in his throat.

Giant clocks painted on crimson walls stood at two minutes to midnight. Words trailed between them, ride till the midnight hour.

Penny stopped, peered into the shadows. "Cody? That you?"

"Yeah. What do you want?"

"How come you're out here?"

Cody tossed his black hair out of his face. "Didn't feel like being locked up like I'm in a fucking zoo."

"Harlon's on his way. You're on the edge with him. He finds you out here, it's your ass."

Cody dragged deep on his cigarette, blew smoke toward Penny's face. "Whatever."

Penny turned to me. "Come on. One more deck down."

I lingered on the steps, feeling as if I should say something.

"What are you looking at?" Cody said.

"Is it bad down here?"

"Bad? No. It's fucking hell." He walked through the holo, slammed the door behind him.

Penny's voice came from below me. "You coming?"

I hurried after him, thinking about the look on Cody's face. I'd do anything to stay off that deck.

# # # # #

Harlon's cabin was small, warm, and so neat; he could put maid service out of business forever.

"Get naked," Penny said.

I froze. Was he the audition before Harlon's main show? Or the warm up?

"Relax, boy. Need to get you out of those wet clothes."

Under his impatient eye, I looked for somewhere to undress.

"Just strip down. You got three of something I ain't seen before?"

I shed my clothes, left them in a soggy pile, and put on the red flannel shirt Penny gave me. It fell past my knees

He took off his wet shirt, revealing the rock-hard arms and chest of a man who'd spent years doing heavy work. He didn't seem to care that his jeans were soaked. "How long he bought you for, kid?"

"Five years."

He let out a low whistle. "Last Cabin Boy made it about six months."

"Where's the body?"

That earned me a long, hard look. "If it was me in Harlon's cabin, I'd lose that smart mouth."

"I didn't mean ..."

"Come out with me. I need a smoke." He grabbed his cigarettes off a low table.

# # # # #

With the door closed behind us, he lit up. "Harlon's ex-MC You know what they do?"

I'd heard of the Mercenary Corps, seen them on holo. "Targeted hits in the war?"

"I put a gun in your hand right now, and tell you I'm gonna kill you, you'd shoot me. That's how we work, self preservation."

"Harlon's different?"

"MC uses Kill Feedback."

"What?"

"Means the harder your target fights, the harder you go after them. The harder the kill, the better you feel. It's no joke. Hypno Conditioning. Never goes away."

"He likes to hurt you?" I couldn't bring myself to say "kill."

"Didn't say that." Penny inhaled a lung full of smoke; let it trickle out between his words. "Harlon's a good man. In a fight, I want him at my back every time. But you piss him off, talking's done. He does what he's gotta do."

Yeah. I heard. "What happened to his last cabin boy?"

"You met him."

Oh, damn. I leaned against the cool metal wall, head back, eyes closed. "Cody? But he's not in Harlon's cabin anymore."

"You don't miss much, do you?"

"What did he do?"

"I'm guessing he pissed off Harlon. Just telling you. Watch yourself with him."

Rapid footsteps echoed on the metal stairs.

"What's he doing out here?"

At the sight of Harlon, it was all I could do to stop myself from taking off at a dead run. But where would I go?

"Needed a smoke," Penny said. "We ahead of the weather?"

"Almost." Harlon lifted my shirt, fondled my balls. "Go on inside and take this off. I gotta talk to Penny."

Him touching me like that in front of another man made my face burn. Embarrassed, I turned my back on them, opened the door.

# # # # #

Those M.C. men used Adrenal Crystal to jack up their reflexes. Their reaction time was in the millionth of a second range. That explained why he didn't care about me being PK. Harlon could throw me overboard before I could more than give him a light suntan.

I stripped out of the red shirt and stopped short. I didn't know if he wanted me between his sheets or on my knees or ...

The floor tilted, then leveled out.

I played it safe, sat in the corner on a thin rug between his bed and the wall.

The floor tilted. Rain lashed the tiny circle of a window. The lights went out.

My breath stopped in my throat. I forced air from my lungs. It came out in a breathless scream.

I jumped to my feet, ran through the dark, heading for the sound of rain on the window. If I could lock out, and see even the dark grey rain clouds ...

I tripped, went sprawling to the floor.

Cold metal under my naked body, blinded by darkness, I felt like I was in a drawer in a morgue, locked up tight.

The door opened, black on black. Footsteps rushed toward me.

Violent bursts of color pulsed in and out to the rhythm of my thudding heart. Oh, God. I didn't need this. The Burn was starting.

"You all right, Boy?"

No, I wanted to say. Stay back.

But I couldn't talk, couldn't stop what was building inside. A river of fire rushed through me, flaming every nerve.

"Rafe." It was Harlon. "Talk to me."

I was burning up inside. I had to let the fire out. I banged both palms flat against the metal deck.

The relief was instant, but I was in a different kind of trouble. Spreading heat turned the deck hotter and hotter under me. I couldn't move; the discharge had exhausted me.

Harlon scooped me up. "Holy shit." He shifted back.

I knew he could feel the heated deck through his shoes. "I would have burned you if I didn't let it out."

"Harlon?" It was Penny, from the doorway.

"Yeah. It's all right. Systems online?"

"I don't know. Engines are still up."

"Go check. I'll be there in a minute." Harlon put me on his bed. "Don't move."

He disappeared into the dark, then I saw the glow of a candle.

"You need anything?" He sat beside me. "It makes you feel sick?"

"No. Just thirsty." I edged away from him. "Guess you want your credit back."

The lights flickered, blinked, then stayed steady.

"I seen more shit than you know, boy. I gotta get up top. You all right?"

I licked my dry lips. "Yeah."

He left. I heard him lock the door behind him.

# # # # #

I slipped into his red shirt, looked out the window. Beyond the double pane, it was grey on grey.

If I wasn't here, I'd be ... where?

Cooking in a dive? Working the street, hoping the Registry Special Forces didn't find me?

I was in a battle to survive, and it felt as if I was on the losing side.

Back in the first half of the Hundred Years Middle East Conflict, our side poisoned the ocean over there. Japan and China dropped out of the war.

Good for our side.

The virus from Operation Black Waters spread, turned the oceans deadly. The poisonous vapors rising off the water killed entire ships of soldiers.

Bad for our side.

Sky Transports and Deep Sky barges slowed the war machine, but it kept cranking out death.

In the second half of the Conflict, a religious nut case slipped Meth Steroids into the water supply.

By the time our side found out, women were already sterile or they were having Meth Babies like me – weird, fucked up.

Failure to Register was a mandatory ten year Work Camp sentence. But Meths who registered faded off the grid. First you're there living a normal life, then you're gone, like you never existed.

I looked around Harlon's cabin, realized an awful truth.

Five years from now, if I joined the grid again, I'd be on the run, hoping I was one step ahead of being kidnapped to whatever dark corner they took Meths.

If I didn't make it on Midnight Hour, then one way or another, my life was over.

The lock rattled before the door opened and revealed the big outline of Harlon's body. When I saw what he was carrying, I thought maybe it was his idea of a joke.

Kicking the door shut, he dropped the box on the low table, and tossed me a bottle. "Here. You said you was thirsty."

I was parched. The Burn always did that to me.

"What's funny ?" he said.

I finished the bottle of water in three long swallows. "I'd have to Burn your whole ship to be thirsty enough for a case of water."

A half-smile smoothed out the hard lines of his face. "I don't get into nothing I ain't prepared for."

I couldn't meet his eyes. Instead I looked at the scorch mark I'd left on the deck. "I got scared. I can't control it."

Harlon made me stand, so we were on opposite sides of the burn mark, facing each other. "You been on that side of things all your life." He pulled me across the line. "Now you're in my world. On this side of things, ain't nothing we can't find a way to make right."

He took me in his arms, kissed me.

It felt like the Burn starting again. But this time I wasn't scared. I wanted Harlon to set me on fire.

His rough calloused hands cupped my ass, squeezed.

I wrapped my arms around him, felt his firm muscled body under my touch.

"Damn, boy. You could drive a man crazy." He sat on his bed, spread his legs. "Come over here."

I shucked out of his shirt, knelt between his legs, and kneaded his crotch softly.

He undid his jeans, took out his hard cock and leaned back on his thick arms. "Suck me."

I cupped his full balls in my hands, licked up and down his dick; let my tongue slide all over his dark flesh.

Harlon lifted his hips. "Yeah, boy. Just like that."

I squeezed his balls gently, licked them, sucked them into my mouth, and played my tongue over them, while I jacked him off slow.

He hissed through clenched teeth. "Damn, boy. Who been teaching you to do that?"

His balls twitched inside my mouth. I jacked him off harder, faster. His hips rose and fell to my rhythm.

Then I let go his balls, and licked him again, slid my tongue under his throbbing cock along the vein, and took him in my mouth.

He groaned, pushed himself deeper

I fought my gag reflex.

He grabbed my hair in both hands, held my face still. "Fuck, boy. Gonna come in that hot mouth."

After that, I learned what it was like to get used like Harlon's cabin boy.

He held me in place, his hips moving fast, his cock stroking in and out.

I was helpless in his grip, forced to take every inch. When I gagged, he moaned, went faster, till his hips hammered my mouth.

No one had ever done that to me, taken me so completely.

He used my mouth like I was his property, and he was going to have every inch that belonged to him.

He dug his fingers into my hair even tighter, groaned deep in his throat. It was the hottest thing that ever happened to me.

My own cock was throbbing, but I didn't dare jack off. Somehow I knew that wouldn't be okay. Not with him.

Harlon groaned, threw his head back. His hips jerked one last time.

He rammed his cock so deep in my throat, he stopped my breath.

His animal grunts of pleasure and the feel of his hot come spurting down my throat filled my world.

"Damn." He pulled out of my mouth; fell back on the bed, breathing hard. "Clean me up."

I licked him, tasted his salty come, took his balls into my mouth again, and sucked.

He let out a long slow sigh, reached down and stroked my hair.

I love the smell of a man after he comes. I rubbed my cheek against his slick cock, kissed and licked him till he was as clean as I could get him.

"Come here, Boy."

I lay on his bed next to him. He ran his fingers delicately over my swelling lips. "I ain't had nothing that good in a long time. Didn't mean to hurt you like that."

His soft touch made me think about his tattoos. It didn't feel as if I was lying next to a pirate, a man who'd done time inside a brutal prison, a deliberate killer who'd been a government-paid hit man.

"What you thinking about, Boy? You're all quiet."

I noticed he didn't ask me if I liked it or if I wanted to come. I thought fast. "How come Penny has a girl's name?"

Harlon laughed. "Used to be a Collection Enforcer. Always got his client's money, right down to the penny. Started calling him Penny Man. Now it's just Penny."

He turned over on his side, hooked one of his legs between mine, and rubbed his rough hand over my chest. "But that ain't what you was thinking about, is it?"

He didn't wait for me to answer.

"Wanna go to the beach?" he said.

Sand sloped down to the sky. White clouds billowed by like a strange sea.

Harlon was lying on the blanket beside me. I was sitting up, staring at the shoreline. I couldn't escape the feeling that we were upside down, hanging between the water and the sky. "How can we breathe this high up? Can you fall off?"

Harlon ran a big hand up my back, caressing. "Force field. I buy oxygen. Chem. system mixes it, makes air."

"Force field keeps you from falling off?"

"Yeah. Pushes you back."

"How come where we landed was windy like that?

A strange look came over his face. "Field's expensive. Only run it where we need it."

"And the sand doesn't blow off?"

"Damn, Boy."

I suddenly remembered where I was and thought maybe I'd been talking too much, more than he liked. "Sorry. I've just never seen anything like this."

"Ain't nothing wrong with you asking. Most boys, they don't even talk unless I make them."

He was on his back, eyes closed. Taking a deep breath, being careful not to let my hand shake, I stroked his bald head. "Harlon?"

"What?"

"You're not scared of what I can do?"

Without missing a beat he said, "No. You ain't scared of what I can do?"

"Yeah. I am."

"I don't know why boys get like that. Act like I'm gonna lose my fucking mind and throw them in the sky."

"You wouldn't?"

He turned and looked at me. "How many times you ditched something that cost you out the ass?"

I ain't nothing but a pirate making a living in the sky, he'd told me. "You have a pretty cool ship." I felt shy all of a sudden, the way I did my first time with a man. "I'll try not to fuck up."

He pulled me down, rolled on top of me. "I ain't gonna have that problem with you."

I spread my legs, rocked against him. "No one's ever made me feel like you do."

"Yeah? How you think it's gonna be, getting fucked in the sky?"

I nuzzled the side of his neck, whispered, "Real hot."

He rose to his feet in a single fluid move, so smooth; he made you believe gravity was for other people.

When he unzipped and took out his cock, I was there, between his legs, licking and sucking his balls, running my lips along the length of his hard dick.

He stood there with his legs spread, watching. "What you like more than sucking dick, boy?"

I stopped, looked up at him. "Swallowing?"

"I'm ready for that ass." He touched my hair. "Better get the lube unless you want it dry."

I grabbed it from the blanket and lubed his thick cock till it glistened.

He brought the blanket from where we'd been, moved it to the edge of the shore.

I peeked over. That close up, the clouds roiled underneath the ship, like a stormy white ocean.

Then his rough hands were all over me, undressing me, touching, feeling, squeezing.

It felt like I was melting. "I want you inside me, up here, in the clouds."

"I'm gonna give you all the dick you want," he said. "Get on the blanket, head down, ass up."

I did what he said, pressed my face to the rough blanket, spread my legs. My fear came back in a cruel rush. Harlon was big and thick.

He fingered my hole. "Best relax, boy. You tense up like this, it's gonna be real bad for you."

I felt the slick coolness of lube against me and pushed back, biting my lips as my ass opened to let in his finger.

"I'm good to my cabin boys," Harlon said. He slid his finger in and out slowly. "But I fuck ass how I like. You feel that burn shit starting, you go on and do it, ain't nothing out here for you to burn."

I felt him guide his dick to my ass. Right before he did it, I knew what was coming.

Harlon sank his cock head into me, got a firmer grip on my hips, then drove deep inside in one long stroke.

I balled the blanket in trembling fists, bucked in his grip, tried to twist away from the pain. "Oh God, you're hurting."

He slapped my ass hard enough to make my muscles clench around his dick. "Quit fighting. I ain't doing nothing you can't take."

Pain seared into me. I held onto one thought, not the red deck, not the red deck.

"That's it, boy," Harlon said, grinding his balls into my ass. "You ain't got no choice. Just take it."

His dick thrust deep into me again and again. I groaned at the feel of him stretching me.

"Nice and tight. Just how I knew you'd be." He pulled out, turned me over, pulled my legs up on his shoulders, and slid into my ass again.

Shards of pain jolted through me with every deep thrust. But every time he pulled out, I lifted my hips, wanted his cock deep again. My God, was I going crazy?

"Fuck, yeah," Harlon said. "Knew you was gonna be like this when I used your mouth. You like getting my black dick up your tight little hole?"

I pressed my hands to his chest, felt his ripped muscle under my fingers. His cock pounded me relentlessly. "I never had it like this before."

He grabbed my clenching ass in both his big hands, stroked harder and deeper into me, watching me squirm and wriggle. "Gonna be a good boy for me?"

I thought back to how he'd mounted me, humped my ass while I was on all fours. "Yeah. I like how you ride me."

Harlon clenched his teeth, fucked me harder. His cock swelled and twitched inside my ass.

Hot spikes of pleasure and pain shot through my body. I thrashed under him. "God. Please." I clenched down hard around his big dick. "Empty your balls in me."

"Fuck." He threw his head back, and let out a deep groan. Then his hips slammed into me, and his cock spurted hot cum up my ass.

I moaned, wriggling, pushing against him, wanting his come deep inside me.

He stroked into me a few more times, kissed my lips, my face, my throat, then he was on his feet, motioning me between his legs.

I rose to my knees and licked his cock, still warm from my ass. The smell of him drove me crazy. I could get used to five years of this.

His powerful hand pressed my face into his come-covered cock and balls. "Jack off and lick me."

I stroked myself, licking and sucking him, lapping up his cum.

"Yeah, that's it. Come with your face buried in my crotch after I pounded your hot ass."

I pushed my face deeper between his legs, and came hard, every gasping breath filling my mind with his scent, as my cock exploded all over my hand.

He let go, but I slid my tongue out to lick him.

Harlon laughed. "You best stop, unless you want my dick up your ass again tonight."

My ass was aching from his hard fuck, but when he pulled me to my feet, I licked his chest, kissed hard muscle.

Harlon smoothed my hair out of my eyes. "No more tonight. You had enough. Come on. Lie down."

# # # # #

I lay next to him, his arm around me, my head on his chest, thinking about tattoos.

"Your heart's beating real fast. What you scared of?"

I looked out at the clouds whipping by, tried to think of something to say. "It's weird being this high up off the ground all the time, I guess."

"Rafe, you ain't gonna be able to hide nothing from me. Get used to it. Tell me what you was thinking about."

Caught. "When you were in Ferron City ..." I swallowed around the sudden dryness in my throat. "You got four spikes for ..."

"That was business." He caressed my smooth ass. "I told you. I do what I gotta do. Give me that ass and suck my dick when I say, and you ain't got nothing to worry about with me."

I closed my eyes, tried to pin down the feeling that eased through me, like a slow moving river.

He kissed the top of my head. "I ain't gonna do nothing bad to you."

It slid into place. For the first time in my life, curled up next to a pirate captain, I felt safe.

Below us, it was midnight somewhere. Up here in the clouds, the midnight hour never came, and that was all right with me.

MAKING ROOM AT THE TOP
Michael Bracken

Little Stevie adjusted his tie and looked at his reflection in the bathroom mirror. He saw my reflection over his shoulder and smiled. I'd spent a lot of my free time behind him, and his smile grew bigger when I reached into my pants.

The smile disappeared when he saw me raise a .38, and a moment later his last thought splattered across the mirror.

"You take care of things?"

I sat with Big Tony in the back room of his restaurant, a plate of cannelloni in front of me, a half-eaten mound of linguini in clam sauce in front of him. Spots of clam sauce clung to each of his double chins.

"I changed Little Stevie's mind," I said. After I'd shot him, I'd called the cleaners, a pair of dykes who made bodies and evidence disappear. "He won't be talking to anybody."

"He give you any trouble?"

"Nothing I couldn't handle."

Big Tony belched into his fist. "Any of this going to come back on me?"

"If you thought that was a possibility," I asked, "you wouldn't have asked me to do this."

Tony glared at me, his little pig eyes black as coal. "You got chutzpah, talking to me like that."

Maybe I did. Maybe I didn't. Big Tony carried a lot of weight, but not near as much as he once had. The gentlemen I worked for tolerated Tony as long as he produced, and lately his revenue had been dropping. He'd blamed Little Stevie, claiming his debt collector had

151

been skimming money and accepting payment in blow jobs rather than hard cash. When he'd confronted Little Stevie about it, Stevie had denied the accusations and had then made vague threats about ratting out the fat man.

Or so Big Tony claimed.

I doubted his story, but I wasn't paid to argue with the bosses, only to find permanent solutions to their problems.

"I need me somebody to work the fag bars now," Big Tony said around another mouthful of pasta. Little Stevie had worked The District for Big Tony, a part of town with a high concentration of gay-owned businesses, many of which directly and indirectly owed their existence to Big Tony's willingness to squeeze a dollar from anything or anyone that drew a breath. "Carmine won't go near them fudge packers, thinks that shit'll rub off on him."

I held my tongue. Political correctness had not infected Big Tony's universe, and it probably never would. I pushed the plate of cannelloni away from me and pushed my chair away from the table. I stood.

"That's your problem," I told the fat man. "I did my part."

I turned and stepped to the door.

Big Tony sputtered. "I didn't give you permission to leave."

"I didn't ask," I said. I opened the door, stepped through, and closed it behind me. I didn't hear whatever invectives Big Tony hurled at my back as I crossed the main dining room.

Carmine – Big Tony's remaining debt collector – was walking into the restaurant as I was walking out. We nodded to each other without speaking.

Austin did not know exactly how I earned my living, but he did know I owned a three-story French Second Empire home and that he had been quite happy overseeing the renovations and the redecorating since joining me in it two years earlier.

He was waiting for me in the living room when I returned home that night at a quarter past ten, wearing silk pajamas I'd given him the previous Christmas, reading the second book in a popular

152

series of vampire novels, and nursing a glass of Chablis. He closed his book and placed it next to his wineglass on the end table. "How was your day?"

"Filled with meetings."

"And how did things go?" he asked as he stood.

"I was very persuasive," I said.

Austin's finger-length blond hair had been styled earlier that day, he was clean shaven, and he had not been long out of the shower because I could smell a lingering trace of his favorite body wash. He was exactly what I needed to see, and I felt my pulse quicken and my cock twitch. I took him in my arms and covered his soft lips with mine.

Our tongues met in a fiery dance of desire, and our kiss was long and deep and hard, and by the time it ended, I had an erection straining against the inside of my boxers.

When the kiss ended, Austin said, "I made chicken and rice. You hungry?"

"Only for you." I pressed up against him, and he noticed my turgid erection.

He slipped one hand between us, cupped my cock through the fabric of my slacks, and whispered hoarsely, "You've had a hard day."

Far harder than he could imagine. I had killed a man I had once fucked on a regular basis, and I had done it because that's what I did. I solved problems.

Austin pushed my jacket off my shoulders and it slid down my arms. He caught it and laid it across the back of the couch. He unbuttoned my shirt and started pulling the tail from my waistband. As he reached around me, he found the holster at the small of my back and the .38 I carried in it. He made a face and my cock began to wilt.

My belt was threaded through the holster. So, I unthreaded it from my belt loops, slipped the holster off, and placed it on the end table next to Austin's paperback and his wineglass.

"Why do you carry that nasty thing?"

"For protection."

He thought I managed investments for my two uncles, which was true as far as it went, and had no idea why I needed protection. We'd had this discussion before, and there was only one way to end it: Remind Austin why he'd been removing my clothes. I slipped out of my shirt and then peeled off the wife beater beneath.

My live-in lover placed one palm on my hairy chest and purred softly. Then he drew one of my hands to his face and wrapped his lips around my middle finger. He sucked it into his mouth and my cock responded immediately.

The .38 apparently forgotten, Austin stripped off the rest of my clothes and then removed his silk pajamas, revealing his pale, nearly hairless body and precise manscaping.

He cupped my heavy nut sac in one hand and kneaded my nuts together while he wrapped the other hand around my cock and stroked his fist up and down a couple of times. Then he winked at me and said, "I'll meet you upstairs."

One of the first things we had done during renovation was convert the third floor into a master bedroom, creating a love nest in hardwood and indirect lighting, and we had spent many hours entwined in one another's arms once the renovation was complete.

I chased Austin up two flights of stairs, my attention riveted on his smooth, white ass the entire way. We both knew I could have caught him without exerting any real effort, but it was a game we played. I finally caught him as we crossed the bedroom from the stairs, and we tumbled across the king size bed, wrestling one another until I had him pinned on the bed.

He lay flat on his back; his arms flung out to either side and held in place by my shins as I knelt above him. I was leaning forward, my hands flat against the wall above the headboard, and my nut sac dangled above his face.

Austin thrust out his tongue and tickled the hair on my nut sac. Then he lifted his head from the pillow and sucked my sac between his lips. He nipped at my nuts and rolled them around in his mouth, soaking my sac with his saliva.

My erect cock bobbed above Austin's face. I reached down and wrapped my fist around it. As he sucked my scrotum, I stroked myself. The faster I pumped my fist, the harder Austin sucked my nuts, and soon he was sucking so hard that pleasure mixed with pain.

I pumped harder and faster and soon couldn't stop myself. I came with a grunt and fired a thick stream of cum across Austin's face and against the headboard. I leaned against the wall for a moment while my cock throbbed and oozed out another few drops of cum.

Then I twisted off of Austin and flopped onto the bed beside him. He wiped his face with his hand, licked his fingers clean, and then bent over my crotch so that he could take my flaccid cock in his mouth and bring it back to life.

As soon as I was hard again, Austin rolled away from me, reached into the drawer of the nightstand on his side of the bed, and pulled out a half-used tube of lube. He squeezed some onto his fingers and painted my erection with the slick stuff.

I took the tube from Austin and pushed him facedown on the bed. After squeezing a big glop of lube into the crack of his ass, I massaged it in. I slipped one finger into his tight sphincter and continued massaging until I could slip in a second.

"Quit teasing me," Austin whispered hoarsely, and I knew he was ready.

I positioned myself behind him, between his spread thighs, and grabbed his hips. I pulled his ass upward and knee-walked forward until I had the swollen head of my cock pressed against his slick asshole. Then I thrust my hips forward and drove my cock deep inside my lover.

He moaned with pleasure and thrust his hips back to meet each of my powerful forward thrusts. I slammed into him again and again and again and soon the headboard was banging against the wall and the wall-mounted lamps above the bed were rattling, and I was grunting with exertion.

And then, I came and came hard.

I fired a thick stream of cum deep into Austin's ass, and I held his hips tight against my crotch until my cock finally quit throbbing and softened enough that I could pull away easily.

I flopped onto my back and Austin rolled over, into the cradle of my arm. After he fell asleep, I slipped out of bed and returned to the living room for my .38 and holster. I put them in the drawer of my nightstand and returned to bed, confident that I could reach the revolver should I need it for any reason.

I spent the next several weeks keeping tabs on Big Tony and his efforts to replace Little Stevie. No one in his organization understood The District and the men who populated it, and it appeared that Tony's heavy-handed tactics were causing one of his key revenue streams to dwindle to a trickle. It didn't help him any that I fomented resistance to his efforts by suggesting to his clients that a gay man could better serve their needs than Big Tony ever could.

The gentlemen I worked for had no idea I was undermining Tony, and they increased their pressure on him to improve cash flow. Tony was old school, but he wasn't stupid, and he figured out what was happening before I was ready to make my move.

I came home one evening after spending a day in the District to find Big Tony sitting in Austin's spot on the couch, Carmine standing on the far side of the room, and Austin in a heap in the middle of the floor, a long cut on his right cheek and blood trickling from the corner of his mouth.

"He hit me," Austin said as soon as he saw me.

Big Tony had a small revolver nearly engulfed by his pudgy hand, and his hand rested in his lap. It was obvious that Tony had backhanded Austin, and the revolver's sight had slashed Austin's cheek.

Carmine stood with his arms folded across his chest. He was accustomed to intimidating people with his size and with a face that looked as if it had been hit repeatedly with the flat side of a shovel and the shovel was the worse for it, and I knew he would be slow to go for his gun if any shooting started. I returned my attention to Big Tony and the revolver in his fist.

He pointed it at me and accused, "You been going around behind my back."

I shrugged.

"You got chutzpah, boy, but you ain't too smart," he continued. He wasn't aiming the gun at me so much as he was talking with his hands. "Ain't nobody crosses me. Nobody."

"What's he talking about?" Austin asked from the floor.

I unbuttoned my jacket.

"We're gonna go for a little drive and settle this."

Big Tony started to heave himself off my couch. He was so big he needed both hands to leverage himself.

I had a brief moment of opportunity, and I took advantage of it. My hand darted behind my back and came out wrapped around my .38. I put a single shot through Big Tony's forehead, turned, and put two into Carmine's chest in the time it took him to unfold his arms.

Austin leapt to his feet and wrapped his arms around me.

I had two dead men in my living room, and my live-in boyfriend blubbering in my arms. The full impact of what I'd just done was sinking in, and I was getting a hard-on thinking about it. With Big Tony out of the way, there was an opportunity for someone to move up, and I was the obvious choice.

Exactly as I'd intended.

"Jesus," Austin muttered as one hand drifted from my back to my crotch. "You're turned on by this."

Apparently, he was, too. He unzipped my fly and unthreaded my turgid cock from my boxers. Then he dropped to his knees and took the head of my cock in my mouth. He wrapped one hand around my stiff shaft and pumped his fist up and down as he painted my cock head with his tongue. The zipper of my slacks pinched my cock skin as Austin jerked me off, a mixture of pleasure and pain that turned me on even more.

When he removed his hand from my cock and began to take a little more of my length into his mouth, I grabbed the back of his head

157

and held it as I drove my cock deep into his oral cavity. Then I face-fucked him hard and fast, my zipper scratching his nose and cheeks.

He grabbed the backs of my thighs and held on until I couldn't restrain myself. I stiffened as I came, and I fired hot cum against the back of his throat. He swallowed and swallowed again, and when my cock stopped throbbing I pulled Austin to his feet and covered his mouth with mine. I tasted my cum and the blood from his cut lip and I didn't care.

I needed to have a long conversation with Austin about how I earned my living and what part he would play in the future. After I called the cleaners, I started by telling Austin, "We'll need to redecorate."

SHARP AS A RAZOR
Barry Lowe

"Fuck you, queer," he screamed as I kneed him in the balls.

"So which one of your gang kissed and told," I said through gritted teeth. This might be Sydney in the roaring soaring 1920s, but it was still against the law to bonk another bloke. And, you paid even more dearly if you happened to be a member of one of the razor gangs that ruled the inner city streets. Make that ex-member. You could stick your cock in a goat, especially if you were a former Sicilian farm boy, and no one would turn a hair, but just try sticking that dick in another bloke, and you paid with banishment, humiliation and, occasionally, with your life. I wasn't sure which choice I was being offered, but I didn't like the odds: two against one, and they both had open cut-throat razors.

I'd tried wit to disarm the situation, but these two gang members had about as much appreciation of humor as genital lice and were just as difficult to shake off. That's why my second approach had been more direct: a painful assault on his testicles.

I thought his agony would have given me time to escape, but his mate was already on me from behind, a position I sometimes enjoy, holding me securely for his injured partner who had balls of steel if his quick recovery was anything to go by.

I felt the razor slice down my cheek. I had just had time to admire its intricately carved ivory handle, it was a beauty, as brutal looking as the two bastards who had attacked me, before the blood flowed.

Don't get me wrong, I was no innocent, and my punishment was no more than I deserved if you lived by the law of the streets. Nobody, but nobody, goes behind the back of the razor gangs. I'd tried it on, and now I was getting my payback. My only hope was that my attackers were trying to scare me off rather than kill me. Mutilation would attract little attention, whereas a murder, well, that would attract attention.

The pain would be swift and the blood copious. The wound I would wear with pride, and the scar would be my ticket to legitimacy, but it stung more than I'd expected and the blood spurted into my attacker's face and on to his thug standard vest and working class hat and trousers. My attacker swore profusely.

I was almost blinded by blood in my eyes, but I was still thrashing out in an attempt to make contact. There was a thud, like the sound of a nose breaking and another like the sound of teeth shattering, and a shower of curses. I knew I had not made contact so while I was waiting for the inevitable punch that would floor me, I wiped the blood from my eyes with the sleeve of my shirt in time to see my two attackers high tailing it down the street with a woman wielding a lethal-looking handbag in hot pursuit.

Okay, there may have been a tinge of hysteria to my laughter, but I bent over double fit to piss my trousers. Clutching my sliced cheek to staunch the flow of blood, I just hoped the bastards were well seen fleeing the wrath of some woman and her handbag. Admittedly she was a big cunt, but they'd never live it down.

Suddenly, light-headed from shock or blood loss, I stumbled but felt strong arms grab for me and hold me up.

"Steady, love," she said in a deep smoky voice that made my balls tingle. "The bastards are gone, but they'll definitely be back. And with mates for back-up this time. I think two's me limit, love, so best if we get out of here quick smart."

"Thanks ... um ... love," I said through pain that was beginning to surge along my body. The attackers had managed a few well-aimed blows to my kidneys and my face as well as slicing me open. I was no sissy, but I knew I was gonna hurt bad, real bad, soon.

"Ruby. Ruby Red. Like the lipstick," she said. "Look, I live near here, why don't I get you home, then we'll decide what to do next.'

I was in no condition to argue. She was a prossie, it was obvious, make-up applied too thick, hair dyed just a little too brassy, a dress that let you see from Sydney almost all the way to Tasmania. I didn't care even as she shouldered me along the footpath shoving people aside to the consternation of gawping bystanders. Down the back streets of working class Darlinghurst to Palmer Street, the unofficial red light area in which women sat in various states of undress in the front doors of their depressed, run-down terrace houses to lure prospective customers, to a modest single story dwelling in a side lane. She kicked the door sharply, and it flew open.

"Lock don't work, love," she said by way of explanation as she bundled me down the narrow hallway to the lounge room. I just had time to register that the building's dowdy exterior in no way reflected the warmth and, yeah, downright class of the interior before she dropped me onto the lounge and banged her fist against the wall to the house next door.

"Timmy! Timmy! Get your flamin' arse in here now," she screamed. And, as if like magic, a few moments later a young man, obviously the Timmy she was hollering at. ran up the hallway. He was a slight lad, maybe twenty, ragged blond hair hanging over his pool blue eyes with a smile so wide it seemed cramped in the room's interior. Until, that is, he clapped eyes on me, and he shuddered involuntarily. I guessed I looked a mess.

"Timmy, go get doc and see if you can hurry him. Here," she said rooting around in a cupboard under the sink, "give him this." She'd found half a bottle of cheap brandy and was pouring most of it into a glass before handing him the dregs. "Tell doc if he hurries, there'll be more where that came from."

Timmy nodded and turned back to look at me again. "He's a pretty boy," he said and then giggled at his provocative behavior before fleeing.

"Don't mind, Timmy," she said. "She held my face up by the chin and began to wipe the drying blood away with an old rag she'd dampened under the tap.

Her fingers were gentle, and I relaxed into their care.

"Is he any good?" I asked.

"The best," she said of the doctor. "Unless his hand is shaking from lack of grog. That's why I always keep some handy. Without booze, he's a mess. With a bottle of gin or brandy, hell anything that's got alcohol in it, and he could operate on the king himself, and no one could do better. But there's gonna be a scar. A nasty one."

She had cleared away most of the blood, and she stepped back to admire her handiwork. "Hmm, Timmy's right," she said. "You are a pretty one." She leaned in and kissed me on the lips. "Just got enough time, I think," she said and slipped to her knees. "Here hold this against your cheek, love," she handed me the cloth and began to unbutton my trousers. They were spattered with blood and street grime, but I didn't think she was intending to clean them. She had other things in mind as she made obvious when she clamped her hand around my cock.

I shuddered at the surprise of it. Sure, I was wary because she sported finger nails that could have gutted a chicken. "I haven't got the makings," I said.

"Love, I'm doing you for the sheer pleasure of it."

My cock was semi-stiff already just from the feel of her hand against my balls, and when she put her lips to my knob it sprang fully hard. She didn't waste any time, and she swallowed me right down to the root. I looked down at her scarlet mouth as she bobbed back up for air and left a snail trail of lipstick on me old feller. It was a real sight as she forced my cock down her throat without even gagging. I'd never had anyone do that before. Usually, I had to hold the back of their head, and then they'd puke. Ruby was a natural. And she was doing things with her tongue that I'd never felt before. She lapped along my shaft as she was sucking my cock at the same time. She must get a lot of return trade, I thought as I tried to hold off from her expert service.

"I don't think ..." I started to say.

"I know, love. When you're ready," she said taking her expert mouth from my knob.

I arched my back, and she pushed her mouth back over my cock and down to my balls. I shot a load into her mouth. Most pull away at that stage and spit out anything that gets in their mouth and then handle you until you blow on the sheets or the footpath. Ruby swallowed every drop and then swirled her tongue around the slit to siphon off the dregs.

The front door opened, and Timmy bounded into the room as I tucked my dick away and my benefactress wiped her mouth in an exaggerated gesture to show her satisfaction. The smile dried on Timmy's face, and he turned and slammed down the corridor.

The doctor appeared shortly after, puffing from the exertion of hurrying, it would be too fine a point to call it running, as he was portly and stank of liquor to the extent it would have been dangerous to strike a match near him.

"This him, Ruby?" he inquired.

"Yeah, doc. This is ..." Ruby began. "Well, names can be dangerous to know sometimes. Let's just call him Pretty Boy."

The doctor looked at me closely. "Good choice," he said as he opened his satchel.

Usually I hated the name, people used it as a put down, but the way Ruby said it, even the way the doc said it, sounded good. The way Timmy said it made it extra special and speared me in the groin.

I don't remember much after that. The pain or some injection the doc gave me and I was in and out of consciousness. I know at one stage I felt for the pain in my cheek and touched stitches before my hand was swatted away. I felt a cloth against my forehead that was cool and soothing. I heard strange piano music that seemed to come from the house itself. I recognized doc's face in my foggy brain, and Timmy, always Timmy, looking concerned, looking pleased, looking ... I couldn't quite place that look. And, of course, there was Ruby and those amazing lips. I woke up shivering with cold to discover a young man in my bed holding me. He was as warm as a blanket, and I snuggled closer.

It was chooks cackling nearby and the sun pouring through the fancy gauze curtains that woke me. Then the cock crowed. I could not remember where I was. Everything was unfamiliar. Someone was holding my hand. I tugged it, and a young man's face hovered over me. He was beaming from ear to ear.

"You're awake," the young man smiled. I scanned my brain for a name to go with the grin. I tried to reclaim my hand, and he let it go reluctantly.

"Tim?" I said groggily. "That's your name, isn't it?" I tried to sit up.

"Yeah," he smiled. "But most people call me Timmy. I like Tim better."

"Tell me, Tim," I tried to recollect what had happened. "Was it you that shared my bed? Kept me warm?"

"Yeah," he said. "You was delirious. Throwing the blankets off, wandering around the room. Someone had to stop you from hurting yourself. Ruby couldn't do it, she has to work."

"Thanks, Tim,' I said and smiled at him. "Could you do me a favor?"

"Sure, anything," he said enthusiastically.

"Can you get me a mirror? I want to look at the damage."

Tim hesitated. "What's the matter?" I asked.

"I don't think you should. You're not so pretty at the moment," he said, and he wasn't smiling now.

My hand shot up to my face. My cheek was swollen and felt red and infected. The sudden movement hurt my ribs. I grimaced. Tim was at my side caressing my face but avoiding my wound. He swept the hair from my eyes with his fingers. "Nice hair," he said and leaned in and sniffed it.

I liked Tim close to me, the smell of him, the touch of him. He was young and would be very handsome in a year or two once he lost his teenage puppyness and masculined up a notch or two. Right now, he was soft and eager to please. Life would toughen him up, or he wouldn't survive. Obviously the lad had been mollycoddled.

"Was that you playing the piano, Tim?"

He looked pleased but also slightly embarrassed and nodded his head.

"I heard you. Even while I was unconscious, I heard you."

"That's what I want to be, Pretty Boy. A piano player."

164

It was like a major confession, and he was surprised by his admission.

"I've never told anyone that before," he said, pleased with himself.

"Any chance of some breakfast?" I asked before the moment between us became too intimate.

"Coming right up," he said and scooted out to the kitchen. I supposed that I reeked, but when I sniffed my armpits and other parts of my body I was comparatively fresh.

"Did someone wash me while I was asleep?" I called.

"Yeah, me and Ruby took it in turns. You were rank, Pretty Boy."

He came to the door holding a heavy metal frying pan. "You sure are pretty all over," he said and before the blush reached all the way up his face, he went back to the stove.

I chuckled and relaxed into the soft mattress wishing I never had to get up. But business called. I had to make my presence felt and mark out a territory if I was to survive. I had to pay back the bastards who cut me because the revenge had been Ruby's, and I had a personal score to settle.

I could smell bacon sizzling and my stomach did a somersault. "How long have I been here exactly?" I called. I heard Tim padding to the bedroom. "Three days," he said.

"I best be thinking about heading off then," I said.

His face fell. "No need to hurry."

We were interrupted by a loud knocking on the front door. It wasn't Ruby; she knew just the right spot to kick it open. The coppers would have announced loudly their presence to intimidate.

"Help me up, Tim,' I said.

"I can handle it," he said with surprising maturity although I doubted it.

He strode down the passageway, and I heard the front door open. I heard him giggle and then a number of brusque voices as men pushed their way inside. I was grateful for Tim's act, he'd perfected Timmy as a shield, and I realized he used it even with Ruby. Three men burst into the bedroom, and I looked helpless lying on the bed. I might win the first skirmish, but I'd certainly lose the battle. My hope was to inflict some serious damage before I went down.

"Okay, queer," the front man yelled. "We don't like your kind. You give the rest of us a bad name."

"Is that why you line up to get your greasy cocks sucked when you think your mates are not looking?" I laughed, and he didn't take kindly to my sneer. I only just managed to duck his fist as I slammed my foot into his stomach knocking him into his bruiser mates. I flung off the blankets and was on my feet. I slammed my foot down into his windpipe. He gurgled and spluttered, and it would be some time before he'd be back in the fray. His mates were on their feet and surrounding me. I went for the closer of the two and had the wind knocked out of me. As I doubled over I was king hit back onto the bed.

One of them leaned forward to grab the front of my singlet to drag me up. I swung my head up and connected with his chin and heard a loud crack, hoping it wasn't my skull and it was his jaw or at least some of his teeth. I was dizzy from the connection, but I saw the third man open his cut throat. "We've been gentle on you so far," he growled. "That's over!"

I was vulnerable. There was no way in hell I could get off the bed with him swinging the razor in front of me.

The thwack to the back of his head must have woken the neighborhood, and he went down. Tim stood there triumphantly swinging the hot frying pan. There was eggs and bacon and cooking fat across the wall, but I didn't think Ruby would be too upset with this addition to her interior design. Anyway, I would pay to have it cleaned.

"Oh my god," Tim was breathing heavily from the exertion. "I'm so fucking hard."

He dropped the pan, conveniently enough on the head of the man he had just whacked, and was on top of me before I could prevent it. He forced his tongue between my lips and into my mouth and I liked this Tim. My tongue went to meet his and they began a competition for dominance. I sucked his tongue gently before pushing it back into his own mouth and fucking mine into his juicy throat.

I felt between his legs, and he was hard. As hard as I was. I heard a groan and remembered we had unfinished business. "Much as I want this to continue, Tim, we have something else to attend to first."

He nodded that he understood I wasn't rejecting his advances and went to find rope as well as cloth for gags and blindfolds. Tim knew of a safe house, and we walked the men along dunny lanes and through backyards to disorient them so there would be no reprisals on those who were about to house the bastards.

Back at Ruby's, Tim looked at me expectantly.

"You're a brave bloke, Tim," I said, and he seemed to grow in stature at the compliment.

"Not like you, though," he said. Then he added shyly, "I like you, Pretty Boy."

"I can see that," I said pointing to the bulge that was obvious in his trousers.

"I guess I can't hide what I am," he said.

"You shouldn't try,' I replied.

"You knew Ruby was a bloke in a dress?" he asked.

"Of course I did,' I laughed. "Not what I usually go for, but she did me a favor, and it sure didn't hurt having her chow down on my cock."

"I was so jealous when I saw what she did to you."

"Then why don't you do it to me now?" I said and dropped my drawers on to the floor.

"Are you like me, Pretty Boy?" There was a hesitation in his voice as he asked the question in case I took offence at the implication.

"One hundred and ten per cent," I said.

"But you could get any girl. You could pass," he said.

I just grabbed him and pushed him to his knees. Okay, his technique was not as good as Ruby's, she was a professional after all, but it was still fine. He played my cock like he played the piano, expertly and gently tugging its length before plunging his wet warm mouth down the length. His nose tickled my cock hair, and I automatically placed my hand on the back of his head, but I had no need to force him. His throat swallowed my cock like a velvet glove contains a finger.

Tim moved tentatively to my arse, and I felt him push against my sphincter. He looked up at me as if not so much seeking permission as gauging my reaction. "It's okay, Tim. I go both ways." He smiled around my cock and almost choked. He doubled his efforts, and soon I was close to shooting a big juicy load into his mouth. I hoped he swallowed like Ruby did.

I groaned that I was close, but he didn't, like so many others before him, take his mouth off my steamy cock and begin tugging at it. I hate that. He sucked until I shot my slime into his greedy cocksucking mouth and it dribbled down the back of his throat. Ruby had obviously taught him well.

"You got grease?" I asked, and he disappeared off the bed and came back with a jar of Ruby's cold cream. I was stiff and sore and wondered how I could keep the pain to a minimum. I dearly wanted to watch Tim's face as he fucked me but that would have to wait. I kneeled on the bed and let Tim grease my arsehole and loosen me up with those long elegant fingers of his. Two, then three, slid into my hole, and he pistoned his fingers to get me ready. My cock was hard again as I felt him kneel behind me and press the tip of his cock against my hole. He pushed gently, a little too gently for my liking. I pushed back against his hardness, and my arse stretched and swallowed his prick down to his balls. He gasped, and I gritted my teeth against the initial pain. It soon passed and Tim fucked into me gathering pace as I squeezed my muscles around his invading cock.

He felt good inside me, and he was so good at it. I wondered how often his cock had been up Ruby's arse as a non-paying explorer.

I groaned. Tim thought he was hurting me and slackened off.

"Don't fuckin' think, mate, because I take it up the arse I'm any less of a man like those bastards in the gangs do," I said.

"Stop your bloody yacking, you're throwing me off." He pushed his cock into me at a different angle and bingo! It prodded that little knob inside my arse chute that made me see sparks. It also made me shoot. My cock twitched and my arse muscles clamped around Tim's cock while my spunk slimed over the bed. He made a grunting sound and shot his wad into my guts. He collapsed on top of me panting and I howled with pain.

"Sissy," he grinned but lifted his weight to the side.

I swatted his arse cheeks and ran my finger along the crease till I found his warm hole.

"You want to be my punk?" I whispered to Tim.

"Do I get equal time with your arse?" he smiled.

"Any time, baby. Any time."

I had big plans but for the moment. I needed to get my strength back. It would take all the balls I could muster to put my plan into action, starting with the bastards that were trussed up like butchers' chickens. I'm make 'em shit their pants when I got together my razor gang of queers. I'd show 'em who the real sissies were.

PUNK
Mark Wildyr

Four hard-bodied convicts pulled the struggling youth from the top bunk, prying his scrabbling fingers from the iron bedstead in the prison dormitory after the 2:00 am headcount. The other fifty cons in the big room remained silent, ignoring the sound of a hapless youngster's brutal rape. The four taking their sexual frustrations out on the new guy were Tall Boys, and you don't fuck with that gang. You quickly learn to mind your own business in a prison ... any prison

# # # # #

An inmate in the first year of a five-year stretch for bank fraud, I was not your typical con, at least not in this federal joint located in southern New Mexico. I was older, mid thirties, white-collar, and Anglo. Most of the guys in here were drug mules, Mexican illegals, or the 'coyotes' that brought them over. The place, built for seven hundred, was just shy of a thousand according to last night's count.

As the head inmate in Receiving and Discharge, I processed every prisoner into the institution and every inmate out of it. I got first look at who's coming in and why. I took his picture, watched him shower and get sprayed for goobies, issued his prison khakis, and then separated him from his personal property. It was a good job for several reasons. Incoming cons recognized a protected position when they saw one, especially the recidivists, so I was accorded a measure of respect from the very first. I was also privy to the gossip between the guards and marshals, a valuable commodity in a prison. In the vernacular of the Mexicans, who make up sixty percent of the inmate population, I was *un gran señor*.

But mostly, it was a prime job because it kept me busy. I worked a regular shift, plus I got called out whenever prisoners are brought in any time of the day or night. While ninety-nine percent of the prison population considered that a bad thing; I gloried in it. Keeping busy in the joint was the hardest thing to do, and not keeping busy made for a long, slow stretch. In addition, the job brought some privileges, such as the cell block where I was moving this morning.

To the uninitiated, a cell sounded like a step backward from a dormitory. Not so. The cellblocks at this FCI consisted of eight, two-man cells. So instead of sleeping with fifty-odd guys at your back, there were only fifteen. The block was locked at night, but the two-man cells remained open, allowing for midnight card games. Also, there was a hell of a lot more privacy. Each cell had its own toilet and basin, so except for the daily shower, everything personal took place in the cell.

Last night's rape didn't surprise me. I'd spotted the kid as fair game when he was brought in with twenty other wetbacks the day before yesterday. Felix Carlos Anda y Cordobles was nineteen, but he had the beardless, angelic face of a seventeen-year-old, the smooth, muscled body of a young adult, and a silky virginal cock hiding beneath a long foreskin. Everything about the kid was sensual. Not much *mestizo* in this youngster. Pure Spanish. With *au lait* skin and dark chestnut hair, the kid stood taller than most of his countrymen at five-ten and weighed in at one-forty.

When I had taken him to the camera for his official photo, he sized me up. "Will ... will they rape me, *señor*?" he asked in a surprisingly deep voice. "Will the guards protect me?"

Taken aback, I looked into that worried face as I focused the lens. "You speak awfully good English. No accent."

"Went to school in New Mexico most of my life." He licked his lips nervously.

"If you went to school state-side, why'd they bring you in as an illegal?"

"'Cause I am. When I graduated high school, everything changed." He sounded as perplexed as I was, but then he went back to his primary concern. "Will they?"

I studied him frankly. "Watch your back every minute, Felix." Bending to the camera, I added. "Maybe you can find somebody to protect you."

"Can you do it?" He sounded like a drowning man snatching at a lifeline.

"Me?" I asked. "Afraid not. Wish I could."

The only other thing I recalled from the processing the kid was the hot eyes of his own people devouring him as he dressed. They got him the second night he was there, but it wasn't his people who did it. It was mine. Or more accurately, the Tall Boys, all of whom were Anglo.

One of the perks of heading up Receiving and Discharge was the privilege of selecting my own cellmate. After I was settled into my new digs in the cell block, I chose Scott Holt, my pinochle partner. He was a tall blond in his late twenties who took a fall for selling meth out of the back of his van in Gallup, New Mexico, earning him five years. Instead of being bitter, he devoted his energy to making life as comfortable as possible.

"I'll clear out whenever you want to bring your punk in," he offered as he made up his bunk the Sunday after the rape. He had the top rack.

"What?" I asked from the commode where I sat to keep out of his way in the small enclosure.

"I said ..."

"I heard what you said. What makes you think I have a punk?"

He paused and looked over his shoulder at me through sky blue eyes. "Scuttlebutt has some kid claiming he belongs to you."

"If I had a punk, it would be you," I shot back at him.

"Other way around, bro! Seriously, there's a kid out there telling everybody he's yours."

"Oh, shit! He wouldn't do that, would he?" I asked rhetorically. "A good-looking Mexican kid who got here about a week ago was worried about getting raped, asked me for advice. I told him to find somebody to protect his ass. Sure enough, they got him the second night he was here. But I never touched him!"

Scott finished making his bunk and sat down on mine. "Smart kid. He's already figured out that none of the guys screw around with you."

"Hell, if they want that kid, they'll roll right over me. He's fucking beautiful."

"That kind makes for trouble," Scott agreed. "Swishy?"

"Naw, just scared. But he's not a cock tease."

My roommate smiled. "I suspect your life around here just changed."

"Not if I can help it!" I got to my feet and strode out the door. Chow was about an hour behind us, so I checked the dayroom closest to Felix's dorm. Nothing. His bunk was empty. I finally found him walking the fence with a couple of other young ones, common exercise in the yard. He saw me and came over to where I stood.

"I hear you've been saying things about me," I opened up on him.

"Sorry, *Señor Robelado*," he mumbled, promoting me from an oak to an oak grove.

"Oaks. My name's York Oaks."

"Oaks," he repeated obediently. "I'm sorry, but I didn't know what to do. Those men ... they ..." The boy shivered. "I couldn't take it again. I just blurted out your name when one of them came at me the other day. I told him I belonged to you. They left me alone after that, but ..."

"But what, Felix?"

"They never see me with you. I don't think they believe me much anymore. Can ... can I come see you. You know, in your cell?"

My irritation suddenly evaporated. He was just a scared kid trying to cope the best way he knew how. He had no idea he could be endangering me. "Yeah, sure. You play pinochle?"

"No, but I play hearts!"

Scott did a double take when we entered the cell. "Jeez!" he exclaimed. I think it came out involuntarily. "Give me six more months in this place, and I'll fight you for him!" I ignored his smart-ass remarks and introduced them.

"*Con mucho gusto, Señor.*" The boy offers a hand.

"Mucho to your gusto, too." Scott glanced from me to him. "This is the kid?"

"This is the kid."

"I'm sorry. I did wrong?" Felix asked uncertainly.

"Go see a man about a dog, Scotty. I gotta talk to Felix."

"Yeah, sure." My cellmate couldn't quite keep a smirk out of his voice.

As soon as we were alone, I invited Felix to sit beside me on my bunk. He hesitated a moment, and then slid his slender butt on the blanket and propped his back against the wall.

"Are you going to do it to me now?" he asked. When I didn't reply, he went on nervously. "I know I'll have to let you do it to me – you know, for claiming to be your boy. But I'd rather you did it than those others."

I let him run out of things to say, and then waited until his roving eyes met mine. "Felix, I've been in this place damned near a year. And I haven't touched one single guy in here."

Curiosity replaced the fear in his eyes. "How do you stand it … you know, for a year?"

"Like every one else," I said crudely. "I jerk off."

"I … I could do that for you," he offered shyly. "You know, to pay you back some for what I did."

"Look, kid, I won't dispute the rumor you've spread around. I won't deny you're my punk. But I warn you right now; I won't fight for you. You've got the protection of my name, but not my fists. I'm not about to take a shank for you or anybody else. You got that?"

"Yes. Thank you. Can … can I hang around some so people will notice?"

"Sure. Now get outa here, okay?" I said, reaching out to tousle his hair.

He grinned happily. "Thank you, *mi cariño.*"

175

We both stood, but he hesitated before leaving. "Can ... can I see you? You know, down there?" I almost laughed aloud as his ears flamed. "If I'm your boy ... uh, punk ... I oughta know what you look like."

"You plan on discussing my attributes with someone?"

His face flushed even darker. "The guys talk sometime. They might ..."

"Oh, for Christ's sake!" I ripped open my trousers ... and my shirt for good measure.

As the boy gnawed at his lower lip while examining me, my cock moved slightly. He saw it and straightened up. "I like the hair on your chest," he mumbled, probably just for something to say. "It's a good chest," he added as he fled, leaving me standing with my shirt open and my trousers around my knees. Fortunately no one passed by before I restored my clothing.

Scott came in with a shit-eating grin plastered on his face. "So you gonna let him put out the word?"

"Yeah. But, I warned him I wouldn't fight for him."

Scott, always a realist, frowned. "If you claim him and don't fight for him, you'll lose a lot of face. You'll get dissed by the Tall Boys, hell, even by the wetbacks."

"Won't come to that."

# # # # #

My first prison anniversary brought an unexpected and fierce restlessness. A whole year without a woman was beginning to take a toll. On the heels of that self-revelation, Felix breezed into my cell and flopped down on the stool. Startled by his sudden appearance and upset by my situation, I shot a thumb in his direction.

"You'd better haul ass out of here," I snarled. "Your butt is beginning to look pretty good."

Those big brown eyes went round as saucers. "What'd I do?"

"Nothing. Get the fuck out!"

176

After he was gone, I regretted treating him that way and decided to look him up after tonight's Toastmaster's meeting. I'd made enough speeches to last a lifetime when I was a banker, but you had to play the game for the parole board. They liked to see 'participation' on your record. It helped with the myth this was a rehabilitation joint instead of a human warehouse.

"Sorry, kid. I'm on edge," I apologized when I found him on the weights. His weeks in the place had done him good. He was beginning to get some definition in that long torso. Just what the good-looking fucker needed, defined muscles!

"Something happen?" he asked with a frown, dropping two fifty pound barbells.

"Naw, I'm just edgy. Been in this place a year today, so I'm down.

His frown deepened. "It's almost lock-down," he commented. "Tomorrow, I come, and you talk to me," he pronounced solemnly, beginning to adopt the patois of the penal system.

"Yeah, sure. Just wanted to let you know I was sorry for the way I acted."

"You good man, York."

"Stop that. You speak English better than I do. Don't let these fuckers take over your mind."

"Sorry," he said, dropping his handsome head. "I'll watch it."

The next afternoon, I beat the shit out of two of the joint's best tennis players on the court, releasing a lot of tension and gaining a little satisfaction. Felix was waiting after the game, freshly scrubbed and looking … different. When he first came inside, I measured him in terms of feminine beauty. Now there had been a subtle change. He looked equally good, but with his masculinity beginning to show. I was suddenly proud he'd turned to me for help.

He waited in my cell while I showered. When I returned to my bunk, Scott and Felix were exchanging tidbits on convict life. Scott promptly got up and claimed to have a week's commissary riding on a pinochle game.

After slipping on a pair of boxers and running a comb through my hair, I stretched out on the bunk. Felix claimed the cell's one chair.

"So what do you wanta do?" I asked when he failed to kick off a conversation. "Movie starts in half an hour. You wanta go?" He shook his head. "No? Then what?"

"I wanta help you, York. Help you like you helped me."

"What help do I need?" I asked, genuinely surprised.

He switched his glance to my crotch. "I think you need something. You mouthed off at me, and Scott says you're getting cranky."

"You and Scott discussed this?"

"Let me help, York. Please."

Strangely moved by his sincere offer, I propped hands behind my head and closed my eyes. For a long moment, nothing happened, and then I heard him get up. I sensed he had lowered the towel tucked beneath the upper mattress to screen my bunk from the outside. Finally, a warm hand rested on the flat of my stomach. When I failed to speak, the hand shifted to my crotch; my cock moved. He tugged down my shorts as my penis slowly crawled up my belly. He grasped me loosely, pausing a moment as his other hand explored my balls. I made a little noise and spread my legs. Very gently, he began to stroke me. It had been so long that I could have busted my nuts without trying, but this demanded time, and consideration.

"Rub my chest," I rasped in an unrecognizable voice. He did better; he laid his head against me while a hand explored my belly. In moments, his tongue touched a nipple; I jumped as if shocked.

Suddenly realizing I was denying myself half of the stimulation, I opened my eyes and watched as he concentrated on masturbating me. His earnestness, his dedication to making me feel good, his incredible boyish beauty drew a bubble of emotion up out of my abdomen into my chest. As his strong young hand stroked the length of my cock, he licked his lips. He moved his left hand to my chest, and noticing that I watched him, gave an embarrassed grin.

"Great," I cooed, moving a hand to his shoulder and kneading hard muscle. I touched his side, feeling the rhythmic shift of his body as he worked on me. His legs scissored involuntarily as I moved to the inside of his thigh. Touching his erection cost me my control. Everything I owned spasmed! I shook like an epileptic in the grip of a grand mal. Cum boiled up out of me and shot over everything, draining me of sperm, of emotion, of feeling. I covered my eyes with an arm. Ever sensitive to my moods, Felix beat a hasty retreat.

Analyzing my reaction, I got up to clean myself off and cursed aloud. Hell, the kid must believe I thought he was a worm or something.

"Lost your commissary already?" I asked sourly as Scott sauntered in.

I caught his quick glance at the towel covering the end of the bunk. "Nope. Cancelled. Feeling better?"

"Cancelled my ass! You set this up, didn't you?"

"Man, I had to do something. You were getting so desperate, I was afraid you'd climb up and fuck my ass or something."

"You actually talked the kid into having sex with me?"

"Naw," he said sitting on the chair Felix had used. "I've got more suave than that! I just told him what your problem was and that I was leaving and would probably stand at the end of the block to stop anybody from coming in. Whatever he did was his own idea."

"Son of a bitch!" I muttered.

There aren't many places to hide on the grounds of a federal correctional institution, but Felix had apparently found one because I couldn't locate him anywhere. I went to bed feeling like a shit, but I slept better than I had for months and dreamed of a pearl of opalescent semen glistening on his dusky flesh.

#

Felix didn't hang around much the next week, and by Friday, I'd had enough. Foregoing my usual tennis matches, I went to the dorm

179

looking for him. As I passed by the showers, I heard some kid yell, "Felix, *tu amorado esta aqui.*"

Following the voice, I found him standing naked outside of a shower blushing slightly, though whether from my attention or his friend's comment wasn't clear.

"York," he responded to my casual greeting as he toweled water from his flat belly. "What are you doing here? Thought you were mad at me. Disgusted with me," he corrected.

I held my answer until he dressed, and we were outside walking the perimeter of the fence. "I was never disgusted with you, Felix. I was disgusted with me for taking advantage of you."

He shook his head and went stubborn. "If me touching you is so bad, I won't come around any more!"

I closed my eyes. "Your touching me was the greatest thing since I got here!"

"Then why'd you hide your eyes?"

"Because I was trying to figure it out. The way I felt took me by surprise. Hell, you took me by surprise."

He leveled an innocent look at me. "Then tomorrow you won't be surprised."

With those words hanging in the air, we completed our circle of the big yard, and I went to the dayroom where Scott and I trounced another couple in pinochle.

# # # # #

The next day, I processed a small Saturday load of new convicts, discharged three, and went for a fresh shower and shave before the 2:00 pm head count. After that, I lounged around restlessly on the bunk in my shorts, refusing an offer from Scott for a pinochle game. He gave me a long, speculative look as he left. Felix showed up thirty minutes later.

"I dreamed about you last night," he said, pulling the chair an inch or two closer to the bunk.

"Nightmare, huh?" I tried to joke.

"No. A good dream. We were … together. Friends. *Cariños.*"

"Lovers," I translated, my cock already reacting to him.

"Sweethearts," he corrected. "You get hard just looking at me, you know that?"

"Because you're one beautiful son of a bitch," I admitted. "Lie down on top of me!" He kicked off his shoes and complied. "How does that feel?" I asked, when we were nose to nose, his erection pressing against mine.

"F … funny," he stuttered.

I put a hand behind his head and kissed that broad mouth. After a moment, his firm lips softened and parted. Shaken, I tried to put steel in my voice.

"Your cock's kissing your belt buckle, so I guess you liked that."

"Yeah, I did."

We tried it again, this time participating mutually. At length, he broke apart with a sob, burying his nose in my chest hair. Then he slowly surrendered to the pressure of my arms and slid down my torso, his tongue setting me afire. When his chin was in my bush, he rebelled. Relentlessly, I pushed him down until his lips kissed my straining cock.

"Do I have to, York?" he asked voice quivering. The vibrato from his Adam's apple sent a tingle through my balls. "Can't I just do it with my hand? I like helping you that way."

"Don't sweat it," I answered cruelly. "I'll get one of the other *muchachos* to do it for me."

"No!" He bobbed up to confront me. "I don't want anybody touching you! Nobody!" The fury in his eyes surprised me. "I'll do it! Me! Nobody else!"

He took me in his mouth then, giving me a jolt as he closed over my glans. He was still for a second, and then he spit me out. "I don't know how to do it!" he wailed.

"Felt okay to me!"

He settled down and returned to his task. I lost the power to protest, to communicate as he experimented. That handsome head awkwardly bobbing up and down on me claimed my full attention.

"Take off your shirt! I want to feel your chest on me."

He shrugged out of the khaki blouse and lay across my legs. Now I had a pair of broad brown shoulders and a long, tapered back to watch. With a sight like that, it didn't take long. Suddenly, I wrapped my legs around his trim hips and thrust at him wildly.

"Oh, shit, Felix! Shit! Shit! Shit!"

I came. I came like a gusher, a geyser, like a Roman candle sending up shot after shot after soaring shot. I hardly noticed that Felix had gagged and come up off me, frantically jacking me with his hand as my pearly semen sprayed us both. When I regained power over my own muscles, I pulled his face to my belly and hugged him hard against me. He stopped coughing and lay quietly.

"Get up," I said as kindly as I could, still in the throes of strange emotions.

He stirred, and then rose, turning quickly to hide the mess I'd made on his face. He fumbled for a washcloth at the sink and cleaned himself. I studied his long back, watching the muscles play as he worked. When he turned to me with a freshly rinsed cloth, I saw the erection pressing against his khakis.

"Take off your trousers," I ordered. "I want to see you." He swallowed hard. "Do it."

The kid was young and hung; his hard cock throbbed against his belly even when he was standing straight. I turned on my side and scooted against the wall.

"Lie down with me," I said. Fighting to keep the panic from his face, he slowly spooned himself against me. I reached around and took his long cock in my hand. "That was the most fantastic thing that's ever happened to me," I whispered in his ear. "Better than with anyone … ever."

I sensed rather than saw his smile. "Truth?"

"Truth! How does this feel?" I asked as I slowly stroked his excited pole.

He snuggled closer. "Good. Great!"

"I can't believe one of your little friends hasn't gotten his hands on it yet. Or his mouth."

"Only you, York. I don't want anyone but you."

I pulled his head back against me and licked his neck as I slowly built the tempo of my rhythmic strokes. He was feeling it. He squirmed a little.

"Lift your leg." He obeyed, and my revived cock nudged his balls.

"That feels good, York," he mumbled dreamily.

"To me, too, lover," I responded, using the word deliberately. "Lean forwards a minute." I withdrew from between his legs and ran my cock up against his crack. He froze. "It's okay. I won't do anything you don't want me to. Stroke yourself."

He began to beat his meat. I parted his cheeks and nuzzled his crack with the tip of my erection. Gradually, he relaxed. The third time I stroked his sphincter, he moaned.

"You want it?" I asked.

"Yes, but I'm afraid!" he gasped. "Those guys hurt me."

"Okay," I said, removing my hand, but leaving my glans pressed between his buns. I took charge of his cock again. Slowly, I ran my fist from the root to the tip. He moaned and shifted his hips. I eased forward slightly.

He gasped and moved away. Then he thrust his butt against me. "Do it! Do it, York!"

Felix impaled himself on my throbbing prick. His pucker string parted; my shaft slid deep into his channel, entering him effortlessly. He bucked against me, fucking my fist and my cock until I was buried completely inside him. Lost in the ecstasy of this beautiful boy, I shifted, putting him beneath me. Parting his legs with my knees, I sought to crawl right up inside him.

"I want to fuck you, Felix!" I cried, slamming his butt eagerly, driving him into the blanket. After a wild, ragged start, we found a rhythm. Long before I was ready to end it, he started mumbling.

"I'm coming, York! I'm coming! I'm coming!"

His tight ass grabbed my cock and his long, drawn out ejaculation carried me to climax. He milked the semen from my balls into his deep, dark channel. He electrocuted me with the uncontrolled snapping of his nerve endings. He drowned me in his sensual, masculine beauty. By the time I was drained of my seed, my energy, my reason, I knew I was lost. This boy was mine! I'd fight for him! Hell, I'd die for him!

Scott brought us back to reason. "Shit, guys, aren't you finished yet? You made so much noise they're talking about it out on the exercise yard."

Felix tried to move, but I remained where I was, my naked body covering his. Scott peeked through the curtain of the towel, and I was inordinately proud he had glimpsed me mounted atop my lover.

"Just … let us … catch our breath," I panted.

We took our time cleaning up, examining one another through new eyes.

"You're mine now, Felix. Nobody else touches you. Nobody sucks you, masturbates you, fucks you. Just me. You don't touch another man's cock. Understood?"

"And you?" he asked solemnly.

"Same for me. You're the only one for me … *cariño*, I'm going to talk to the head Tall Boy. He owes me a favor. I'll see that nobody bothers you. Okay?"

And so it was until the day he left, a day so full of pain that I feared I could not endure it. But as difficult as it was, I wouldn't allow anyone else to process him out. Then I watched the bus carrying him back to Mexico until it was out of sight, not certain I could survive the night.

I did, of course. And eventually a little feeling began to return to my numb extremities. I knew I'd be all right the day I took a little

184

interest in a youngster we were admitting. Eventually, I found other handsome, young partners to make life bearable.

But I never found another like my first punk … Felix Carlos Anda y Cordobles. Never!

NIGHT IN HELL
Wayne Mansfield

It was hot. No, it was worse than that. It was sweltering. Even at ten o'clock at night, the heat was oppressive. My new apartment had no air conditioning, and the fan above my bed did little to cool my naked body. I lay on the mattress sweating, soaking the sheet beneath me and wishing I was somewhere cooler. I was glad it was Friday. At least I didn't have to get up in the morning and go to work. I could sleep in, assuming that I ever got to sleep in the first place.

Finally, after rolling around on the damp sheet for an hour, I got up and opened my bedroom window. There was a slight breeze, enough for me to risk leaving it open. I didn't know this city very well. I didn't know how safe it was, but the heat was making me crazy enough not to care.

After opening the window, I didn't go back to bed. I went, instead, into the bathroom and turned the shower on. The first splash of icy cold water on my naked flesh made me gasp. I held my breath and waited for my body to get used to the change of temperatures. I leaned against the tiled wall of the shower recess, my arms stretched out and my head bowed beneath the cascading water. I closed my eyes, and immediately, all my other senses were heightened. The smell of the heat coming off my body filled my nostrils. I could feel the rivulets of water snaking their way down the muscles of my back, running along the crease of my arse and over my arse hair, tickling as they went. I lifted my head, my mouth open to receive the water, which I gulped down thirstily. I wished I had a bath.

Finally, after I noticed that the pads of my fingers had begun to prune, I turned the water off and dried myself. I switched the bathroom light off and padded back to the bedroom. The sheets were still damp, but I couldn't be bothered changing them. I was tired and all I wanted to do was sleep. At least now the tiny breeze created by the fan had some effect. I closed my eyes and waited for sleep to take me.

My mind drifted to the edge of the place where dreams are made. Vague images floated through my mind, pulling me further and further towards unconsciousness. I wished they'd hurry up.

Then I heard a noise. I ignored it at first. Just another product of Dreamland I told myself, but I heard it again. A knocking sound, followed by hushed voices. I opened my eyes and stared into the darkness, my ears pricked. Footsteps. On the floorboards. My eyes were wide now. I turned over, switched on the bedside lamp and was immediately pinned down by a large beefy man.

I went to cry out and felt something woolly shoved into my opened mouth. A sock perhaps. It sure smelt like one. I struggled against the man, but he was much larger than I.

"Keep your mouth shut and I won't be forced to hurt you," said the brute.

"Where's your money?" said another voice from behind him.

The sock was removed from my mouth.

"Remember," said the brute, "one false move and the lights go out."

He shook his fist in front of my face. I could smell alcohol on his breath. I was intelligent enough to know that he meant business.

"My wallet is in the back pocket of my jeans. They're on the back of the chair over there."

I heard the other guy walk over to the corner where the chair was.

"You're a pretty young thing," said the guy pinning my arms to the mattress. "How old are you?"

"Thirty," I replied. "At least I will be next week."

"There's a fifty and a credit card. You want me to take the card too, Jake?"

Jake frowned. He looked over his shoulder at his accomplice.

"Remember when we said no names, fuckwit! I meant no names, you dickhead."

188

"Sorry Jake," said the second guy.

Jake rolled his eyes.

He was a big guy, rugby build. Since he was only wearing a tank top I could see the thick hair on his chest and the oversized muscles in his arms. He had a rose tattoo on the bicep I could see, and some Chinese characters tattooed on his neck. His head was shaved although his face wasn't. It was covered in dark whiskers. He looked rough. He smelt as though he hadn't showered in days.

His mate, who I later learned was called Dash, was average build, just a bit larger in frame than I was though not as toned. He had blond hair, just bristles, and sideburns which framed a hard looking but handsome face. He was shirtless and wore only jeans. His body had once been defined, there were still traces of a six-pack, but he had let it go. His chest was lightly haired, but his treasure trail was thick and led down to a bulge that was quite large.

"That all you got?" asked Jake. "Fifty bucks?"

"Yes. I've just moved here and that's all the money I have."

I was nervous and that made me chatty. I had to reign myself in, not give these guys too much information.

"Well I guess that'll have to do," said Jake, his voice deep and masculine, authoritative. "But I guess this little break in of ours doesn't have to be a complete waste of our time."

He looked over his shoulder again, at Dash, and the two of them burst into laughter.

I could feel my heart pounding in my chest. My breathing had become erratic. I saw Dash move around to the other side of the bed, rubbing his crotch and smiling a smile that would have been perfect except for the one missing tooth. I was naked and feeling vulnerable against the bulk of these two men.

"It sure is hot in here," said Jake. "Are you hot, Dash?"

Dash looked at Jake as though he didn't know how to answer. Jake nodded his head, slowly and deliberately.

"Yes I am."

It wasn't difficult to see who the brains of the outfit were.

"What are we going to do about it?" asked Jake. "You got any air conditioning?"

I shook my head. "No," I said.

Jake removed his hands from my wrists and took his singlet off. He used it to wipe the sweat off his brow, and when he had finished, he tossed the garment onto the floor.

"One sound out of you, and I'll rip your tongue out," he growled. He stood up.

His fingers twisted the button on his jeans out of its hole and then he unzipped the zipper. He pulled his pants off, revealing that he hadn't been wearing any underwear. Between his legs hung a slab of uncut meat that could best a showground pony. It hung from a thick thatch of dark wiry pubic hair and over a set of low hanging balls the size of seagull eggs. Two thick veins twisted their way up the shaft and tapered off in the large hood that covered his cock head. It smelled but it was a manly smell of pheromone, sweat and perhaps dried cum.

I was so taken by Jake's meat, dangling just inches from my face, that I hadn't noticed Dash undressing. He was less impressive. His body was alright, smoother and less rugged than his partner's. He had shaved his pubic hair, which made his cock look slightly larger than it probably was, yet larger than average. His balls also hung low but were in no way as impressive as Jake's. His butt was rounder than his friend's, and I did notice a small tattoo on his right arse cheek as he pulled his trousers off, but I couldn't see what it was.

"Let's get him into the bathroom," said Jake. "It'll be cooler in there."

"What are you going to do to me?"

I felt the stinging aftermath of a slap. It was a backhander from Jake. I cried out and was slapped again. This time it was the other cheek that throbbed. I brought my hand up to my mouth and dabbed it. When I could see the faint trace of blood from a split lip.

"I told you to keep it shut!" growled Jake.

My eyes watered. I felt so helpless. It was a frightening feeling to lose control. I was used to being in charge of every part of my life, both at work and in my private life, and now I'd had that power taken away from me. I blinked back the tears and told myself to be strong. I certainly didn't want to show them my fear.

I was led into my bathroom and pushed into the shower cubicle. I hit the wall hard and slid to the ground. My shoulder started throbbing, and I brought a hand up to rub it.

I had so many questions, so many things I wanted to say to try and convince these thugs to leave, but I dare not open my mouth again. I wasn't stupid.

"Look at him," said Jake. "Such a pretty face. Such a pretty boy."

Dash stood beside him, cock in hand, nodding like an idiot.

"Time to make the boy a man I think," said Jake, taking his cock in his hand. "Don't you think?"

Dash nodded and then frowned. "Hey, what did we say about no names?"

Jake smacked the guy's face with the back of his hand.

"Don't get smart with me," he snarled.

Then without any warning, Jake aimed his cock at me and let loose a stream of golden piss, which hit me square on the chest and sent splashes of the salty liquid into my mouth. I spat as much of it out as I could, my face screwed up in disgust.

"Open it," Jake demanded.

I looked up at him, my lips securely closed. I shook my head. Yet all he had to do was lean forward, and my mouth was open. He seemed to be quite easy with his slaps, and I certainly didn't want to be on the receiving end of another one.

"That's the way," he grinned. "My nice little toilet slut."

Then Dash followed suit, aiming his cock at me and before long I had two streams of piss splashing into my mouth. I tried to spit as much of it as I could out, but I inevitably swallowed some, nearly choking on it as it washed down my throat.

"That's a good boy," said Jake.

I didn't like being called a boy. He may have been in his forties and his mate not far behind, but that didn't make me a boy. I would have protested, but my mouth was too full of their salty urine, and the ever present threat of a smack to the face was a pretty strong deterrent.

Finally their piss streams became dribbles that soon became drips.

"Now get over here and suck our cocks dry," said Jake. "And be quick about it."

I scurried across the tiles of the shower cubicle and took Jake's cock into my mouth. I sucked it til it started hardening, nearly gagging me with its monstrous girth.

"Don't stop sucking 'til I tell you," he ordered.

I took the length of it as far down my throat as it would go, but it was so thick and so big that my jaw was soon aching even though I hadn't come anywhere near deep-throating him. He seemed to be enjoying my efforts, though. It didn't take long for his cock to harden to its full nine-inches.

"Now suck mine," said Dash.

I took my mouth off Jake's cock and slid my lips down the length of Dash's prick. His cock was easier to manage. It was about eight inches and thick, though not as thick as Jake's. My mouth slipped up and down his shaft with relative ease and soon I was taking him so far down my throat that I could feel the head of his meat blocking my esophagus. I grabbed his arse cheeks to steady myself and soon got a good rhythm going. He put his hands on my head, helping me to keep the rhythm going.

"I'm gonna come, Jake. I'm gonna blow," he said.

I felt a third hand on my head. It grabbed a handful of my hair and tore me off Dash's cock. It was Jake, of course. He threw me against the tiles.

192

"You're not going to come, yet," he told his friend, frowning and casting his eyes down at Dash's leaking cock.

I huddled where I had landed.

"Better get him to work on the other end," Jake said with a sly smile.

He turned around and thrust his hairy arse forward.

"Lick it, bitch," he demanded.

I paused. I don't know why. Maybe I hoped he meant Dash, but I knew he didn't.

"Now!" he growled.

Again I scurried forward on my knees. I cupped a hand over each cheek and pulled them apart. I could smell the musty, earthy stink of his unwashed hole immediately. The dark pink, puckered skin was surrounded by a forest of thick black hair. I closed my eyes, stuck my tongue out and pressed it against the skin of his arse.

"Good boy," he said, almost with a groan. "Get right in there and lick that shit hole."

I began by running my flattened tongue up and down the length of his crack. I could taste the remnants of his last visit to the toilet but that soon disappeared. I worked my tongue into his hole, pushing it as far past the sphincter muscle as I could, licking the inside of his arsehole and sucking on his arse lips. I tensed my tongue and began jabbing it into his hole, tongue fucking him and making him moan with ecstasy.

Above me I heard movement, so I opened my eyes. It was Dash. He was leaning over and pulling Jake's arse cheeks further apart, so I could concentrate on rimming him. And I did. I had temporarily forgotten that I was being forced to lick his arse. I had done it so many other times, to so many men whose names I never got to know. It was easy to forget that this wasn't just some anonymous pick up.

I kept on tonguing Jake's hole, kissing it and sucking on his thick, juicy arse lips, because I hadn't been told to stop. I was sweating like a pig. So was he. Every now and again, a trickle of his sweat ran down the groove above his arse and onto my tongue. By that stage, I didn't care. I had probably swallowed a lot worse.

I reminded myself that if I did what they said then they might just blow their loads and leave me. I kept my tongue in his hole. He was relaxing more now. I could feel him pushing out, his pink pucker flaring out into my mouth. I kissed it like I would a lover's mouth, using my tongue and my lips in unison. Passionate and eager.

"Hey Dash, you wanna sit on his face?"

"Not after your dirty hole has been on it," I heard him reply.

I almost laughed.

"Well let's get the lad back to bed."

Jake grabbed me by the arms and spun me around so that my back was to him while Dash scrambled into the cubicle and grabbed my legs. Together, they carried me carefully into the bedroom, dropping me onto the mattress. Jake then grabbed my legs and pulled me to the edge of the bed. I felt his finger burrow into my tight arsehole and despite myself I felt my own cock begin to harden. I stared unblinkingly at the ceiling, willing my cock to go down but it kept growing, jerking to life.

"Well what do you know? The boy likes me," beamed Jake. "Sometimes it takes one man to show another what he likes."

"I don't like it," I spat back, forgetting myself. "I think you're a sick fuck!"

Jake leaned forward and for the third time that night I felt the sting of his hand across my cheek.

Dash, eager to get in on the action, climbed onto the bed and squatted over my face. He settled on it, pressing his hole onto my mouth, demanding that I lick it, which I had no choice but to do. I ran my tongue up and down the lightly-haired arse crack, flicking the hole with the tip of my tongue and chewing gently on his arse lips. I did think about biting the fuck out of them, but where would that get me? A bed in a hospital, or worse.

Jake pressed the head of cock against my tight hole, wriggling it past the sphincter then pushing the remaining length in centimetre by centimetre. I was surprised by the consideration he was showing me. He could have rammed it in and split me from cock to crown, but he didn't.

My hole was stinging from the girth of the man's cock. I gasped but any sound I made was muffled by a face full of butt. I spread my legs wider, I don't know why. I guess part of me wanted to know what something that size would feel like, deep inside me. I didn't have long to wait. He pushed his cock deep into my arsehole making me writhe beneath him. It was uncomfortable even though he was taking his time, but what could I do? Sharp bolts of pain radiated out from my sphincter, stretched taut by the immense circumference of Jake's horse cock.

And then he began to fuck me.

At first he used gentle thrusts but that didn't last for very long. Soon he was ramming into me with a force that made Dash lean back on the mattress to keep his balance. I was glad of that though because the new position meant I could breathe more easily.

"Nice tight hole you got, bitch." Jake grunted. "Gonna be a pleasure creaming your little hole."

My own cock was rock hard and slapping against my stomach. Jake's huge prick was massaging my prostate. It was torture not being able to take my hard-on in my hand and milk it.

I felt Jake lean forward. Next I felt his tongue on mine as I licked Dash's hole. He licked my lips, his broad flat tongue making a sweep of the bottom of my face. Then he pushed Dash back, dislodging him from my face, so that he could kiss me properly. The kisses were passionate. I breathed in his warm breath, taking it deep into my lungs. He sucked my top lip and then my bottom, running his tongue over it as he held it gently between his teeth.

All the while his hips thrust into me, easing off for the duration of the kiss and then starting the assault again when he'd had enough of my lips.

"Get back on him," he said to Dash. "I wanna suck your cock."

Dash climbed back onto my face, grinding his arsehole onto my mouth, demanding that I lick it and lick it good. I felt Jake lean

195

forward again but I couldn't see what he was doing. I guessed from the moans coming from Dash that he was sucking his mate's cock.

Suddenly Dash began to rock back and forth on my face.

"I'm going to come, buddy," he panted. "Oh keep sucking. Keep sucking."

I felt a sudden pressure on my face. I couldn't breathe. I could hear Dash moaning and grunting, and feel him thrusting his hips into Jake's mouth but all I could think about was drawing breath. My arms were pinned to my sides by Dash's legs, so I began to kick. At first Jake just slapped my legs. His mouth was still on Dash's cock, swallowing a load of his mate's cock cream. I was getting desperate. I began to rock my whole body, trying to knock Dash off my face. Finally it worked. Dash slid off my face. I had just enough time to see Jake suck in a small dollop of cum before he smacked me across the face with a force that dazed me.

"Fuckin' interrupts me when I'm getting a mouthful of cum," he snarled.

I lay there staring into a blurry space. I could hear his voice, but I couldn't make out what he was saying. There was a ringing in my ear and all the time my arsehole was being raped by the sadistic bastard otherwise known as Jake.

I was just realizing what had happened when I heard Jake grunting. His hips were really slamming into me now. His hands around my ankles were hurting me and my arsehole felt like it was on fire.

"Oh fuck. Here it comes. Gonna cream that tight slut hole!"

I closed my eyes and clenched my teeth. The pain was becoming almost too much to bear.

"Open your eyes, boy!" he snapped.

Before I had a chance to do as I had been told Dash was on the bed again, his fingers at my eyes, pulling the lids open so that I could see Jake's face above me. His teeth were clenched, white against the shadow of his whiskers. The ligaments in his neck were taut. He looked more like he was in pain. And then he exhaled, closed his eyes and let his head flop back. I could feel the force of his ejaculation deep inside me, and for a moment, the sensation took my mind off the pain at my arsehole.

After he had blown his wad inside me, he stayed still for a moment, rubbing his hairy chest and belly and looking very satisfied. Then he looked down at me and the smile left his face. He looked at me as though I were something he had trodden in. He indicated with a nod of his head that Dash should leave me alone and Dash obeyed. Then without any warning he pulled his cock out, the pain causing me to gasp. He looked down at it and my eyes followed his. I could see the cum glisten on it in the lamp light.

"Get down here and suck it clean, whore" he snarled.

I shook my head.

His eyes bored into me.

"It's your fuckin' mess so get down here and clean it up."

"You want me to ...?" Dash began.

"You shut up!" he said pointing at Dash but keeping his eyes on me.

For the first time that night, I felt truly terrified. I knew I couldn't suck his cock after it had been inside me, and I also knew that he would probably kill me if I didn't.

"I'm going to count to five, and if your mouth isn't sucking my cock by the time I get there then you are going to wish you'd never been born. One."

I shook my head.

"Two."

His eyes stayed on me. His cock was soft now and a dollop of shit and cum fell off onto my sheet.

"Three."

I pushed myself into a sitting position, my lips closed and my head still moving from side to side.

"Four."

197

I crawled towards him and leaned towards his cock.

"Fi ..."

I closed my eyes and pushed his cock into my mouth with my hand. I was relieved to see that at least it was clean and surprised myself that I only gagged once. As I continued to suck his cock I felt something warm on my back. I looked over my shoulder to see Dash standing on my bed pissing on me.

"Now what did you do that for?" said Jake. "You've ruined his mattress now."

Dash let his flaccid cock fall out of his hand. He stood looking at Jake; waiting for a smack in the head was my guess. But Jake smiled.

"Get down here and clean the boy's arse up. It's a bloody mess down there."

Dash was obviously no stranger to his friend's perverse desires. He wasted no time in pushing my legs apart and licking at cum that was drying in the hair around my hole.

"Now kiss him goodbye."

While Dash kissed me, his tongue invading my mouth, licking the back of my teeth and the sides of my mouth, Jake disappeared and came back with an electrical cord. My eyes widened and my breathing turned into a series of short gasps.

"Please don't," I whimpered.

"Please don't what?" grinned Jake. "You don't know what I'm going to do, yet."

I sniffed back my tears, and my breathing became more measured.

"What are you going to do?" I asked, my voice so timid it could have come from a ten-year-old boy.

"Grab his arms," he said to Dash, who was only too eager to oblige.

Jake straddled my chest, his cock just inches away from my mouth as he tied my wrists together with the cord. He pulled the knot tight so there was no chance of it becoming loose. He then tied the cord around my elbows, disabling me completely.

"Hold this," he said to Dash, holding the remainder of the cord out to him.

He then pushed my legs together and drew them up over my chest. He pulled my arms through them then took the cord from Dash. He tied my knees together and then tied my wrists to my ankles. Having finished the bulk of his work, he reached in and pulled my cock and balls out between my legs.

"Now ain't that a pretty sight? A nice cock and a beautiful pink arsehole."

Dash nodded.

"Put your clothes on," Jake whispered even though I could hear him as clearly as if he had barked the order.

Dash hurried to the side of the bed and got dressed. I watched him the whole time, my face pleading to him. But he didn't look at me once. I saw him take one final look at Jake, and then he disappeared out through the window they had used to enter my apartment.

"Now what are we going to do with you?" I heard Jake say.

I couldn't see him. I was trussed up like a Christmas turkey and he was standing directly in front of me, looking down at my exposed arsehole no doubt.

"I won't tell anyone," I said, ashamed that I should utter something so inane and predictable. "I'll stay in bed, go to sleep and forget that the whole thing ever happened. In fact, if you wanted to you could come back and fuck me again."

I cringed. Had I really said that? I couldn't blame myself though. I would have said anything to get him to leave without further harming me.

"Is that a fact? Well I might hold you to that."

I rolled my eyes. My mind cursed my mouth. "Shit, shit, shit, shit, shit!"

"That hole is mighty inviting and you did take my big old cock pretty well. Let me think on it for while. And by the way, it looks like I got something else to give you."

He moved to where I could see him and spat into his hand. He wiped the spit onto his semi-hard cock and then disappeared in front of me again. I felt him push his cock head into my still stinging arse, but this time it was just the head. The next thing I knew I felt a bloating sensation.

"Can you feel that, you dirty little slut?"

"Yes," I replied. "What is it?"

"Piss, of course," he said with a guffaw. "You don't think I'd be as uncouth as to piss all over your bed like that dickhead out there did, do you?"

Did he expect me to be grateful?

When he had finished pissing, he leaned over my legs.

"Now I am gonna pull my cock out, get dressed and leave. If I see one dribble of piss escape that tight arse of yours then it's gonna be all over for you. You understand me?"

"Yes," I said.

He slipped his cock out slowly, probably made more difficult by the fact that I was clenching my anal muscles down as hard as I could. I could hear him in front of me, obviously dressing.

"I'm still watching you," he said.

I gritted my teeth and clenched even harder. All I wanted to do was let it all gush out, but I had to hold it in. I had to do what Jake said. I was too afraid not to.

Jake walked towards the window and when he got there, he turned, looked at my arsehole and then at me.

"Now, keep your arse and mouth shut. We know where you live remember."

I nodded. My face was probably purple from the strain of clenching my arsehole shut tight.

He took one last look at my arsehole and disappeared out the window.

Even though he had left the room I didn't dare let his piss out. It might have been a trick. If he came back and found a big mess on the floor he might kill me. Or that might have been what he wanted me to think. Either way I had to keep his piss inside me for as long as I could.

I don't remember how long I managed to hold my arse lips together, but I woke up in the morning feeling battered and bruised and with a large mess at the foot of my bed. The second problem was how to get myself untied. I didn't want to have to call for a neighbor, but then again, I couldn't be more humiliated than I had already been.

NO LOITERING
Bearmuffin

My partner Mick Rocca was a rough Italian cop from New Jersey. He broke the rules and scared the hell out of a lot of people, but he got the job done. Nobody fucked with him.

He was so awesomely built that his uniforms were specially tailored to fit him. The first time I saw him naked in the locker room, I was amazed. I'd never seen anybody with such a wide chest; huge biceps and mammoth thighs all covered with a thick pelt of curly black hair.

It was around 3:00 in the morning when Mick and I were cruising the park on the north side of town on the lookout for this street hustler called Spike. We'd heard that he was hustling in the park again and ripping off tricks.

We patrolled around for about an hour but didn't see him. I had to take a leak, so I pulled up by the men's room.

Mick lit up a cigarette and watched the men who were cruising the park lurking in the shadows. "I love this fuckin' job," he said. He grabbed the hefty bulge between his legs and squeezed it hard. "Ya know, I bet there's some fucker out there who wants to suck my dick."

Mick stayed in the car, and I went inside the john. It was musty and stank of old piss. Someone had scrawled the words NO FUCKING on the NO LOITERING sign. I heard the whirring of the ventilation fan on the ceiling and the steady dripping of a leaking faucet.

One of the urinals was flooded with stale piss. I pulled out my fat prick and the piss flowed out of my big piss hole. Then I heard this heavy grunt followed by a steady, smooth pumping sound that seemed to be coming from the last stall in the back. As I got closer, the moans and grunts got louder. I went in the adjoining stall and sat on the toilet. I noticed a glory hole that had been stuffed with a piece of toilet paper, so I poked it out and looked through the hole.

Homo Thugs

There was Spike. He was moaning and grunting lustily while he fucked the shit of this guy who was holding on to the toilet seat. Spike's jeans were pulled down to his knees, and I could see his chunky muscular butt gyrating wildly as he plowed his cock up the guy's sweaty asshole.

You could feel his dangerously seductive power. It shined within his magnetic jade green eyes. An appealing boyish handsomeness made him look younger than his supposed eighteen years. He had long golden blond hair that flowed around to his broad shoulders. I wondered how his smoothly curved lips would feel around my cock.

After a few years on the street, your average hustler is so full of drugs and booze that he can barely stand up let alone get a hard-on. But not Spike. He had a firmly muscled body underneath his black leather jacket. His broad chest and huge biceps bulged provocatively against his tightly stretched T-shirt, and his well-muscled thighs were firmly packed inside his faded black Levis. Those smooth rounded pumped up pecs of his were capped by thick nipples that had been pierced by heavy steel tit rings.

My eyes were glued to Spike's bucking ass, and my cock was getting hard. It was the kind of full ripe stud butt that I wanted to ram my cock into and fuck for a couple of hours.

Spike finally shot his hot punk wad up the guy's ass. Then he took a bandanna out of his pocket and wiped the cum off his dick. "That fuck'll cost ya fifty bucks, dude" he told the trick.

When the guy took out his wallet, Spike pulled out his switchblade and flicked it open in the guy's face. Spike grabbed the wallet and ran out only to crash into Mick who had just walked in. Spike bounced off his burly chest like a rubber ball against concrete and fell into a piss puddle by the sink.

Spike's trick looked worried. I guess he thought he was going to get busted for loitering. But we gave him back his wallet and he left.

We handcuffed Spike. Mick glared down at him, his piercing coal-black eyes were taking in every hot inch of Spike's superbly muscled body. He reached down and gave his bulging crotch a squeeze. "I'm gonna teach this punk thief a fuckin' lesson," he said.

Mick popped the buttons off his shirt and rolled his T-shirt up over his pecs. Thick curly hairs ran across his huge pecs and traveled down over his washboard abs until they swarmed around the thick root of his uncut cock and massive hanging balls. Mick unzipped his fly and his cock poked out. Spike's eyes bulged out when he got a good look at the thick, uncut Italian cop dick bobbing in front of him.

Mick raised an arm and exposed the slimy tufts of hair swirling inside his armpit. "Slurp up that stinkin' cop sweat!" he barked.

Spike immediately obeyed and nuzzled his face into the thick hairs that swirled inside Mick's hot, musky armpits. He wrapped his fist around Mick's spasming cock and fisted it hard as he lapped at the smelly pit hairs. When I looked down between Spike's legs, I saw that he was getting a hard-on, too. He was really getting off on licking Mick's raunchy armpits.

Mick groaned. "Like that fuckin' man-stink, don'tcha punk?"

I pulled Spike's jeans down and his meaty, chunky butt was exposed. I took my cock out and slowly circled it around the hot puckered ridges of Spike's butt hole.

"Dat's right," Mick said. "Tease 'em wit yer stick a little. Fuck! Lookit dat fucker squirm."

Spike was running his tongue all over Mick's hairy pumped up pecs. He took one of Mick's thick nipples and sucked it in between his lips.

"Fuck, yeah!" Mick grunted. "Suck them tits, punk!"

Mick grabbed Spike's head and held him steady while Spike chewed on his protruding nipples. Then he guided Spike's head down along his hairy, sweaty abs. He made him stoop lower, so he could kiss and lick the washboard ripples of his muscular belly until he finally got Spike's face down to his groin.

Mick thrust his cock and balls against Spike's bobbing face. He was filling Spike's nose with the strong stench of his manly, sweaty body. Spike's probing tongue slurped noisily at the cop's smelly crotch. Spike was really getting down now. He mashed his face into Mick's stinky pubes and worked his tongue up and around his big thighs. He licked the sweat off Mick's big hairy balls and then landed his hot tongue on Mick's huge cop prick.

Mick cupped his hands behind Spike's head as his cock quivered violently. The doorknob-like tip of Mick's precum oozing cock hovered just an inch away from Spike's trembling lips. Spike's eyes glittered when he saw the piss slit yawn and one huge drop of precum slowly trickle out. Spike stuck his tongue out and brushed the tip against the cop's oozing piss slit to let the salty drop of precum ooze onto his tongue.

"Yeah," Mick moaned. "Lick it. Stick out that punk tongue. I want ya to get a real good taste of my dick 'cause I'm gonna shove it up your fucking punk hole!"

Spike's face was buried in Mick's groin. His nose and lips were lost in the thick musky nest of pubes. When Mick hunched forward his big sweaty balls slapped against Spike's chin.

Hot foaming spit drooled out of the corners of Spike's mouth as he sucked in his cheeks and slurped on Mick's bull cock. Spike's cock was spasming wildly between his legs, and thick drops of punk precum began to ooze out of his piss hole.

Spike ran his hands up and down the cop's hairy thighs and slipped his fingers in between the crack of his meaty sweaty buttocks. When he wiggled his forefinger inside Mick's hot and sweaty bunghole and churned it around, Mick went berserk.

"Awww, fuck!" he cried. Mick tossed his head from side to side and his muscles trembled wildly. His eyes glowered as he rammed his cock all the way down Spike's cocksucking throat. "C'mon punk," he yelled. "Eat that cock. Yeah, I'm gonna fuck your face but good!"

After I gave Spike's punk bunghole a good warming up with my nightstick, I pulled out my cock which was ripe and ready to shove up his hot little ass.

"Okay, punk!" I rasped. "Let's see that hard punk butt!"

I grabbed his firm meaty buttcheeks and wrenched them wide open. Spike's puckered hole was jutting out, and it looked like two big lips waiting to suck around my big fat dick. When I nudged the blunt tip of my cock against his puckered bunghole, Spike started to squirm.

He turned around and looked at me. The sheer terror in his eyes sent another hot jolt through my cock.

"PLEASE, MAN. NOT UP MY ASS!" he wailed.

"What d'ya mean you can't take it?" I barked. "Open up, punk. I smacked his juicy butt until it was red hct.

"You're gettin' this cock all the way up that fuckin' ass of yours, punk whether you like it or not."

My cock plowed up Spike's bunghole. Spike broke out in a cold sweat. "AWWWWWW FUUUUCX!" he screamed. His body went rigid for a split second. I got a firm hold around his waist, and with a hearty grunt, I rammed hard into him. Spike's slimy punk bunghole suddenly snapped and gave way as I sunk my fat cock in to the hilt.

Spike was getting it from both ends. I was fucking his hot punk ass, and Mick was pumping his hot Italian cop dick between his trembling, frothing lips. But Mick's beefy hairy butt started to itch, and he wanted Spike to give him a rim job. He spun around and stuck his butt in front of Spike's face.

Mick reached around and spread his own cheeks as he butted his big hairy ass against Spike's bobbing face. His hole opened wider, and Spike's fluttering tongue slipped inside. Spike's cute, boyish face was smothered in hot stinking Italian cop stud butt.

"Yeah! Fuck!" Mick howled, wiggling his hairy butt against Spike's flickering tongue while he fisted his own hot spasming cock. "Tongue dat butt, punk! Work dat tongue up my hole!"

Spike gripped Mick's sweaty boulder-like ass cheeks and tore them apart, so he could jam his wiggling tongue all the way up the cop's smelly bunghole.

Mick groaned loudly, grabbing onto the sink for support as he shoved his smelly butt into Spike's ass eating face. "SUCK MY ASS!" he barked. "EAT IT!!!"

Spike sucked harder, licking and rimming until the cop's butt was slick and shiny with hot frothing punk-spit.

Mick reached behind him and grabbed Spike's tit rings and yanked them. Spike groaned and jabbed his funky tongue up all the way up Mick's musky butt.

Mick was trembling. Hot streams of funky cop sweat ran down his muscles. His hot pulsing cock was just about to shoot its spunk. "I got a hot load for ya, punk." he grunted. "Wanna take that hot load?"

"Gimme that load!" Spike shouted.

Mick looked straight at me. His face was flushed and his eyes burned with lust. "How ya doin' buddy?" he asked. "Are ya ready to fill this punk's ass with your hot cop load?"

"Let's come together" I panted. "Yeah, we'll give him two hot loads at once."

Mick spun around and shoved his cock into Spike's mouth.

"Swallow my load!" Mick barked. I heard Spike's stifled groans when Mick's cock exploded and hot squirts of Italian stud semen gushed down Spike's gurgling throat.

I leaned forward and gripped Spike tightly around the waist and slammed into him. Spike's tight hole clenched around the root of my spasming cock as huge jets of cop sperm squirted out of my cock and hurtled up his asshole.

"UNNNGH, UNNNGH," Spike groaned. "I'M GONNA SHOOT MY WAD, MAN. I'M GONNA FUCKIN SHOOT!" A heavy fuck spasm shook Spike's entire body as his cock erupted, and he squirted his hot wad all over the floor.

We got back to the car. Spike sat in the front seat between Mick and me. Spike's head was bobbing under the steering wheel while he sucked on Mick's spasming cock.

"Listen, punk," Mick said. "We're going to my place. If ya don't like it, ya can go to jail. There's a whole cell full of mean horny fuckers who could use a pretty boy like you. So whad'ya say, punk?" But Spike couldn't. His feverish lips were locked around Mick's throbbing cop prick.

"What's the matter, punk?" I said. "Can't you talk with your mouth full?"

"Yeah. I can't hear ya," Mick said. He grabbed one of Spike's tit rings and yanked on it. "Ya comin' wit us or not?"

"Yes, sir!" Spike cried out, wincing with pain.

"Dat's more like it!" Mick said. "I'm gonna make a man out of you yet."

So Spike moved in with Mick. And why not? Spike never got into trouble again. After all, Mick may have had an unusual way of doing things, but he sure got results.

THE CONTRIBUTORS

BEARMUFFIN has written for many gay magazines, and his fiction appears in anthologies from STARbooks, Alyson and Cleis Press. A devotee of raunchy, anonymous sex, he lives in San Diego and hangs out in adult bookstores, sex clubs, and bathhouses in a never-ending search for grist for his pornographic mill.

MICHAEL BRACKEN's short fiction has been published or is forthcoming in *Best Gay Romance 2010*, *Biker Boys*, *Black Fire*, *Country Boys*, *Freshmen*, *Hot Blood: Strange Bedfellows*, *The Mammoth Book of Best New Erotica 4*, *Men*, *Muscle Men*, *Teammates*, *Ultimate Gay Erotica 2006* and many other anthologies and periodicals.

H. L. CHAMPA has been published in numerous anthologies including *College Boys*, *Like Magnets We Attract*, *Skater Boys* and *Hard Working Men*. If you prefer your erotica in electronic form, shorts stories can be found at Dreamspinner Press, Ravenous Romance and Torquere Press. Find more online at heidichampa.blogspot.com.

GARLAND CHEFFIELD is the pen name of a full-time actor and writer living in Hollywood, California, whose stories have appeared in numerous anthologies including *Tight Ends*, *The Mammoth Book of the Kama Sutra* and *Frat Sex II*. He also has several stories slated for numerous anthologies coming out later this year. www.myspace.com/hiphopjoe or JFilip4675@aol.com.

LANDON DIXON's writing credits include *Options*, *Beau*, *In Touch/Indulge*, *Three Pillows*, *Men*, *Freshmen*, *[2]*, *Mandate*, *Torso*, *Honcho*, and stories in the anthologies *Straight? Volume 2*, *Friction 7*, *Working Stiff*, *Sex by the Book*, *Nerdvana*, *Ultimate Gay Erotica 2005*, *2007*, and *2008*, and *Best Gay Erotica 2009*.

PETER EROS has been published in many STARbooks Press anthologies.

JAMIE FREEMAN lives in a small town in the red state of North Florida. His work is featured in *Cruising for Bad Boys*, *Video Boys*, *Special Forces* and *Hard Working Men*. He's hard at work on more darkly erotic stories, so stay tuned. Check out his blog http://nickdreamsong.blogspot.com; jamiefreeman2@gmail.com.

MARK JAMES is a writer of gay erotica with several published short stories, and two published novels, *The Iron Hand* and *Escape from Purgatory*. He resides in Dallas, where summers are hot, the land's flat, and the cold winters lend themselves to long days spent indoors writing.

BARRY LOWE is a Sydney writer whose short stories have appeared in *Hard Hats*, *Surfer Boys*, *Cruising for Bad Boys*, *Time Well Bent*, *The Mammoth Book of New Gay Erotica*, *Flesh and the Word*, *Best Date Ever*, *Boys Meet Boys*, and others. He is also the author of *Atomic Blond: The Films of Mamie Van Doren* (McFarland). www.barrylowe.net.

WAYNE MANSFIELD lives and works in Perth, Western Australia. He has had several stories published in STARbooks Press collections, most recently *SexTime*, *Service with a Smile*, and *Boys Caught in the Act*. He is also published in *Biker Boys*. He's also the best-selling author of *Highway Patrol* – a short story released in paper back. Find out more about his work in his blogs at http//www.myspace.com/darknessgathers

CHRISTOPHER PIERCE is the author of *Kidnapped by a Sex Maniac: The Erotic Fiction of Christopher Pierce*, as well as the novels *Rogue: Slave* and its sequel *Rogue: Hunted* (STARbooks Press). His short fiction has been published in more than thirty anthologies, including *Rough Trade* (Bold Strokes Books), *Surfer Boys*, *Leathermen* (Cleis Press) and *Ultimate Gay Erotica 2005, 2006, 2007* and *2008* (Alyson). Visit him on-line at www.christopherpierceerotica.com.

Published in dozens of gay erotic anthologies, **JAY STARRE** grinds out fiction from his home in Vancouver, Canada. His short stories can be found in STARbooks titles like *Love in a Lock-Up*, *Don't Ask, Don't Tie me Up*, *Unmasked I* and *II*, *Boys Caught in the Act*, *Pretty Boys & Roughnecks* and *Service with a Smile*. His steamy gay historical novels *Erotic Tales of the Knights Templar* and *Lusty Adventures of the Knossos Prince* are also published by STARbooks Press.

Born and raised an Okie, **MARK WILDYR** presently resides in New Mexico, the setting of many of his stories, which explore developing sexual awareness and intercultural relationships. Approximately fifty of his short stories and novellas have been acquired by Alyson Publications, Arsenal Pulp, Cleis Press, Companion Press, Green Candy Press, Haworth Press, STARbooks Press, and *Freshmen* and *Men Magazine*. He has a full-length historical novel scheduled for release in May 2010 by STARbooks, *Cut Hand*. His e-mail address is markwildyr@yahoo.com.

LOGAN ZACHARY lives in Minneapolis, MN, where he is an avid reader, writer, and book collector. His stories can be found in *Hard Hats, Taken by Force, Boys Caught in the Act, Ride Me Cowboy, Service with a Smile, Surfer Boys, Ultimate Gay Erotica 2009, Time Travel Sex, Best Gay Erotica 2009, Biker Boys, Unmasked II, Unwrapped, College Boys, Boys Getting Ahead*, and *Queer Dimension*. He can be reached at LoganZachary2002@yahoo.com.

ABOUT THE EDITOR

Shane Allison has had stories published in over a dozen anthologies including, *Muscle Worshipers*, *Boys Caught in the Act*, *Teammates*, *Wild and Willing*, *Any Boy Can*, *Best Gay Erotica*, *Best Black Gay Erotica*, *Ultimate Gay Erotica*, *Leathermen*, and most recently, *Biker Boys*. His first volume of poetry, *Slut Machine*, is out from Rebel Satori Press. He would like to thank the writers, editors and designers that have made this anthology possible. He hopes that the late great John Patrick is smiling down upon him from a bathhouse in heaven.

aring any underwear. "Excuse me," I said, having a hard time loc
inded by that bulge in his crotch, "but don't I know you?" "Mayb
ind of t   bout
with Ra   God,
t loser?   in?"
id. "Lik   s stro
ce body   e on
lly, he l   I ev
up to t   any i
staking   e sa
, I coul   ery l
ood raci   me s
ing with   e in
we go   beh
ill see   in p
ed?" he   vent
rivacy.   graf
hard. I
k, traci   t, sc
ed it, ha
with m   bing
bbing, I   n co

he sound of unzipping filled the small space. I don't know who's
, but before I knew it, I had his rod in my hand, and mine was in
t to do?" he asked, his tone challenging. I knew exactly, and san

Cover Image Courtesy of Cocksure Men

http://www.CockSureMen.com

www.ingramcontent.com/pod-product-compliance
Lightning Source LLC
Chambersburg PA
CBHW051646260626
47170CB00004B/1369